The Gos~~:~~ ~~_____~~

Sara Read

Wild Pressed Books

First Edition.

This book is a work of fiction.

The publisher has no control over, and is not responsible for, any third party websites or their contents.

The Gossips' Choice © 2020 by Sara Read.

Contact the author via twitter: @saralread

Editor: Tracey Scott-Townsend

Cover Design by Tracey Scott-Townsend, based on Michael Sweert's 'Head of a Woman' (c1654) now in the Getty Museum's collection.

ISBN: 978-1-916-4896-8-4

Published by Wild Pressed Books: 2020

Wild Pressed Books, UK Business Reg. No. 09550738

http://www.wildpressedbooks.com

For Beth, who became a new mother in the same year this book was born.

The Gossips' Choice

Gossip: *noun, Female friends invited to be present at a birth.*

Gossip: *noun, A person, mostly a woman, of light and trifling character, esp. one who delights in idle talk.*

Chapter One

'This day I laid the daughter-in-law of Lord Calstone of a son.'

Sixteen-year-old Lady Eleanor Calstone lay on her bed, drifting into sleep. It had been a gruelling two days and nights as she had struggled with every ounce of her being to give birth to the much desired Calstone heir. Her face was pale with exhaustion, her hair matted, and her eyes glistened whenever she was roused to open them. Midwife Lucie Smith had been a little intimidated by the bed when she first arrived. Large, ornately carved and draped in expensive tapestries, it was unlike any furniture she had seen before. She'd heard it came to Calstone Manor as part of Lady Eleanor's dowry, and boasted Charles II amongst those who had reposed in it – not that this was on either hers or the young woman's mind at present.

'Eleanor, wake up, my girl,' her mother urged. 'The midwife says you mustn't sleep for the next few hours. Your humours need the chance to settle. Do try harder, my dear. We don't want you falling into sickness.'

At her side in the dimly lit and stiflingly hot room, Lucie Smith worked busily and efficiently with a practised ease that came with years of experience. Her intractable rule was that a woman should not sleep until four hours after giving birth, and her calm authority set the tone for the gathered women present in the chamber who went about their various occupations discreetly. Lady Eleanor's maid and companion was seated on a stool at the side of the bed, leaning on to it. She must have been weary from sitting behind her mistress, propping her up as she'd pushed her son into the world. Lucie felt for the girl, she was surely no older than Lady Eleanor and had been a great help at what was probably her first gossiping. Glancing up from her charge, Lucie noticed that the two fashionable waiting women from the Countess's entourage had retired to a table in the corner to play cards, and was grateful for the space to work without a crowd of onlookers. Lucie had sent her young deputy, Mary Thorne, to attend to the newborn child at the far side of the chamber where she was working while chatting to the wet and dry nurses who had recently been summoned.

Lady Eleanor's mother looked more like her daughter's sister than her parent. The servants had told Lucie how Lady Eleanor's family were kin to the King, and Margaret Trust, the new grandmother – only yet in her mid-thirties – was less than keen to trouble herself with the dirty side of the birthing process, considering it beneath her rank. The Countess of Northerton, as she was properly styled, fancied that she favoured her cousin Mary, the late Princess Royal, with whom she was of an age. She seemed aware of her royal blood at every moment, never passing an occasion to glance at her reflection in a glass. She had worn a fine silk dress of pale blue throughout the birthing, and had refused the midwife's offer of a sturdy apron to protect it.

'Listen to your mother, young lady. Begging your pardon, my Lady.' Lucie had never dreamt she'd live long enough to be in such grand company and had no notion what the proper way to address a countess might be, so she had taken her lead from the household servants. She refrained from curtseying though. Apart from anything else, her knees would never forgive her.

'You're a mother now, too,' she continued. 'You have new duties. We need to keep you well. You really must stay awake

4

for a little while longer. I've ordered you some caudle which'll help revive your spirits.'

In truth, Lady Eleanor's duties for her child were not like those of common women, since she would not be responsible for its care, for its education, for its upbringing: in fact, she would barely be consulted. Her role in the matter was largely over. However, she obediently tried to hitch herself up higher on the pillows.

'No sudden movements, my lady,' instructed Lucie. 'I've got to stanch this small tear the young man made on his way into the world. Just lie still while I make you neat and tidy.' She pressed a folded linen cloth firmly on the wound.

Lucie was in her later fifties, of middling height, with a waist that had thickened over the last decade or so. Her grey hair was tucked neatly into her cap with only the silvery strands at the front showing, and although she'd lost a number of teeth over the decades, she still looked somewhat younger than her years. Her plain woollen suit of clothes was protected by a thick apron, enhancing the difference in rank between the midwife and the women by whom she was now employed. One thing that stood out about the ageing midwife was her gaze. Her blue eyes had the ability to draw people in and elicit their trust, and they still had a brilliant twinkle on occasion. Women bedded by Mistress Smith always remembered those eyes, and not the gentle wrinkles now surrounding them. Having delivered hundreds of babies, she was well-liked and respected by women for miles around. The female attendants, Lady Eleanor's gossips, all sensed that this country midwife deserved their confidence.

Unusually, there were men in the birthing chamber, too. Dr Thomas, a physician, was standing at the back of the room with his assistant, not playing an active role but issuing directives from time to time, which the midwife discreetly ignored as she went about her work. Lucie had never worked under the direction of a physician, but then she had never delivered a child of this quality before either.

A tap on the door caused Lucie to look up from her work. A nervous-looking page entered the room with apparent reluctance. He carried a package at the sight of which, the doctor demanded imperiously, 'What is this here?'

Lucie walked over to the boy and took the proffered parcel, and one of the maids showed the relieved young man out of the birthing chamber.

'Well?' reiterated the male voice.

Lucie turned to him, replying, 'It's just the hare-skin I sent for, Sir. We always lay the skin of a freshly killed hare on the belly of a new mother to help settle her humours. My Lady will benefit from its application, by your leave, Sir.'

'Indeed.' The eminent physician seemed slightly affronted by the older woman's obvious ability. 'But in future, pray consult me before sending for any remedies. Lady Eleanor is my patient, after all.'

Lucie agreed for the sake of keeping the peace in front of the new mother, but several of the ladies present glanced at one another anxiously. Lord Calstone's decision to have his London physician at the delivery of his first and much anticipated grandson (for his Lordship had never for a moment doubted that a man-child would be born) had caused much of the conversation amongst the gathered gossips in the early stages of the young woman's labour, before the doctor had deemed his continued presence necessary. By contrast, Lucie's services had been engaged by Lady Calstone, who had made discreet enquiries as to who was the nearest local midwife of highest repute. The good doctor raised no objections to Mistress Smith doing the practical work; in truth he was likely relieved to be spared the practical parts of his latest commission. Lucie had been hoping he would now take his leave, but he was occupied examining the newborn child, watching as one of the nurses swaddled him and then introduced him to his wet-nurse. There was clearly nothing wrong with the baby, who suckled heartily on the local woman's dug.

Satisfied that the child was likely to thrive, Dr Thomas walked over to the bed to examine Lady Eleanor. Taking the young woman's pulse, he commented that since Mistress Smith, a name he pronounced with unmissable condescension, appeared to have everything in hand, he would look in on his patient later that evening, but was to be called immediately should there be any cause for concern.

Dr Thomas was just about to take his leave, his assistant having packed his medical bag, when Lord Calstone burst into the room, bringing with him a sudden glare of bright light as his entourage held lamps aloft. His son, the new father, followed just behind. Lucie was startled by his Lordship's appearance, since when she had first sight of the man, on her arrival at the Manor, he had been wearing his long dark curled periwig in the manner of the King. Now he was sporting a velvet cap instead of a wig, leaving strands of his shorn but obviously grey hair on display. His Lordship and his retinue nodded to the young woman on her bed, Lucie having scarcely had time to cover her decently after the door had opened yet again. The midwife was obliged to bite her tongue as she swallowed down the urge to chide his Lordship to have a care for the tender eyes of his newly lain daughter-in-law, who, as everyone knew, was meant to repose in dim light for the first few days after delivery.

'Good work, my dear child,' he said to his overwrought daughter-in-law. 'I knew your belly was filled with my grandson. I have decided the boy will be named Charles James after our good monarch and his brother. I trust you have no objection?' Lucie felt he had added the question rather pointlessly, for his mind was evidently set.

Lady Eleanor shook her head, almost imperceptibly, as her father-in-law walked away to see the baby. Her mother, Lady Margaret, clapped her hands and beamed at his Lordship's announcement and declared how delighted she knew her cousins, the King and the Duke of York, would be at this news, especially as the baby shared the birthday month of May with Charles, who would be thirty-five on the twenty-ninth. Sir Robert, Lady Eleanor's young husband, seemed timid and clumsy in his father's presence, and only had the courage to glance over at his wife and shrug as if to apologise for his father's domineering presence.

Seeing the babe suckling well on the nurse's ample breast, Lord Calstone declared everything satisfactory and announced that he and his men would be away to sup.

'Be sure to follow the advice of Dr Thomas, my dear; young Charles will need a playmate as soon as possible and I'll be looking to you to repeat this task within the year!'

The baron strode across the room laughing loudly at his own comment, as the young girl's already wan face visibly blanched. A single fat tear stole down her cheek, of which Lord Calstone was entirely unaware, already congratulating the doctor on a job well done, patting him hard on the back, and insisting that the physician join him in the main hall for the celebration supper. He took a quick glance over his shoulder to where both his wife, Cecilia, and Lady Eleanor's mother were standing, and boomed that he would be expecting all the ladies down to supper shortly too, as household order must be maintained even on days as special as today.

Sir Robert held back from his father's entourage as it left the chamber, the light levels at last receding to the gloom Lucie thought fitting for her patient's recovery. The sound of the baron reminding the physician to submit a full bill for his services to his steward with all haste echoed in the corridor as his voice trailed off. Lucie had never seen such a flamboyantly dressed young man as Sir Robert, even in the days of the old King. His periwig was tied in scarlet ribbons, so that the hair gathered in bunches fell nearly to his waist. His sleeves were tied in ribbons of the same colour, his breeches were augmented with a deep lace frill, and his shoes were tied with extravagant bows. A father now, only just in his majority, and not yet possessed of a full beard, he

8

walked over to his wife's bed and kissed her cheek with some tenderness. Theirs was a dynastic match, and Lucie had heard they had known each other for most of their lives, since Sir Robert had been brought up in her father's household for several years, following the death of his mother. The couple appeared to have a degree of fondness, which would mean the marriage wasn't entirely without affection. In truth, Sir Robert seemed more than a little overwhelmed, Lucie guessed both by becoming a father and the realisation that his young bride had produced their child. Glancing up from her work, she sensed Sir Robert was looking at Lady Eleanor with fresh eyes.

'Thank you, little Nelly. Thank you for my son. He'll one day be a fine man, I'm sure! You don't object to his name, do you? We always knew my father would name him for the King, I suppose.'

Silent tears slowly slid down Lady Eleanor's face.

'What is it, Nell? Are you in pain? Was it ever so bad?'

Without waiting for an answer, Sir Robert impulsively leant over and took his wife in his arms.

'Talk to me Nell, please. What is it?'

Utterly exhausted, Lady Eleanor couldn't seem to speak.

'Perhaps it is your father's words,' Lady Calstone said gently. 'No woman having been safely delivered wants to be reminded so bluntly that she must suffer all this again, even if it is true.'

Sir Robert nodded to his step-mother but whispered in his wife's ear so none of the women milling round the room save Lucie could hear. 'You'll say when the time is right, my love. I'll not press you, I promise.'

The midwife saw her young charge's body relax. She smiled approvingly at this gauche young man who had grown up in front of her eyes in that moment.

'Perhaps it is time for you to join your father, Sir,' she prompted, 'and leave her ladyship to begin her recovery. She'll be more herself when you look in again tomorrow, I'm sure,' she added, making sure the young man knew his presence was not required again this day.

As soon as Sir Robert and his man had left and the room had again become the female-only space that was proper, it erupted in whispered chatter. The presence of a physician at the delivery had been a new experience for all of the women present, even the grand Lady Margaret. Tales of doctors or surgeons summoned to births that had gone wrong, in which mother and baby were in grave danger, were well known, of course, but to have a physician attend for no reason was a new precedent, and one that none of the dozen or so women approved of. Lucie busied herself once again with applying pressure to the tear the girl had been left with, to make sure that the bleeding had completely stopped. She washed down the girl's privy parts with warm, herb-infused water, all the time chatting in soothing terms to the young woman, explaining as she went along what she was doing. Satisfied that all was healing, Lucie folded a fresh linen cloth several times and placed it between Lady Eleanor's swollen labia to encourage the womb to rise back to its normal position.

It was testimony to Lucie's skill and not that of the expensive physician that the young woman had only a small tear. That the upper ranks insisted on breeding so young was not something Lucie approved of, but luckily births of mothers at this age were few and far between. Satisfied that all was in order with the new mother, Lucie turned her attention to the womb-cake, which had only just been delivered before the interruption of the page. Luckily it was whole and neat, which meant it had come away cleanly and would not cause any problems. Lucie checked Lady Eleanor's abdomen under the hare-skin and was satisfied that here, too, all was progressing as it should. She applied a clean cloth to the young woman's face to mop the tear stains, and sat on the edge of the bed.

'I'm very proud of you, young lady. You did very well indeed and will make a full recovery. Your pains were long and hard because you have barely finished growing yourself, and you have produced a lusty son that took some getting out. You should be very pleased with yourself, so no more tears.'

It might not be mannerly for a commoner to speak so freely to a woman of Lady Eleanor's rank, but in Lucie's eyes she was no more than an exhausted girl, who needed reassurance.

The young woman responded with a watery smile.

'I am so very sore, though, Mistress Smith, and so, so tired.'

'Of course you are, my dear, but tomorrow it won't be so bad and you'll feel much better after a night's sleep. The new man will be taken to the nursery and well cared for, so you won't be disturbed.'

Since the hare-skin had now been in place for an hour or so, Lucie decided it was fitting to remove it, and began gently cleaning Lady Eleanor's belly with some warmed oil infused with St John's wort, passed to her by Mary Thorne. Mary brought some cloths that had been warmed up by the fire and applied them to Lady Eleanor's nipples, to keep any milk at bay. Even if a mother were to nurse her own child, the breasts had to be discouraged from producing milk for at least twelve hours, until the woman's blood had settled. The midwife nodded to Lady Eleanor's maid, indicating that it was time to offer her mistress some caudle, and the maid began spoon-feeding the exhausted younger woman, who revived a little on receiving the warm food. When she determined that the young woman had had taken enough food, Lucie motioned for her mother to come and sit a while on the side of the bed and try and get her daughter to take a draught of wine, after which it would be permissible for the girl finally to sleep.

Across the room the future heir of the recently created Calstone title and its estate slept peacefully. A dry nurse, whose job was to change the infant's clouts and swaddling bands, was rocking his crib gently as Lucie went over to check on him.

11

'He is a fine looking young man. We are not privy to God's will, of course, but I don't think we have much to fear for him.'

She looked up at the proud grandmothers, both of whom had, as tradition demanded, supported the young mother in her labour. It was a shame that his own mother had not asked to see him, but it seemed that babies held no fascination for Lady Eleanor; in that respect, she resembled many girls of her age.

'What do you propose to do now, Mistress Smith? Would you like me to send for the coach to take you home, or would you prefer to stay the night here at the Manor to better attend my daughter-in-law?' asked Lady Calstone.

'I think I'll stay another night as it is getting late. If you could ask the maids to make up a truckle bed here again, I'll stay near at hand, should my lady need any attention in the night.'

Lucie had seen the day she'd have made for home regardless of the hour, but her years insisted on being acknowledged, and the hard work of attending to women in labour was getting more wearying with each passing year. A coach would take nearly three hours to make the journey to Tupingham, a horse an hour less, but she was too tired to ride. It wasn't just Lucie who had changed of course; she had received her midwifery licence when England was a different place, before the Civil Wars, before the Commonwealth years, and when Charles Stuart, now Charles II, kin to the new babe, was still in petticoats. Sometimes, in the small hours, Lucie would reflect on the most recent national news, the King's trade war with the Dutch, and wonder if the turmoil would ever end. Things seemed to weigh more heavily on her as she aged. As a confident young midwife starting out thirty years before, she'd paid no mind to news, and political events on a large scale seemed remote and irrelevant to a country midwife. It was day-to-day life that absorbed her attention. Of course, events over the second half of her life had changed her way of thinking. She remained steady, reassuring and professional – a dignified, God-fearing midwife, townswoman, wife, and mother in the eyes of all who knew her – but she felt a keen sense of foreboding in her very bones as the year 1665 drew on. This was not entirely without cause, for there'd been a comet in the skies over London the Christmastide past – her husband had seen it with his own eyes – and everyone knew this strongly suggested God was displeased with them.

The orders for a temporary bed for the midwife were duly given and the room slowly divested of people as the wet and dry nurses took the baby off to settle him in his own quarters in the nursery along the corridor. Ladies Northerton and Calstone and their women also took their leave in order to change for supper. Housemaids bustled into the birthing room to set up a bed for the midwife, who in truth was almost as tired, after continuous attendance on the young mother, as the girl herself. A meal of ale, cheese and cold meats was laid on the table nearby and instructions given to call out should there be anything else she required. Lucie washed her hands and checked on the sleeping Lady Eleanor, before settling herself to enjoy the meal. Lady Eleanor's personal maid, who had gone down to the kitchen to eat, taking Mary Thorne with her, was also going to lodge with her lady but instead of sharing her bed, as was their normal arrangement, she would sleep on a mattress next to the bed. The midwife was amused to see that Lady Eleanor's small spaniel, Dash, who had cowered under the bed for most of the last day, unable to comprehend what was happening to his mistress, had climbed up and snuggled at his lady's feet. She in turn let out a contented sigh in her sleep, at the familiar sensation.

In the morning, satisfied that both mother and child were like to continue well, Mistress Smith showed the attendants how to dry the redundant milk in Lady Eleanor's breasts, dispersing the excess humours in them by applying a sponge soaked in a special topical medicine. It consisted of meal of beans, bitter vetch, comfrey powder, mint, wormwood and various other ingredients boiled in vinegar. Lucie's husband, the local druggist, had made it up in the shop where he and Lucie lived and worked. She then prepared to take her leave. She didn't hold with the custom of some high-born ladies of employing other women to nurse their children, but sensed Lord Calstone would never have allowed his daughter-in-law to do menial work, which was what he no doubt thought nursing was, and it was known that nursing delayed the conception of the mother's next child. Following the family's losses in the wars and the years they had spent in exile with the Stuart court, Calstone's whole attention was taken up with augmenting the dynasty he was now intent on building, following his elevation to the peerage.

As she left, Mistress Smith issued her usual instructions: 'Let my lady eat no flesh till two days at least be over, for she may not use a full diet after so great loss of blood suddenly. As she grows stronger she may begin with meats of easy digestion, such as a little chicken, boiled not roasted. You could let her drink barley water, or boil one dram of cinnamon in a pint of water, dissolving two ounces of fine sugar in it, and if she will drink wine, mingle twice as much water with it, but let it be white wine in the morning, and claret in the afternoon; she may sometimes drink almond milk.'

Lady Calstone made careful notes of this advice, which Lucie took to be testimony to the regard in which she was held. Noticing that the new father was loitering in the doorway seeking permission to enter the chamber, Lucie reminded the room that, since the child was a boy, Lady Eleanor must lie in for thirty days, and that until she had done this and been churched, her husband must abstain from her. Sir Robert's appearance was even more startling to Lucie in the morning light. She smiled to herself, thinking

14

that he should have a care dressing like that in this season lest he be mistaken for a maypole. Although he'd absorbed the aristocratic demeanour of his foster-family, the Northertons, whose rank far exceeded his own, he was nothing like his overbearing father. Lucie couldn't help but notice a slight air of relief in his face that his promise to leave his lady until she was ready was officially sanctioned. As she left the room, with her deputy, Mary carrying her bundle, Mistress Smith lowered her voice so that only the women near Lady Eleanor might hear, and said, 'Pray send for me without delay if you are troubled. I'm sure Dr Thomas will be along as well, but I'd be more certain of her Ladyship's recovery if I knew my instructions were the ones being followed.'

Chapter Two

Back at home, Lucie took in a deep breath of the familiar herbal-scented air and crawled into the bed her husband Jasper had lately vacated to go to his apothecary shop in the front of their house. She pulled the curtains around her bed tight shut. Even though it was daylight and there was much to do, she knew from experience that she needed to take the chance to sleep. Her bed at Calstone Manor was comfortable enough, but when she was in the room with a newly lain mother she always had one eye and ear open, and the night before had been spent watching as Lady Eleanor struggled. Pulling up the bed covers, which still held some residual heat from Jasper's body, she smiled at the thought of some well-deserved rest. Poor Mary would, she knew, value it even more since no truckle bed had been provided for her apprentice, and she'd had to sleep on a mattress on the floor with Lady Eleanor's maid.

As she dozed, Lucie considered the great contrast between the formal but faded elegance of Calstone Manor and the cosy apothecary shop at the sign of the three doves. She had never taken much notice of Calstone Manor in the past as it had been shut up, quietly decaying, for many years during the wars and while Cromwell was in power. Attending Lady Eleanor and supping with the servants had revealed much about the family's business. It appeared that income from its land and from the Calstone property in the North had been sequestered by parliament and not used for the maintenance

17

of the family or their homes. His Lordship had eventually been successful in his petition for the return of his land and properties, but his rise, at the King's Restoration, from the gentry to a minor peerage had not come with funds commensurate with this elevation.

The boastful and indiscreet steward had told the midwife how the receipt of Lady Eleanor's considerable dowry had turned matters around and this money was funding refurbishment works. It was going to take all that money, for it was a substantial property built in the time of Queen Bess by the present Lord's grandfather, using profits from his wine importing business.

When it was built, the Manor was considered very modern and stylish with ornate Tudor patterned brickwork, and a dozen chimneys, of which the steward bragged as if he had personally built them with his own labour. The brickwork incorporated what was then the family's newly-purchased coat of arms in its design. The house even had a brick gatehouse, not now in use, and elegant walled gardens. In the time of Lord Calstone's father, the Manor had hosted both James I and Charles I. Unfortunately, the wine merchant's talents in trade had not been inherited by his male descendants who had been reliant on his fortunes, instead of adding to them.

The Manor was situated about eight miles west of Tupingham, the thriving but small market town where Lucie had lived her whole married life. While the Calstones had been resident in the area but a few generations, the family of Jasper Smith, the chemist, had lived in the country town as long as anyone could remember. He himself had only left for the years of his apprenticeship with an apothecary in Deptford, where he met his future wife; although he made the two-day journey to London annually, and so had many contacts and connections there, he was very happy to have built a successful business in his home town. The shop they'd made their home in was modest but perfect for their

18

needs. The Three Doves was of old-style timber construction – like all the properties on that side of the high street – but the front had been modernised to be enclosed by a large window, made of many small leaded glass panes, rather than being open-fronted like many other shops yet were.

Flagstone flooring ran throughout the ground floor, and the main living room was a good sized kitchen with a wide stone hearth, a large table and benches, and a pair of armchairs where the master and mistress could sit in the evenings. It was much darker than the shop area, not having the large window the shop enjoyed. On the rail in front of the hearth there was almost always some linen drying or airing. From the timber beams there hung pots and pans, some posies of dried flowers to help keep the air sweet, and shelves to hold the family's pewter cups and plates lined the walls. Several rush mats covered the flags to make the room cosier, and on the wall behind the table was a painted scene that the Smiths' son Simon had done as a youth, of the riverbank with Tupingham high street in the distance. It was not the most accomplished piece of artwork, but it held a special place in the Smiths' hearts and reminded them of their son, now a business man in London. The walls were otherwise whitewashed and plain, with dark wood shutters folded back against the wall during daylight hours, ready to be closed over the window at night.

Through the small scullery where their housemaid did the copious laundry Lucie's job provided, the house had a good sized herb garden which supplied many of the apothecary's needs, edged with hedgerows upon which linen dried in the fresh air whenever the weather was fair. In the corner of the scullery, under some sack cloth, there was a most unusual-looking piece of furniture. Well-worn wooden knobs rose from the front of each of its arms, and it had a large hole cut in the seat. This was one of the main tools of Lucie Smith's trade, her birthing chair, on which dozens of women had brought forth their children.

When the shop was closed, callers normally came down the

ginnel at the side of the house and rapped on the back door. This was the entrance Lucie and Mary had just used, being the most convenient for dropping off their bags of linen and other equipment from their stay at the Manor.

At noon, Martha knocked on her mistress's bedroom door and went in, placing a tray with a cup of small beer down on the table next to Lucie's bed. The Smiths' bedchamber was up the first pair of stairs, taking up most of the first floor. It was neat with plain but good quality furnishings. In the corner was a large wooden press filled with clouts, sheets, linen towels, and knitted blankets which Lucie used in her role as the town's midwife. There was a desk at which Lucie often wrote in her journal, for the light was better there than in the darker kitchen. She would rest her feet on a brass box which could be filled with smouldering coals in the winter months to keep her warm without the trouble of asking for the fire to be set. She also had a large trunk containing the several volumes of journals she had filled over the years and some knick-knacks and trifles saved from the years the house had been filled with small children. The master also had a locked cupboard, containing his purse and personal accounts, to which he held the only key.

Drawing open the shutters, Martha told Lucie, 'The master will be closing the shop for dinner soon, Mistress Smith, and I expect you'll want to join him. I know you don't like to sleep too long in the day. I have laid your day dress out for you and I've already soaked the aprons and clouts from yesterday's birthing in some cold water and salt ready to wash later.'

'Thank you, Martha; you've saved me a deal of trouble as usual.' Lucie sat up and drew open the bed curtains. 'Is Mary awake? It might be best to let her sleep on a while and waken in her own time.'

'I'll look in on her, Mistress Smith,' Martha replied, heading towards the narrow pair of stairs to the attic bedroom and the bed Martha Jones shared with Mary Thorne. Their quarters were small but light enough, due to a window cut in the roof. The women were especially grateful for them since the apothecary's apprentice Ned was obliged to sleep in the kitchen in order to be available to answer the door to any callers needing medical or midwifery services in the night.

In the three years Mary had been apprenticed to Mistress Smith the two women had grown close, and Lucie knew that Martha would be looking forward to hearing Mary's account of her time up at the Manor House, assisting the birthing.

Physically, the two women who worked in the Smiths' household could not be more different. Martha had fierce red hair, testament to her Celtic heritage, which was not showing any signs of dulling now she was in her forties. She was a tall, solid woman who laboured long through the day to keep the house in good order. The deputy midwife (as midwifery apprentices were generally known) was almost half Martha's age, and much slighter. Her mousey brown hair was as fine and lank as Martha's was thick and wavy. Her small frame and unremarkable complexion should fool no-one, however, for Mary was a diligent, hard-working woman, for whom nothing was too much trouble. In sum, she was a pleasant and capable young maid, quick to learn and a credit to Mistress Smith's training. She had already gained a good reputation amongst the teeming women she helped to deliver. Martha had told Lucie that she was much happier to have this apprentice as her bed-mate than a couple of others who'd occupied the position over the twenty years she'd worked in the household.

When Lucie got down to the kitchen, Jasper and his apprentice Ned were already seated and supping a cup of small beer each. Martha busied herself serving a dish of rabbit which she had cooked in liquor thickened with eggs. It was big enough to make a meal for the whole household with bread dipped in the sauce.

'I'll put a plate aside for Mary; she showed no signs of rousing when I looked in on her. No doubt she'll be ravenous when she comes down,' she said.

Table talk was about the three days Lucie and Mary had spent at the manor house; it was the grandest birthing Lucie had been called to undertake – Lady Calstone having borne all her children at their London home.

'I thought I'd delivered mothers in all ways and of all degrees, but this was new to me.' Lucie described the comparative opulence of the birthing-chamber, and how the ornately carved bed she'd worked upon had been patronised by His Majesty during its lifetime. She said that the girl who had given birth seemed a pleasant enough wench, but that her mother was pride-sick.

'My Lady Northerton is kin of His Majesty, and a similar age to him, being five and thirty.' She described how the young grandmother had worn a shimmering gown with lace sleeves in the birthing chamber and refused an apron. She was celebrating being out of her year-long mourning for her husband, the Earl, and not minded to put on dowdy apparel again. It was a strange set-up, with the new mother and father being raised almost as siblings, and then married off to one another at their parents' command. She'd warrant that his Lordship would never have dared hope for such a match when he'd secured a place for his young lad in the Trusts' household. Lucie did not dare begin to describe the new father's costume to her husband, whose choler would rise to dangerous levels at hearing about such a peacock of a man. Instead, she went on to list her frustrations at the interference of the London physician.

As supporters of parliament in the late wars, the Smiths would not have volunteered to work for the Calstones in any capacity – and indeed, Jasper would have supported his wife had she refused the command to attend – but the midwife's oath made it clear that a licensed midwife must attend anyone who needed her services, regardless of wealth or rank, or lack thereof. But to have been summoned to attend the labour, only to find she had to be deferential to a man who had clearly got his learning from books and not from touch and experience, wasn't something she had expected when the order came. A man in charge of the birthing room was not something she was in a hurry to experience again.

'I've been working as a midwife more than thirty years now, licensed before the past wars, even. I can count the times we have had to send for a physician on the fingers of one hand. A chirurgeon many times more, but a book-taught doctor, full of fancy words, but no sense, who's never laid a hand on a teeming woman . . . well, I'm lost for words!'

She saw her husband smile. Probably because it was not often his wife found herself in that condition. Lucie did not react well to having her authority in the birthing chamber questioned, and with good reason, for she was the most experienced midwife in the region, nicknamed the gossips' choice because it was Mistress Smith whose name came to the lips of expectant women throughout Tupingham, and beyond.

'But this physician left you unmolested to attend to your duties, I hope, my dear?' Jasper said. Lucie was aware he knew of Edward Thomas from his London trips and thought he was particularly pompous and not very affable to the many people he considered his inferiors. 'What you don't know about births is surely not worth knowing,' he continued.

'Well, we had to mind our manners before Dr Thomas – he is one of the King's physicians, after all. But the best thing was to see Lady Eleanor's mother-in-law, Calstone's wife, noting down my parting instructions – which is another new thing, I'm sure. She says that many fine ladies keep commonplace books, and so does she. Apparently, she writes down all her recipes, and advice, household and spiritual, and other odd ends. And she means to put in my instructions, so that she might follow them on another occasion if she is called upon. Lady Calstone can be as fine a lady as any, if she pleases, but she doesn't let that hinder her from being a good woman. She spoke knowledgably and seems wise, too. And she was always ready to hear what I had to say.'

The Calstones had a remote property in the far north, where there was not a midwife to be had for miles, it seemed; Lady Calstone was sometimes called upon to assist at deliveries in families belonging to the household and estate, and to provide remedies, so no doubt Lucie's advice would be put to good use in the future.

After the meal was over, Lucie asked Jasper, 'What do you mean to do this afternoon, husband?'

'I have some distillations to finish, and some deliveries of supplies to enter in the ledger, but then I thought I would leave the Three Doves in Ned's hands for a couple of hours while I repair to the coffeehouse to read the news sheets and see that all's well with the world.'

'Very good! While you are mixing ingredients, can you prepare me some more oil of St John's wort? My bottle's almost empty.'

Lucie went upstairs to her desk to write up the case notes for the Calstone baby. Not many midwives went to this trouble. Indeed, many would not have the literacy to do so if they'd wanted to, but Lucie liked to keep records and detailed notes to refer to and as aids in teaching her apprentices. Her journals now ran to five volumes. This set her thinking. Mary Thorne was in the final months of her training, for three years was generally judged sufficient for midwifery, with Ned in the fifth year of his seven-year indenture. The Smiths would have to have a conversation about whether they were to take on more apprentices soon, so they weren't left without help when these two spread their wings. Lucie was not sure she was ready to take on another deputy, as she wanted to wind her work down in the next few years and start taking life a bit easier, perhaps concentrating on supplying the shop from her beloved garden and not the hard, physical work that midwifery could be. Besides, she could not rid herself of the creeping melancholic humour with which she had been so beset recently. Something seemed to be telling her Mary would be her last apprentice. The foreboding she felt would have seemed so very odd to the steadfast, easy-going woman she once was, and that no-one must learn of it Lucie was adamant. In any case Mary was the most capable and gifted of all the apprentice midwives Lucie had trained, barring perhaps Alice Shore, now Mistress Wallis, of course.

Ah, dear Alice, she mused. *I'd love to hear how she does; it has been a good while since we had a letter from her.* Alice had moved away from the area after her marriage and Lucie wondered, not for the first time, if Mary would be the one to take over as the leading midwife in the neighbourhood in due course, with herself as support when needed.

Moments later Lucie realised she could hear Martha and Mary's chatter from downstairs as they boiled up the cloths from the most recent delivery. She hadn't heard the younger woman rising but was pleased to note how she applied herself to work; nothing was too much trouble and she was a sunny presence around the house. Mary *was* the natural successor to her practice.

'Mary, might I have a word?' Lucie called down the steps, beckoning her assistant up when she appeared. 'Martha can hang the cloths and clouts on the bushes outside to dry: it doesn't need both of you. We need to talk through the Calstone case.'

Mary stood beside the desk as Lucie proceeded to ask her questions about why she thought Lady Eleanor had had such a gruelling time and what further steps might be taken in such another case, to help the mother through her ordeal.

'Well, Mistress Smith, you've taught me there are great differences in women's constitutions and education. Lady Eleanor has been brought up as a fine lady unused to exercise and hard work, meaning her body wasn't equipped for an easy labour.'

'Quite right. Anything else?'

'Yes, she was a slip of a girl. I know she was fully sixteen, but it seems, from what her mother was saying, her monthly flowers began less than a year ago. She said her daughter had been betrothed to the Calstone heir for some while, but the minute and hour my Lord heard she was fit for breeding they were wed and bedded before her body could ripen to womanhood.'

'Indeed, I wish the Quality would not be in so much haste to continue their lines. Lady Calstone is still breeding, after all, so the Calstone nursery will be filled with his Lordship's children and grandchildren all at the same time, as is their way.'

Lady Calstone's last girl-child was beginning to walk and had been trundling about the nursery with the support of a wheeled baby-walker when Lucie looked in on the new-born. Perhaps, she mused, now Calstone had a grandson he'd be minded to leave his wife alone and consider their family complete. Stories of his fondness for actresses when he went to London to serve as one of the Grooms of the Bedchamber to His Majesty circulated through the district with monotonous regularity, as did talk of at least one child born from this.

'So, what are the differences in how we manage fine ladies compared to country women? For you may kill one with that which will preserve the other; a tender lady that is bred delicately must not be governed after the same manner as a hardy country woman.'

'Well,' Mary replied with confidence, 'a fine lady is commonly weak stomached, but the other strong, so if you should give the weak woman presently after delivery strong broth, or eggs, or milk, it will cast her into a fever, but the other that is strong will bear it. So tender women must be tenderly fed, and nothing given them that is of hard digestion nor yet what they have no mind to, provided that what they desire be not offensive.'

'And for country women?' Lucie pushed her deputy on.

'A country woman will besides her ordinary food like mutton broth, and may take ale-berries with bread, butter, and sugar. Let her drink her beer or ale with toast, and she may drink a decoction of liquorish, raisins of the sun and a little cinnamon, if she can get ingredients like this.'

'You have done well, Mary. You are skilful at your handiwork and earnestly given to book learning, too. I've seen you, in your quiet times, reading back through my journals of the women I have laid and how they fared.'

'I can read well, but I wish I could write, too. I can barely make my mark,' Mary now looked ill at ease. 'There was no money for me to stay on at school once I'd learned to read.'

'Perhaps we could ask Ned to give you lessons, if that wouldn't make you bashful, Mary? He's a towardly lad who went through grammar school until he was fourteen, when he began his apprenticeship with Mister Smith. But it's no matter, truly! You have my journals, after all, and it's not hard words that do the work in midwifery; it's touch and experience. I've been thinking that at the next birthing we attend, if it is fitting, you should lead, as you are coming to the end of your years with me. I'll help and advise, but you should take charge.'

Chapter Three

'This day I laid the wife of Samuel Jones.'

Lucie and Jasper were roused by a rapping at their chamber door, as apprentice Ned woke the couple to let them know there was a caller downstairs. It was still dark, not quite yet dawn.

'What time is it, Ned?' asked Lucie, sitting up.

'The church clock has just struck four, Mistress.'

'Who calls?' asked Jasper.

'Sam Jones: he says it's his wife's time.'

'Oh, I didn't think that was due for a little while yet! Go fetch Mary, would you Ned? And rouse Martha – she's kin to the Joneses and they'll likely want her to be a gossip again. Then bid Goodman Jones return to his wife and we'll follow presently. I'll need you to come with us, Ned, and hold a lantern.' Lucie could picture Ned rolling his eyes at this instruction for she knew how much he disliked this sort of task. Nevertheless, she could tell by the creaking of the boards that he was using his candle to light those on the table in the bedchamber in order that she would be able to see to dress and that he'd go obediently enough up the next pair of stairs to wake the two women.

The home of the local weaver, in a closely packed row of cottages on Warley Lane, could not be more different from the Manor or even the Three Doves. Whereas in the Manor the servants had servants, or so it had seemed, here the family lived and worked in what was little more than the one

29

room. A loom was at the end nearest the window to make best use of the light, a fireplace in the middle, and a partition wall affecting an alcove, with an opening rather than a door, to make a bedchamber of sorts. None of the windows in the row were glazed and the internal shutters provided the only defence against the elements, which made working in bad weather even more of a challenge. There was just one entrance, a door on the back which opened onto the communal yard, and was the same door the occupants of the small attic rooms above used. The other Jones children, the youngest in their parents' bed and the older two on a straw mattress at its side, hadn't stirred at the comings and goings, and in her fifth labour Anne Jones was making no noise that might waken them. The main room was cluttered and cramped but it was clean enough and the family, while poor, seemed robust.

An elderly neighbour had been waiting with Anne for the midwife to arrive, and then the women agreed that she should carry the young sleeping Joneses to her rooms on the floor above. Sam helped rouse the older ones, saying he would see them tucked in the neighbour's bed, and warn them to mind the younger ones and not to disturb their mother, before taking his leave of the birthing.

'Call me as soon as anything happens,' he said, as he left the cottage to begin his anxious wait.

Lucie had attended Anne before and was not anticipating any problems, so had asked Mary and Martha to carry her birthing chair, while she carried her bag and Ned both the bundle of cloths and the lantern to light the way. If she'd known the baby was due now, she would have had Ned deliver the chair in advance, ready and waiting. Ned was obviously not pleased to be made to trudge through the dark town in the night, carrying the midwife's things and holding up the lantern, but seemed relieved he didn't have to lug that birthing chair for the half hour walk. Lucie knew the other apprentices made his life a misery when he had to deliver it

30

here and there through the town, mocking him by screeching and swooning and arching their backs to stick out their bellies, asking for a turn in the "groaning chair" as Ned struggled with the cumbersome object, such a potent symbol of women's business. It was big and heavy, and awkward to carry. He regularly grumbled to Martha that the handles the teeming women used for grip were forever catching him when he tried slinging it over his shoulder to ease the burden.

Other midwives had birthing stools that were not much bigger than milking stools, and Ned had cheekily remarked more than once that his life would have been infinitely improved if Mistress Smith had invested in one of those. He seemed to care not that the comfort of the labouring women wouldn't compare, for as Lucie explained, at least with a back-rest, the woman might have ease between pains.

The women carried the chair between them this night, an arm each, and still struggled as it bashed into their skirts while they tried to hurry along. They were hindered not only by their burden, but also by the trials of balancing on the four-inch iron pattens attached to their shoes to keep them and their skirts away from the muck of the street. Ned left the women in Warley Lane and set off to return to the shop under the now light skies of the early summer dawn.

'Anne, my dear, if you agree, Mary will examine you and we shall see how long we are likely to be waiting for this babe,' Lucie said.

Mary had just finished putting layers of sheets on Anne's bed, ready for when they put her to bed after the delivery. She'd already set out all the clouts and childbed linen they'd be likely to need, and went on to anoint her hands with almond oil and motioned for Anne to lay on the bed for the internal examination. Young as she was, Mary showed no signs of hesitancy.

Thrusting her hand and forearm confidently inside her patient, Mary tried to loosen the vagina as was customary. She felt that the neck of the womb was opening nicely, and the child seemed to be in a good position. All seemed well, she reported. The coats were still intact, meaning the waters had not come down, which was ideal, for when they burst they would help the baby slip out.

Anne's labour progressed as expected, and she alternated between walking round the room, supported by neighbouring women Jane Croft and Anne Allen, and resting between the pains. When the pangs were coming thick and fast, Mary asked Anne to sit on the birthing chair so she could examine her once more. The baby was ready to come, she announced, so, having sought Lucie's consent, Mary tore the membranes with her nails to release the waters. Anne groaned as the baby lurched downwards. Mary massaged the opening to the vagina with more almond oil to help it expand and in the hope of keeping it from tearing as the baby's head put pressure on the perineum.

Lucie meanwhile prepared a draft of wine infused with mugwort, pennyroyal and sugar.

'Have a sip of this to keep your strength up and help things along. Not long now, I warrant.' The atmosphere in the small room, cramped and hot with the six women, was charged with anticipation. Anne Allen jabbed at the log on the hearth rather more vigorously than was strictly necessary. The party knew that this was the most dangerous point in the delivery but that it meant also the end of the ordeal was close. Jane rubbed her friend's back as the labouring woman leant forward in her seat, white knuckled from gripping so hard on the chair knobs, grunting loudly as she was suddenly overwhelmed with the urge to bear down.

The baby's head emerged and Mary, kneeling below the birthing chair, carefully guided it out. A gush of water and other humours splashed from the womb immediately afterwards, soaking Mary's apron. 'Gently stroke Anne's belly downwards,' she instructed Martha, while still keeping a firm hold on the head. 'This will help the body come forth presently.'

With a little manipulation on Mary's part the shoulders were out, and the child fell into her arms. Martha let out a little sigh of relief at which Lucie laughed. 'No wonder you're gasping, Martha, you were holding your breath like Anne here as she pushed.' Martha had not had a child herself but, unusually for a spinster, had acted as a gossip many times as a consequence of living with a midwife, and was always visibly relieved to hear the newborn's first cry. Mary passed the baby to Lucie – the midwife and her deputy's roles reversed – so that Lucie would attend the babe and Mary the mother. Lucie quickly twisted the navel string in two places and cut between them with a pair of scissors. Since the baby was a lusty man-child, Jane and Anne joked ribaldly with the new mother about asking the midwife to leave the navel string long enough for the boy's yard to grow a good size. Normally the best length was thought to be four or five inches for boys, less for girls so their secrets remained tight shut. Many myths and superstitions circulated about the properties of the cord, and like most midwives, Lucie was anxious that it should not drop on the floor while attached to the child, for then he would not be able to hold his water and would inevitably be a bed wetter.

Having cut the cord, Lucie applied a few ashes from a burned linen rag to the open end and sealed it with a fresh piece of linen.

'We don't want the cold getting into your belly, do we, young man?' she cooed to the baby, as she went through the necessary processes.

In the corner of the room the Jones's dog had recently whelped and was busily licking her pups to toilet them.

'Twould be much simpler if we could bring forth our babes as easily as the beasts do,' Jane said ruefully.

Lucie looked up.

'That's very true,' she said, 'but as we know, the curse from our first mother's sin means the burden of childbirth falls much more heavily on us.'

Her next task was to bathe the infant gently in warm wine, and then she stroked down his belly to encourage him to pass his first water, and examined his fundament before wrapping him in soft clothes. In swaddling him, Lucie made sure all his limbs were straight and in the right places. Having had the filth picked from his nose, the infant was deemed ready to be placed in his cradle.

Mary had also finished attending to Anne, who was quietly jubilant, looking forward to telling her husband he had another son. Due to Mary's fine care she had not torn or injured herself, so was likely to recover quickly.

'Who will suckle the baby while your good milk comes, Anne?' Mary asked.

'I will,' replied Jane Croft. 'My boy is four months old and I can easily nurse this new lad alongside my own for a couple of days. Anne will return the favour next time, I'm sure.'

Living hard-by one another in the weavers' cottages, the women of Warley Lane rarely had to resort to feeding water or asses' milk to their newborns while they waited for their good milk to come in.

'Ah yes, Jane, how does little Matthew do?' asked Lucie. 'He was a fine boy when we birthed him and I thought he was like to do well.'

'Oh, he is strong and very contented, Mistress Smith. Last month he was troubled with some sores on his breech. But Mister Smith sold me some unguent for sixpence for them, and now he's as happy as a king.'

'Sores? Did you change his clouts often enough? Piss and dung burns the skin, you know.'

'Yes, but you see the life I lead. I have the other children to care for, too, and I must help my husband with his work, so I did it as much as I could, but perhaps not often enough.'

'I know you are all busy women, with so much to do. But now Matthew is four months old you can unswaddle him to the waist and let his arms free. You can also start washing him twice a week, if you please to, and this will help his skin.

When you change him, remember to sing to him and dance him on your lap, to help his legs grow strong. You can set the older children to do that.'

Lucie noticed Jane bristling a little at the unsolicited advice. The younger woman had been dandling infants on her lap since she was a girl and evidently didn't take kindly to the insinuation she wasn't raising her latest boy properly.

'I'm sorry, Jane, I'm given to prating,' Lucie said. 'It's a bad habit, one I'll pray for the Lord's help in remedying. Your brood are happy and healthy, thanks to your care, and in future I'll wait to be asked before coming in with my five eggs.'

Jane laughed, 'No, you're right, Mistress Smith! Goodness knows you have seen all. I value your advice, but with money to earn and the big children to look after, I don't seem to have leisure for dancing little ones. Still, it's true they don't stay babes for long and I'll try to find more time for Matthew. Truth be told, I was ashamed to own he had sores. It made me feel like a slattern and a cruel mother.'

'Not at all, Jane,' reassured Lucie. 'Come here and have a hug, my girl. It's not easy without your own mother to turn to, I know.' Lucie had delivered Jane and knew her mother well. She had died of a cancer on her breast, many years ago; Lucie had helped Jane nurse her to the very end.

Mary motioned for Lucie to come over to the bed where Anne was now tucked in, sitting up and drinking a dish of broth that Martha had warmed. 'Do you wish to examine her,' asked Mary, 'or are you satisfied that I've done what was needed?'

'I'm satisfied if you are. Just let me observe the womb-cake, and check it came out in one piece. Then we've nought to do but take our leave.'

'Thank you with all my heart, Mistress Smith, and especially you, Mary,' said Anne. 'Sam will come to the shop to talk about the bill. We'll have to pay it week by week like last time, but you will get it all.'

'Don't trouble yourself with that now. We'll call back soon, but remember to send for us if you have any pains or fever in the meantime. When Sam comes up, he can tell me what name you've chosen and when the christening is to be. Mary and I will be there to stand in your stead as this lovely babe is welcomed into the family of the church, of course. I find it one of the pleasantest parts of my calling and I never tire of it. Thank God for your safe deliverance, Anne.' Lucie took off her apron and folded it up neatly. Passing it to Mary to bundle with the other childbed linen in need of washing, she cast an experienced eye over the room. All seemed in order and the new baby was sleeping contentedly, making adorable little snuffles as he did so.

'Now, see that you do rest. I remember last time you were up and about as soon as my back was turned, but for a childbed woman it's a matter of more haste, less speed! Indeed, no doing too much until we have you safely churched.' With that she motioned for Mary to step outside with the bundles, and made to follow her. 'Martha, you don't need to come home yet. We can do without you a day or two, if you want to stay here and help your cousin. No doubt Anne and Jane here will want to get back to their broods. Ned will come to collect my birthing chair later today, so pray have it wiped down and ready.' Lucie was about to step into the fresh air, but Anne Allen grabbed her arm, to stay her.

'Just before you go, Mistress Smith, I'm teeming again, with number three. I'll have to call for you in autumn, most likely November, by my reckoning.'

'Oh, that's good news, Anne. You know where to find me if you have any troubles,' Lucie replied with a warm smile. She walked into the communal courtyard at the back of the cottages to join Mary, and mused that as a skilled and well-reputed midwife, she had never lacked employment, that was for sure.

It was fully daylight now, and it had rained overnight, so Lucie was pleased she and Mary had taken the trouble to fasten their pattens back over their shoes. The women discussed their hope that the arrival of summer would mean drier streets, so that they would soon have a few months' freedom from these awkward appendages. The main street in Tupingham was cobbled but the rest were still dirt roads which soon became muddy after any downpour. It was hard to know what was worse: maintaining your balance on the cobbles in your pattens on High Street, or getting covered in dust, mud and other filth everywhere else.

'You know, Mary, you did a fine job there and I think it meet that you begin your ledger, ready for your licensing application in due course, with a line to say you laid the wife of Samuel Jones. I'm sure Anne will vouch for you.'

Mary smiled at this. Although only four and twenty, and thought by some to be young for the trade she was learning, she'd said that she knew it was her calling, and was resolved to succeed. 'That's pleasing to hear, Mistress Smith, but begging your pardon, I won't be able to write the list and Ned's unwilling to give any lessons. He's become so wayward of late that I'm not sure . . . '

To Lucie's relief, Mary's voice faded out, for it wasn't seemly for her to find fault with Mister Smith's apprentice in front of her. Lucie tactfully changed the subject.

'I always fear for weavers' wives while they are pregnant, Mary. 'Tis a dangerous trade for breeding women, especially when they're as short as Goodwife Jones. So much bending and stretching. Mind you, she never seems the worse for it and doubtless will be back at her loom in a couple of weeks, as she was last time.'

Both women knew poorer women didn't have the luxury of keeping to the woman's month like noble ladies, more was the pity.

Chapter Four

'This day I unhappily laid Farmer Bromfield's
Wife of a dead maid.'

Mistress Smith, accompanied by Mary, arrived at the small
farm an hour's ride outside Tupingham; the farmhand who
brought the message begging for her aid had come red-faced,
sweating, and anxious. His mistress, Jenny Bromfield, had
been in labour from Thursday past and it was now Monday.

Her attendant was a local hand woman, Mother Henshaw.
She appeared to be well past sixty years of age but still
active, and was one of the many untrained women who
worked informally as midwives throughout the country.
Lucie's path had crossed Mother Henshaw's many times over
the years, but since the hand woman mainly attended births
outside the town limits, they generally avoided one another.

An obviously annoyed Mother Henshaw told Lucie there
was nothing anyone could have done better and that there
was no call for Farmer Bromfield to have sent to the town for
Mistress Smith. She did, however, confirm that Jenny had not
felt the child move since Friday, and that it might have been
dead longer, judging by the smell in the room. Anger rose in
Lucie, and her guts griped into a knot of pain, causing her
to clutch her belly for a moment. She had been increasingly
troubled with this problem over the last few months at times
when her passions were high.

'And you didn't think to send for help? For me? For a chirurgeon, even, to get the child out?'

The hand woman had the grace to look somewhat abashed but defiantly snapped, 'I know what I'm about! Clearly the due time had not come for the child to be born.'

'We don't wait when the mother's life is so clearly in danger, you foolish woman! Unless you mean you think that God intends both lives be lost when the mother may yet live. Now move and let me see my patient.'

Lucie adjusted her tone and spoke to the exhausted mother. The pains had stopped and she was visibly ailing.

'I am sorry you had to hear that. You are in good hands now. I'll take over, with Mary here. God willing we'll have you out of this plight and like to recover, but you must follow my instructions without question.'

Her calm voice carried more conviction than her instincts suggested. It was in truth unlikely the woman would survive. Jenny nodded weakly.

Examining her patient, Lucie confirmed that she had all the signs of a dead baby. The blood and waters flowing onto the sheets were indeed thick, clotted and smelled appalling. Jenny's breath was as smelly, her skin pale, and her eyes sunken. A small grey pebble lay on her belly, so Lucie promptly removed it.

'It is far past the point where applying an eagle stone would be of any use,' she said, addressing Mary primarily.

'I've never known the eagle stone to fail,' muttered the hand woman.

The idea that a hollow stone with a smaller stone inside would encourage the womb to deliver was still prevalent in many parts, and Lucie wasn't at all against their use when appropriate, but this was now a case of extremity.

'If we give her some white hellebore powder to make her sneeze, would that hasten the labour?' asked Mary, greasing her hands with duck fat ready to examine the womb.

40

'She hasn't the strength left to push this child out,' replied Lucie. 'There's nothing for it but surgery, but there's no time to send for the chirurgeon. Mister Collins lives too far away.'

Mary, having conducted her examination, reported that the child was lying face up, rather than face down as it should be. She then anointed Jenny's secrets with some garden tansy juice, which Lucie had told her was the best thing she knew to help a woman birth a dead child. Jenny groaned at the examination, and her attendant mopped her brow. Mary then stepped aside, knowing this case was beyond her skills at present.

'Mary, you go one side of Jenny and you,' Lucie commanded, addressing Damaris Todd, Jenny's only gossip, 'are to take the other side. Now we need to raise her middle up with pillows. You two must hold her firmly so that when the child comes, she does not rise with it.'

A male voice broke into the tension: 'Let me assist my wife, Mistress Smith. I've been birthing heifers from a lad and nothing of this nature can appall me.'

With no time for debate, Lucie agreed that the strong farmer might indeed take the other side and help to hold his wife. She only conditioned that he should face his wife and speak to reassure her, without observing the operation. Next she arranged blankets over the mother's bottom half and took another which she beckoned to Mary and Mother Henshaw to hold up, blocking the sightline of the couple.

Lucie stepped up to the bed with her instruments and began her sad task. She used one end of her serrated iron hook to efficiently puncture the skull to reduce its size, and then the other end to remove the arms from the corpse with assured movements, being as gentle as possible under the circumstances. Removing the limbs one at a time and placing them on the sheets at the end of the bed, the smell from the corrupted humours flowing from Jenny's womb rose in the air. She wished there was another person in the room to light a chaffing dish with herbs to counter the stench, and

41

keep the company free of infection, and chastised herself for not thinking to do this before she started work. Still, in less than half an hour from her arrival at the farm, the babe was out, and all attention could turn to the poor mother. Lucie decided it was safe to apply the eagle stone now to encourage the after burden to come forth quickly, which it did presently. Although deteriorated, it seemed to have come out completely and was not likely to be a danger to the mother. Lucie offered up a quiet prayer of thanks for this mercy.

It was essential that Jenny had a medicated bath, so a large metal bowl was placed in front of the fire and filled with warm water. Lucie added bay leaves, sage, betony, lady's mantle and various other dried ingredients to the water. With a lightness of touch which belied his burley farmer frame, Farmer Bromfield lifted his wife from the bed and gently sat her in the soothing waters, while Mistress Todd held her shift up out of the way. She hadn't the strength to support herself, and Lucie was fearful of the outcome. After Jenny was bathed and tucked into a clean, dry bed, Lucie took a flask from her bag and instructed that Jenny was to be given a draught in wine, morning and night for the next few days. She also left an ointment, thick and greasy, which was to be applied to Jenny's privities daily.

Before Jenny had been moved, Mary had scooped up the little bundle containing the baby's body, and was attending to the dead infant with as much care as if it were a lusty child. Lucie was occupied in attending to the mother, but was so proud whenever she looked across the room to see Mary working with such compassion. The smell was terrible but Mary cleaned the corpse with great tenderness, singing a nursery rhyme to it under her breath, displaying a maturity well in advance of her years and experience, never once flinching. Farmer Bromfield asked what sex it was and Mary gently told him that it was a maid. Because of the way Lucie brought the body forth she knew Mary would not want the farmer to see the poor creature, so quickly spoke up

42

'We'll take her and see she has a proper burial,' she told him.

Even though midwives could baptise babies in cases of urgent need, it had not been possible that day as the child was long dead by the time Lucie and Mary arrived. This meant burial in consecrated ground was out of the question, but the sacred oath Lucie had sworn decades ago when she began to practise her trade had foreseen this and ordered that midwives personally saw to it that children born dead be buried discreetly in appropriate places where they would not accidentally be dug up by a dog or pig. Because of the actions of some unscrupulous or desperate folk, the oath specially forbade the disposal of these poor babes in the jakes, Lucie recalled with a shudder, her eye drawn to Mother Henshaw, probably unjustly, she chided herself.

'No,' said the farmer. 'I'll see the little scrap is buried in the meadow and I'll fashion a cross to her myself, if you give her to me.'

Mary had lain out the child as Lucie had taught her and had wrapped the creature in a sheet of waxed cerecloth so that she formed a tiny parcel, with her arms swaddled against the body as with any other child, and tied it securely at the top and bottom,so the father would not discover its true state. The young woman placed the bundle into her father's arms, and Lucie saw that the tear glistening in his eye as he trod heavily away to perform this solemn duty was matched by an identical one in the eyes of her deputy.

Lucie and Mary soon had set everything to rights and had done all they could; Jenny Bromfield's recovery was in God's hands. She had seen to it that a bundle of dried sage was now burning in the grate to purify the air. The signs were as promising as they could be. Lucie took a bottle of the dispersing medicine from her bag to be applied on a sponge to Jenny's dugs, to relieve her of the milk for which there was now no use. With a pang, Lucie remembered leaving a supply at Calstone Manor in happier circumstances so recently.

43

Lucie reminded the women that the room should be kept dark for three days, since daylight offended the eyes of a newly laid woman. Lucie had insisted the shutters were opened just to help her extract the child, but it wasn't best to leave them open now. After giving her usual instructions for the aftercare of her patient and a promise to come again later in the week with more medical supplies, Lucie took her leave.

Moments later in the yard, the farmhand helped Lucie mount Dapple, her trusty mare – a tricky process made even more difficult by the fact that, being a woman, she used a sidesaddle – meanwhile, Mary was bracing herself for the long trudge home alongside her mistress. Suddenly they saw the hand woman coming towards them with a sprightliness no one who had not witnessed it would have believed.

'Hey! Before you sneak off. Don't think that because you thrust in here with your irons and took over, that you're to have my fee. The Bromfields are my people and I shall be expecting payment. I've been here four days, not an afternoon like you. Whatever bargain you strike, don't think I'm going without my due!'

Lucie and Mary looked at one another, before Lucie adjusted her reins and replied curtly, 'As you will, Mother Henshaw, as you will. Although with a patient like to die in your care I don't know how you can think to ask these people for money. You should be ashamed.'

With that, she kicked the horse into action with her one free leg and trotted off, leaving Mary struggling to keep pace.

———————◆◆◆———————

It was almost dark when the women arrived back in Tupingham, and the streets were quiet. Lucie sent her deputy home ahead of her and walked the mare to the blacksmith's forge on Market Street where it was stabled. The blacksmith's lads would attend to it, used to the midwife being called out at all hours. Back at the Three Doves, Jasper had been asleep in his armchair in front of the

44

embers of the fire as he waited up for Lucie. Martha had thoughtfully laid out some ale and cold cuts of meat, with a dish of pease pottage under a linen cloth.

'Not a happy delivery then, wife?' Jasper enquired, as Lucie took off her cloak. 'Young Mary refused any supper, just washed her hands and face and carried a cup of ale up to her chamber.'

'Well, we saved the mother, God willing, so that is something. The child was long dead before we were called. The husband insisted on holding his wife while I brought out the child from her body. It is most unusual to have a man in the birthing room and this year with him and the physician at the Manor, and his man, that's three in all! Mary had to lay the baby out, a tiny maid child, and it's been a long day. She'll be worn out. But I wish she'd taken some food all the same; she needs to be mindful of her own health.'

Lucie washed her hands and then picked at her food. 'It gets no easier despite the years, Jasper,' she reflected. 'Of course, we accept God's will, though. Please pray with me for the little mite's soul and for the Bromfields. May they be blessed with a healthy child by this time next year.'

'Indeed, I will. Come here, my love. Never doubt that you are doing God's work.'

The next morning, Lucie sat at her desk in her chamber writing up her case notes and drafting her bill to send out to the Bromfields' farm. She resolved to send Mary on their horse in a few days' time to deliver the bill, which would give her occasion to observe Mistress Bromfield's progress. She fervently hoped there would be good news. Martha busied herself washing clouts and the instruments and making sure the midwife's bag was in order. Since she had worked for the Smiths nearly twenty years, she understood the routine and rhythms of the household, and few instructions were ever needed.

Mary was in the shop, a large room lined with shelves stacked with bottles, jars, boxes of herbs, spices, and other ingredients of the chemist's trade which she was running a dusting clout over, trying to keep busy. Jasper was behind the counter, busy conversing with a customer. Scents of rosemary, frankincense, and lavender filled the air. A cupboard on the wall was made up of many small drawers, and there were barrels of liquids in front of the wooden counter, which stood in the middle of the room. A huge pestle and mortar stood on a cylindrical stand, making it the right height for the apothecary's apprentice, who spent hours grinding ingredients. There was also a smaller pestle and mortar, some delicate brass scales, and a chaffing-dish on the top of the solid counter as well as an assortment of the items most regularly called upon, such as ointments-filled gallipots, and bottles of tonics, which Jasper always had ready mixed.

Ned was busy in the small anteroom off to the right, behind its own lockable door, where he was putting away the items of stock which had been delivered that morning. This room also served as a space for patients seeking a private consultation. It was where the expensive glass distillation cups were kept and it contained piles of papers, correspondence, and printed books along with Jasper's bulging recipe book and locked spice chest – for the valuable and rare ingredients, without which he would be unable to work.

'Here is your sixpence change, Goodwife Gilbert,' Jasper said, handing over a coin and a parcel to the local woman. Staying at the counter in the shop, he waited until the door closed behind his customer and then decided to engage Mary in conversation to attempt to draw her out of her reverie.

'I often reflect on how those girdles I manufacture to treat the itch are the main thing that keeps this roof over our head,' he commented, in a cheery tone. 'Like the one Goodwife Gilbert just took?' he added, not certain Mary was listening, but deciding to plough on nevertheless. 'I wonder at her and others not bringing in her last one to have it refreshed for a shilling and save herself sixpence from the cost. It is wasteful, to my way of thinking, to buy a new belt each time.'

As he stopped speaking, Jasper fancied he heard a stifled sob from behind him but decided it best to say nothing and let Mary give vent to her grief. She had attended only a few of these sad cases and it would be a good while before they ceased to be such a torment to her. Still, from what Lucie had said, Mary had discharged her duties well and even readied herself to examine the mother without being asked. Not something every apprentice-midwife would choose to do in such a case.

'Mister Smith?' Mary spoke after some time had passed in quiet companionship.

'Yes, my dear?'

'The ointment Mistress Smith left to anoint the secrets of Mistress Bromfield yesterday,' Mary said, her face flushing despite herself. 'Can I ask what it is made from? I mean, what should I be thinking of in a case like this?'

'You don't need recipes for unguents such as this; you can buy them from any druggist of good repute.'

'No, I know, but I should like to learn what it is comprised of. If you don't mind, that is?'

'Very well, let's see.' Jasper called through to Ned to bring him his enormous notebook from the back room. This tome was filled with recipes and Jasper was extremely methodical in his work, numbering each recipe, with a short description of its use, and adding each new entry to a list at the front of the volume so he could swiftly locate every one. Taking it from his apprentice, Jasper consulted the contents page, and then leafed through to find the right entry.

'It is not something I make often enough to recite from memory. Right, here we are... It's an unguent made from oil of lilies of the valley, mixed with ground earthworms and the boiled up flesh of a still-blind puppy. That's the base, at least, then it has to be pressed through a cloth and a few further ingredients added to the straining. Things like calamint, frankincense, and mastic. Then I mix it in enough wax for it to come to the right consistency.'

'So it lasts a long time, if you don't have call to mix it often?' Mary asked.

'Oh yes, it lasts a good while in a sealed jar. I make some once a year, at most. You would just ask for the ointment to help mend the womb after a dead birth and any apothecary would sell you a jar.'

'Thank you, Mister Smith. I am grateful that you take the time to talk of these things with me. Some chemists would chase an apprentice midwife out of the town for probing into their secret recipes.'

Jasper smiled to see signs of the young woman's natural cheery demeanour reappear.

Chapter Five

A bright July morning saw life in the apothecary's household keeping its accustomed order. On average, Mistress Smith and Mary Thorne attended a couple of births a month, in Tupingham and the country roundabout. Sometimes they came in clusters and sometimes, like now, there hadn't been a birthing for a few weeks.

Lucie had taken herself for a walk around the town to look in on some of the women whose time was coming soon, and who had already taken the precaution of securing her services. Arriving back in the Three Doves before dinner was due, Lucie glanced up at the sign that gave the shop and her home its name – marking it out as the apothecary's place. Having hung outside the shop ever since they began leasing it many, many years ago, the sign was due for renovation, for it looked faded and battered. It wasn't a priority, however, since the reputation of the Smiths' skills in medicine and midwifery spread by word of mouth: only strangers looked to identify the shop by the three doves. Still, it would be pleasant to have it looking bright again, with the doves' feathers sprucely white, instead of grey and bedraggled. Next year would be the thirtieth since she and Jasper were wed. Maybe she could commission a painter to make a new sign as an anniversary gift.

As she entered the shop, Jasper called to her and said, 'A gentleman named William Pardoe has been looking for you; he'd like a word when you are free, my dear.'

'Pardoe? I'm not sure I know that family. Are they customers of yours?'

'No, they are newcomers, as I understand. They have taken lodgings in the boarding house on Park Street, but I don't know what business they have here. He mentioned that he wanted to speak to you on the recommendation of his landlady, so perhaps his wife is big-bellied and looking to retain your services?'

'Most likely. I'll go there and seek them out after dinner.'

'No,' replied Jasper. 'He made a strange request. He bade me send young Ned to tell him what time was convenient for him to come back here and talk with you. We were to send a message that the medicines he had ordered had been mixed and were ready for him to fetch, but not to mention you at all.'

'Really? Most odd. But then, every one after his fashion. We've seen all manner of odd things in the last thirty years!'

With that they shut the shop and went through to sit at the large kitchen table and wait for Martha to serve dinner – she was preparing a household favourite, a dish of collared eels – after which they could dispatch Ned to inform Mister Pardoe, in the indirect manner he had chosen, that Mistress Smith would be home all afternoon and he could call in whenever he chose.

So it was that a very nervy young man – Lucie guessed he was about thirty – stood in the Smiths' kitchen a couple of hours later. He was dressed in the manner of a business man, with a modest periwig, and a doublet with plain breeches and buckled shoes, thus appearing to be a man of some means but not of the gentry: much like her own son, Simon, a printer and bookseller in London.

'The matter requires nice handling, Mistress Smith,' said the young man.

'It usually does,' replied the midwife. 'There is very little you could say that would shock me, so please speak freely. But Martha and Mary, if you could take yourselves off to tend the garden for a little while and leave Mister Pardoe and me

50

to our chat, that would probably be best.'

When the pair had left, Lucie pulled the door to the shop tight and dropped the latch so that no-one would disturb them.

'So what is on your mind, Mister Pardoe?'

'Well . . . the thing is . . . ' the young man began hesitantly, 'my wife and I have a child. A fine son who is two and already walks well. We, well I, and I believe both of us, would like more children, naturally, but my wife won't let me near her. She cries and cries if I try to, well, as Scripture says, give her due benevolence.'

William Pardoe blushed to the roots of his hair at speaking so freely to the midwife.

'I see. And why do you suppose this is? All was well before your son was born?'

'Oh yes, we were very fond of each other and dealt with each other kindly, but this is unbearable! I have been most patient, Mistress Smith. I waited while she nursed our son for a whole year, and not wishing to spoil the milk, didn't press her. But now he is weaned, we are no further on. I am at my wits' end.'

'I'm sure. Can you think of anything that happened that might account for this change in your wife's affections?'

'Begging your pardon, Mistress Smith, my wife insists she loves me deeply still: she just cannot submit to my embraces. She won't give me a reason, just cries at the thought, as I say, and I don't know what to do any more. One of the reasons we moved to Tupingham was I thought a change of air would remove her fears.'

'Did something go amiss during the pregnancy? Or during her travail?'

'She carried our son easily and bloomed throughout. I know she had a hard time birthing him, as he came forth arsewise, but more than that, I couldn't say. The secrets of the birthing chamber are not open to the likes of me, after all.'

51

'Oh, that can be hard for a first birth! But most women recover well and go on to have more children the right way round. I take it you'd like me to speak to your wife and see if we can resolve this matter?'

'Yes ... well, yes, if you think it would help? If my wife thinks I've been talking about her to strangers she might be hurt, but I don't know what else to do. The tavern keeper's wife is big-bellied, and he says he'll call on you when her time comes, and that you're the best midwife for miles around. I don't know if there's aught you could say or do, but I plucked up my courage to come and talk with you. I hope that wasn't too presumptuous?'

'Of course not. You can tell Mistress Pardoe you met me and Mister Smith in the shop and that I said I should like to come and meet her and that son of yours. I can walk back with you now if that suits?'

'Truly? Oh thank you, thank you, Mistress Smith.'

'Don't thank me yet, for I might not be able to get to the bottom of this, but I am willing to try.'

Lucie decided to dispense with her pattens, since the day was fine. She wrapped a light cloak around her shoulders, and set out with Mister Pardoe to meet his little family.

They had taken two rooms in Mister and Mistress Turner's house in Park Street. Mister Turner worked as a book-keeper for some local businesses, and Mistress Turner kept the house running beautifully, therefore she was at home or around the town most of the time. Mistress Smith and the Turners were of long acquaintance, so Mistress Turner saw nothing amiss in Lucie's arrival; in fact, she naturally assumed that the little family of Pardoes would be expanding soon, which pleased her well, since she loved children.

William showed the midwife to the rooms and they found the toddler playing while fastened to a small wooden close-stool.

'Ah, you are trying to train this young man to use a chamber pot, Mistress Pardoe? How goes it?' Mistress Smith enquired when the introductions were complete.

Isabelle Pardoe replied that the baby was doing well and as long as she sat him over the pot regularly they had but few accidents in the day, although at night time he still needed tying in clouts or he would bepiss the bed every night. Lucie reassured her that this was common, but if she became anxious she could ask Mister Smith for a cordial to soothe the child's bladder, and then he might start to have dry nights.

The toddler was a bonny, well cared-for young man and his mother obviously doted on him. Lucie explained that she had heard the couple were newly come to town, and thought she would take the opportunity to introduce herself, in case the couple needed advice about the baby, or the services of a midwife, in the coming months. At this, she noted the shadow that passed over Isabelle's face.

'It's a warm afternoon, my dear. Could I trouble you for a cup of small beer, if you have any to spare?'

'Of course, Mistress Smith. Forgive me, for I should have offered. You are our first visitor since we removed to Tupingham and my manners have quite deserted me. My husband says I am quite given over to the mulligrubs recently, and am no company. '

'Come now my love. I am sure the midwife here will agree with me that the fine country air in this town will have your spirits and cheer restored before we know it.' With this declamation, William took the opportunity to make his excuses and leave, claiming he had no interest in women's talk. He gave his son a little chuck under the chin before running down the stairs.

Isabelle poured them each a drink and offered the midwife a biscuit she had cooked on the griddle that morning. She also gave one to William junior to chew on while he was imprisoned on his stool, until he had soiled the pot. Shifting on her seat, Isabelle took a deep breath to try and keep her voice steady, before asking Lucie if she normally called on newcomers to the area, since she had not known midwives to do this where she came from.

'I think perhaps my husband asked you to call? Am I right?'

'Yes, my dear,' replied Lucie gently, 'but don't be hard on him: he longs for you to live together as a young married couple should. Can you tell me why you refuse him? There is absolutely nothing you could say to me, with my age and experience, that I won't have heard before.'

The younger woman struggled to hold back her tears but Lucie sensed that she understood the midwife was someone in whom she could indeed confide. Isabelle explained that it was impossible for her to countenance ever having another child and that, as much as she had wished that she and William could be blessed with a larger family, baby William's birth had rendered it out of the question. Lucie coaxed Isabelle to talk her through the story of her experience. The pregnancy had been unremarkable. As she described the start of her travail and how her throes came upon her, Isabelle noticed that the child on the close-stool had begun to doze. She lifted him off and pulled down his skirts, before gently laying him on her own bed and drawing the curtains around him so that he could nap undisturbed.

That done, slowly Isabelle revealed that she had been attended in her delivery by a number of gossips, including William's mother. They had all been very kind, and the baby had been in an awkward position, coming out backside first, but that wasn't the main cause of her troubles. The midwife had insisted that to widen 'the inner-gate', as she called it, she must necessarily widen 'the outer-gate'. Isabelle paused again, seemingly overcome by shame.

The truth finally dawned on Lucie when Isabelle blurted out that the midwife had stuck her hand into her fundament and opened it to at least the size of her palm to encourage the front passage to widen to ease the birth. Lucie was enraged. She had heard tales of unskilled midwives doing things like this, but never met a woman who had endured it.

'I assure you, midwives have absolutely no business meddling with the back part, unless it is to protect it from further injury, which wasn't the case here!'

Isabelle then told Lucie that when her labour began the midwife had torn the membrane at the opening of her womb: although it had taken a long time to heal, she was prepared for that. But she could never again endure to have her fundament torn asunder. She revealed that she had had a deal of trouble holding in her stools for some months after, and that the whole place had been bruised and swollen. She had felt humiliated in front of her attendants, and had since had harsh words with her mother-in-law, who did not know the full horrors Isabelle had endured, despite being present, and thought her daughter-in-law lingered over long in her recovery. In short, nothing would induce her to suffer that again.

Lucie explained that this was not proper practice, and neither she nor her deputy Mary would dream of subjecting a mother to such absurd and brutish dealings. She knew, though, that Isabelle's terrible sufferings had all but broken her heart. Lucie would need to win her trust before she would run the hazard of conceiving another child. She mulled it over for a few moments while she drank her small beer, then hit upon a plan. The next time she attended a birth in the town, she would ask if the mother would invite Isabelle to be a gossip: most women welcomed an extra pair of hands and friendly face. Seeing Lucie at work might restore the young woman's faith in midwives. Isabelle didn't seem entirely convinced, but agreed to think about it, at least, and the pair parted on friendly terms.

Chapter Six

'This day I laid the wife of George Dill, at the Black Bull.'

In the event there wasn't time for Isabelle Pardoe to come to the next delivery, for Peggy Dill the alewife went into labour that very afternoon. Up till now, Peggy had had quite an easy labour for all of her large and robust brood, but with each pregnancy she had become more corpulent, which made Lucie fear things might be different this time. The word that Peggy's time had come reached Lucie as she strolled back to the Three Doves on her way home from the Pardoes', for the Dills' cellar boy met her as she turned into High Street. She asked him to let the Dills know she was on her way and went to the shop to gather her things.

'Mary, make sure to let the butcher know I'll need a hare skin in the next couple of hours. Alewife Dill won't take long, I'll warrant,' she said as she was making her way out of the door. 'Then meet me at the Black Bull. You'll remember the steps to the living quarters are around the back on the outside and not through the alehouse, which saves you running through the noisy crowd. The drinkers will be making merry with knowing Peggy is labouring above the stairs.'

'The alewife's in travail again, is she?' remarked Jasper. 'Send word if you need any drafts mixing, for if I remember right, she complains a great deal of her pains.'

'Ha! Yes, she does! One of these days, she'll bring the alehouse down about our ears! She should thank God for giving her such an easy time of it, compared with so many women.' Lucie was, of course, thinking about her chat with Isabelle. Having a first-born come breech down would be hard enough without an incompetent midwife adding to her troubles.

Peggy was tramping around her bed-chamber when Lucie arrived, trying to walk the pains away, while all the time drawing heavily on her ever-present clay pipe of tobacco.

'Oh, Mistress Smith, I can't believe we're here for this again! I'll tell you what: if George even thinks to look at me again I'll chop off his yard with my best kitchen knife. You see if I don't!'

'From what I've heard, Peggy, matters are quite the other way about and you can't help but jump on the poor man whenever the chance presents!' one of her gossips remarked.

'Well, a woman needs her due benevolence, ain't that right, Mistress Smith? And as God knows, working in this alehouse from dawn to dark and raising this endless herd of kids, I've little enough time for pleasures out of door.'

'Mother!' exclaimed Lucy Dill, Peggy's eldest daughter, now in her teens and acting as a gossip for her mother for the first time.

The girl was named after Mistress Smith, who had delivered her, like all the Dill children. For all the girl had been raised and now worked in a alehouse, in often rowdy and even bawdy company, Lucy had grown quite prim, and so very unlike her own mother.

Peggy laughed and then let out a long groan as another of her throes took hold.

'They are almost making me toes curl, Mistress Smith. You'll give me something to ease them?'

'Not until Mary has examined you and seen what's what, I won't,' was Lucie's answer. 'Come lie on the bed, lift your skirts and we'll soon see how far things have gone.'

Mary had greased her hand and arm with oil of almonds and, examining Peggy, found that things were pretty well advanced.

'There won't be any need for drafts to help you rest, Peggy. This baby will be out in the next hour or so, and you'll be sat up having your supper before night.'

Peggy rolled about on the straw mattress as if in unendurable agony, yet still found breath to demand young Lucy run down and fetch a fresh tobacco pipe. Mary asked Lucie if she could have a word apart, and reported that the alewife's substantial frame had made the examination difficult, and that she feared the baby might be suffocated in the birth. They had last been here only three years before, and both remembered Peggy birthing on the chair, but neither thought it would be safe this time.

'Right, Peggy! If this baby is to come out presently, you'll have to give birth in a grovelling posture. Come on, over you go,' Lucie ordered.

The gossips helped Peggy to get on all fours, while Lucie considered what to do with her namesake, who had just returned from her errand and now was being berated for not having asked her father to light the new pipe ready for her mother to drink from immediately. Lucie did not want the girl frighted into perpetual virginity by the sight of her mother's broad backside, with the humours and other substances of birth in open view.

'Lucy, you stay up near your mother's head and mop her brow when she needs it, will you?'

Mary re-examined Peggy. 'Ah, that's much better,' she reported. 'The passage is clearer and the head is well down. A few strong pushes and this baby will be here.'

True to Mary's prediction, within the hour, a large and lusty boy was safely delivered into the world. Peggy immediately ordered Lucy downstairs to tell the tapster of his new son's safe arrival and to demand he bring up a flagon of celebratory groaning ale. Against the midwife's command, Peggy drank down a tankard full without pausing for breath. She then demanded another, as well as a fresh tobacco pipe, which she claimed would speed her recovery. Despite themselves, Lucie and Mary enjoyed the convivial surroundings and joined in, taking a cup each to toast the new babe. Even accounting for the aftercare and the merrymaking, the midwife and her deputy were walking home by eight of the clock. A good result.

'Another one for your list of cases, Mary. Well done indeed! If you take over the task of looking in upon Peggy over the next few days, we can then set it down that you know how to tend mothers in their upsitting, after having their babies.'

When they got back to the Three Doves, they found Martha had laid out a cold supper as normal, but there was no sign of her.

'She'll be at the Joneses, I expect,' Lucie remarked.

Lucie bade Mary serve the supper while she popped into the scullery to put the various cloths and bands from the labour into cold water to soak. Stepping back into the kitchen, Lucie let out a squeal of delight as she clapped eyes on the tall young man she saw standing before her.

'Simon! Simon, I can hardly believe my eyes! Why ever didn't you write to let us know to expect you? Oh, never mind! Come here and give your old mother a hug.'

Simon was a handsome young man of seven and twenty, his looks only slightly marred by the marks left on his face and hands by a childhood bout of smallpox. He was fashionably dressed in the latest London fashions. He wore a long wig in the court style, and was, as his mother said, 'a sight for sore eyes indeed.'

'Does your father know you are home?'

'He does, yes. We spoke this afternoon. That's when he told me you were engaged at the alehouse and bade me call in again later.'

'Call in? This is your home,' replied Lucie, with a break in her voice.

Simon looked down and muttered, 'I've taken a room at the Boar.'

Despite herself, Lucie approved her son's good sense in choosing Tupingham's best coaching inn, rather than one of the rowdy taverns, and stroked his sleeve, signalling that she understood.

'I think it best,' Simon continued, looking directly at her now. He took her hand from his arm and squeezed it in his larger one. 'You know Father and I find it hard to stay on good terms. This afternoon, I had been in the shop scarce two minutes, when he took exception to my new periwig.'

Jasper wore his hair naturally, shorn at the collar, without a periwig at all, let alone an array of past-shoulder-length curls like Simon's.

'Well, it is a little bold, I admit, and here in the country we don't care for the fashions, do we?' Lucie's tone was conciliatory. 'I can't say I am not sad you're not staying here, but as long as I have your company while you're back, I'll content myself.'

'He said he hadn't set me up to be a tradesman in the city of London to have me come back a town fop,' said Simon, with a rueful smile.

'Oh dear,' Lucie replied, while thinking that Jasper would not be the only observer to look askance at Simon's travelling suit with his frilled shirt cuffs: true, such attire was not unknown in Tupingham, but it was more likely to be worn by the nobility and gentry in the great houses round about than by an apothecary's son in the kitchen of the Three Doves.

'You'll eat with Mary and me, won't you?' Lucie asked when she had finished hugging her boy.

'No, I've supped at the inn, but I'll tell you all the latest city news while you both eat.'

Simon told the midwives how London was emptying, as everybody who could was fleeing to the country to escape the contagion, for the plague was back and with unprecedented severity. He had passed homes marked with the cross, warning people not to enter. The King had ordered playhouses and all other public entertainments to be closed on the fifth of June, and since theatre was a passion of Simon's, he now found London a much duller place than before. There was not much trade around so he and Mister Miller – his former employer and now, thanks to the Smiths' investment, his business partner – decided to shut their print house and follow suit.

'The pest is taking so many souls that I can't fully describe the sights and smells all around,' he said. 'Everyone looks so mournful.'

Lucie later learned from Henry, the elderly neighbour who often helped her in the garden, that what had prompted Simon's final decision to leave the city was the sight of a naked corpse, dead of the plague, and left in the street like a dead dog. He had encountered it as he walked home from a happy afternoon at his good friend Robbie's house. He was far from the only one fleeing, as he'd described to Henry just how long the queue was at the Lord Mayor's office to obtain a travel pass and the certificate of health you now needed to leave town. Simon had queued for over three hours in the summer heat with other anxious citizens, during which time rumours ran wild about how even with the certificates, some inns wouldn't admit Londoners, and how turnpikes had been set up to stop travellers altogether at several points. Simon could vouch for the first part of this claim, having himself seen people turned away, but his stage-coach had not been stopped at any unusual turnpikes, thankfully.

Lucie gasped. 'Oh, Simon! Why in God's name didn't you leave sooner?'

She had lost her other three children, Sarah, Hannah and Peter, to a smallpox outbreak many years before. To have buried three children made the thought of the plague carrying off her remaining child all the more terrifying. Simon explained that the contagion had not long arrived in his district and there had been hopes it would pass by their neighbourhood.

'The King has done all he could to limit the disease. He has issued many orders, like closing the playhouses. And a couple of months ago he sent orders to the College of Physicians, that they should review the old recommendations for treating the pest and see if they could be improved upon. They brought out a new book presently: we didn't get the contract to print it, but I made sure to buy a copy for Father.' He reached into his pocket and brought out the book, published in May, entitled: *Certain Necessary Directions, As well For the Cure of the Plague, As for Preventing the Infection: With Many easie Medicines of small Charge, very profitable to His Majesties Subjects.*

'I brought you these sheets, Mother, too, so you and Father could see what was going on.' Simon took out a number of printed papers, known as Bills of Mortality, which were reckonings of the number of deaths across the parishes, together with the cause of each. The deaths from pestilence outnumbered all the others by ten to one.

'His Majesty's fled by now, I expect?' Mary asked.

'Oh, yes, the King and his court repaired to Salisbury a couple of weeks ago. Soon only the poorest, who have no choice, will remain.'

'And who will attend them in their sufferings?' Lucie asked.

'The Lord knows. Physicians, chirurgeons and apothecaries are flying for their lives. But a few have stayed behind. There's Thomas O'Dowde, for one, he's one of those that call themselves chemical physicians and he's still working in St Clement Dane. He's even one of the King's Grooms of the Chamber, so could have been safe at Salisbury, but he makes a great show of staying and serving even the poorest in the parish. Says it's his Christian duty. I believe Father knows him? They say he has his daughter Mary working with him now, and that she's as good a physician as her father.'

'Really!' cried Lucie. 'I believe your father knows of him,

for he was an apothecary back then, but he would have been on the other side in the late troubles, so not a near friend any more. I'm not sure we even knew he had a grown daughter.'

Mary interrupted to say that as much as she loved hearing about London and all the gossip, she was tired from the hard work of delivering Peggy Dill that afternoon, and was ready to retire. Lucie and Simon continued to chat, exchanging news for a good hour longer, before Jasper came out of the shop, where he claimed he had been profiting from the long summer evenings to get aforehand with his work.

It was just starting to get dark, so he lit a candle and lodged it in a crack in the wood of the door frame. Without looking directly at the young man, Jasper announced gruffly: 'Well, it was good to see you, son, but I am sure you will want to be getting back to your bed at the inn now.' Simon dutifully noted his cue to leave and rose, accepting without question his father's dismissal.

'Come back tomorrow!' Lucie implored.

'I certainly will, Mother,' he replied, kissing her on the cheek. 'Goodnight, Father,' he added with a nod, as he retreated through the shop and into the night.

'Pray try to stay on good terms with our son while he is back at home, Jasper, I beg you,' Lucie said when Simon was safely on his way. 'Goodness knows we see little enough of him. He brought you this new book of cures for the plague. 'Tis published by the College of Physicians and is given out free to those in need, he says. A great act of charity.'

'I think you'll find me properly paternal, wife,' replied Jasper tersely. 'He's my son, too, and for all his faults, I'm not unhappy to have him home a while. It is indeed a charitable thing to give the book *gratis*, to stop the poor falling into the hands of quacks and poisoners, but he might have given me the book himself when he called this afternoon.'

'He probably had it packed in his trunk,' Lucie said, again conciliatory, while thinking, perhaps if you hadn't rebuked him about his dress as soon as he stepped into the shop, he would have.

'I hope he's not implying my cures are old fashioned,' muttered Jasper, always quick to take offence at anything Simon did.

Lucie ignored that. There was nothing profitable to be achieved by challenging him. 'He brought these Bills for us, too, Jasper. They show the shocking number of plague deaths and also what else Londoners are dying from. Perhaps it is worth getting as many preparations ready as we can in case, God forbid, the pest visits us in Tupingham.'

'A good notion,' Jasper replied, glancing at the documents. 'These figures are like nothing I've seen before! The King is fled, I take it? I heard some talk in the coffeehouse, but I suppose Simon would know for certain.'

'Oh yes, they are repaired to Salisbury, he says. London is quite desolate by all accounts.'

'I'm not surprised the court has fled. No doubt they were the first to run,' Jasper said cynically. 'I have to say, though, that my mind misgives me. I think you're right to suggest we make up as many remedies and preventatives as we can, in case it spreads this far. I'll read this book and thank Simon for it. Not that there is any true remedy once the plague has fully taken hold of a patient, but we must try something, I suppose. I'll refer this matter to the other aldermen and see if they wish to call an extraordinary council meeting. Perhaps we should look to locking the town gates, at least at night.'

As a respectable tradesman and pillar of the community, Jasper had served many terms on the town council, so Lucie knew his advice would be taken seriously.

'A good thing our boy came home to warn us, I'm sure you'll agree, husband.'

Jasper grunted in agreement and declared it time for bed.

Chapter Seven

It was now high summer, Lammastide, when all those who could made themselves available to work in the fields to help bring in the wheat harvest. Simon had decided to work on the land too, not only because he was free, but to help him drive the worries of the plague in London from his mind. Even though he had been home only a week or so, Lucie knew he missed the bustle of London and felt out of place in the small town where he had not spent any length of time since his teens, and therefore had a lot of pent up energy to spare.

Lucie was serving in the shop, although it was quiet, in order that Jasper could attend to correspondence in the back room. He presently wandered into the shop to consult Lucie about one new missive, which was from a worried father asking for advice about his daughter's lack of courses and her overall lethargy. The writer was concerned because she was now seventeen and it was normal for girls to flower into womanhood a few years earlier than this. Lucie agreed with Jasper that the best reply was to send a bottle of steel waters to give the girl as a tonic, and to advise that if that did not resolve matters, then the father should send for a barber-surgeon to have the girl let blood from her ankle to encourage the blood to flow down her body, fill her womb and allow her monthly courses to start.

Since it was a fine day and the shop was quiet, Lucie offered to walk down to the postmaster's office to drop off his mail, rather than send Ned, but Jasper explained that he would to run the errand personally as he needed to pay a visit to Alderman Robbins to discourse on a council matter. When he returned less than an hour later Jasper wore a troubled expression. He held a package which had been waiting at the postmaster's, addressed to Lucie. It looked like a matter of some importance. Jasper told Lucie of his shock when, turning it over, he saw it bore the King's own seal, and how the package had clearly piqued the curiosity of the postmaster, who'd raised a quizzical eyebrow as he noted the apothecary's amazement.

'What in the name of God could His Majesty want with you?' he asked Lucie sharply, his abruptness exposing his disquietude at this turn of events.

Lucie was as surprised to see the King's seal as her husband had been.

'I wonder if we should wait for Simon to come home before we open it,' she said, before the cross look on her husband's face made her wish she could bite back the suggestion. Jasper insisted it was better to determine the contents immediately rather than spend the rest of the day in puzzlement. He locked up the shop and then he, along with the whole household – Martha, Mary, and young Ned – all gathered around the kitchen table as Lucie broke open the seal. Inside was a small leather purse and a note. It read:

> *To Mistress Smith, Midwife, Wife to Mister Jasper Smith, Apothecary, at the sign of the Three Doves, Tupingham*

> *Salisbury, August 1, 1665*

> *His gracious Majesty the King commands me to write to convey His thanks for your kind ministrations to His GodDaughter, the Lady Eleanor Calstone, in Childbed. He would have made this Acknowledgement earlier, if the Court had not*

*prudently retired to Salisbury in light of the great
Contagion sadly spread so far throughout London
and other parts of His Realm.*

*His Majesty wishes you to know that he has heard
nought but good Reports from the Countess of
Northerton, at which He is well pleased.   He
understands well the Part Midwives play in looking
after the Women of the Nation.   In Witness of His
Gratitude, and for the Sake of the Child, for whom
He is also pleased to stand as Godfather, He
commands me to offer the enclosed Token of his
Approbation, to wit 2l. for your Services and 5s. in
respect of the Service of your Deputy.*

*Your obedient Servant,
Joseph Williamson,
Under-Secretary of State for the South to His Majesty
King Charles II.*

Jasper looked up at his wife, with a scathing expression
which suggested his choler was rising.

'Prithee, who might this countess, no less, who's gone
about commending you to His Majesty be?'

Lucie clasped her hand over her mouth, 'Oh my goodness!
That will be Lady Eleanor's mother, Lady Margaret. She is
the Countess of Northerton. You remember, from the birth I
attended at Calstone Manor in spring. She barely spoke to me
the whole time, and now this! Who'd have thought it?'

Jasper snorted incredulously.

'Well, here's a wonder. His Lordship has not yet settled our
account for your services and yet His Majesty has supplied a
reward. Well, well, well. Did you know how close the Manor
was to the King when you were working there?'

'I knew his Lordship was one of the grooms of the King's
chamber, but I hadn't the least notion His Majesty stood
godfather for Lady Eleanor, nor that he would do it again for

69

baby Charles. Goodness! He must have had a proxy for the christening: the whole town would be bursting with the news if he had attended in person.

'Indeed, the coffeehouse and taverns would be speaking of little else, I'm sure, not that he'd have had such a warm reception here,' Jasper replied. 'I'd advise you to keep your distance from the whole pack of them; we don't want to be keeping company with courtiers and the like. No good will come to ordinary folk like us.'

Lucie ignored her husband's comments. The King had been back on his throne for five years now, and while she knew Jasper retained some hopes that the King's new reign might not be the end of the matter, it seemed clear to her that the restoration was obviously God's will, so they must make the best of things. And, in any case, as Jasper knew very well, the midwife's oath did not allow her to pick and choose her patients. A childing woman in need must be helped, and that was that.

'Oh, Mary,' she cried, 'here is your present from the King!' She opened the drawstring on the purse and took out the silver crown piece meant for her apprentice, along with two bright golden guineas for herself, each one newly minted, and stamped with a tiny African elephant, to remind the King's subjects where the gold came from. 'What will you do with it?'

'Oh dear, I'm not sure,' Mary answered in a flustered tone, 'but I can't wait to tell my mother when I see her next!'

'Why don't you go tomorrow, dear? It is to be the fast day after all,' Lucie said kindly, thinking that, since Mary's parents lived in a village about a ten-mile journey away, she could get there in a just a few hours' brisk walking. 'This is not something that happens every day, and if you care to, you may take the letter to show your mother and father.' At church the previous Sunday, Dr Archer had read out a royal proclamation that on the first Wednesday of August, there was to be a day of public fasting throughout the land to atone for the populations' collective sins that had brought the plague upon the realm. 'Everyone will be staying at home, quietly thinking on their sins, and while babies are no respecters of proclamations, we are not expecting any births this week, and the shop will be closed for the day.' She paused for breath. 'So if you leave at dawn you can walk home in time to greet your parents as they rise. We'll sup heartily tonight in advance of the fasting tomorrow. You may stay the night with them and walk back here as soon as you have broken your fast on Thursday.'

Jasper had been seated at the table, his fists clenched, as his wife's excitement caused her tongue to run away with her. As she at last stopped speaking, he banged the table and stood up, his eyes glistening in temper.

'While addressed to you,' he snapped, 'this Stuart money came into *my* house. I'll thank you not to assume I am content for you to accept it. Since the Calstones have not yet condescended to pay for the delivery, if we do keep it, then it will have to be used against that charge before anything else. I'll make my decision later and let you both know.'

With that he stalked back to the shop, beckoning Ned to follow him, for, as fond of Mary as he was, Lucie knew he did not hold with doling out random holidays, and she felt quite fearful that her prating had increased her husband's ire. She had recently prayed hard to cure her of this habit, but it seemed to no avail. She saw her husband catch Ned's eye as he chided, 'Don't you think on holidays, my lad! You'll be spending tomorrow with me and Mistress Smith, in quiet prayer and reflection.'

'Don't worry about the master,' Lucie said to the women with more confidence than she felt. 'He'll come round. His bark is always worse than his bite. And Martha, you must share in our good fortune! After all, you laundered the clouts and prepared my bundle, as you do for all births. I'll give you five shillings from my coins, so you are the same as Mary, and I suppose I'll give young Ned a shilling for his errand running or we'll never hear the end of it.'

'That is kind of you, but maybe we should think of a gift of some item Ned will need when he completes his indenture, rather than giving him the coin, Mistress Smith,' replied Martha. 'What do you think you'll do with the rest of your reward?'

Lucie was somewhat puzzled by Martha's comment but could see the sense in starting Ned gathering his own tools of the apothecary trade. Unlike her housemaid, she didn't know the extent of Ned's carousing, or she would never have suggested supplying him with a coin which would not last long when he got to the alehouse with it.

'I'm not sure yet, but think I might have a little maggot in my brain,' she replied with a smile. She was thinking that she would strike a bargain with a painter not just for renewing the decoration on the shop sign, but painting the frames, door, and timbers to give the shop a general smartening too. Ever since she'd determined to have the sign re-done as a present for Jasper for the thirtieth anniversary of their wedding next year, the idea had pleased her more and more, and now, thanks to the King's gift, it might just be possible to have a full refurbishment of the shop front to set the sign off well. She would mention it to Simon when he called in next.

The following morning, the family rose early and made their way to church with the rest of the parish. The Rector of All Hallows, the Reverend Dr Ralph Archer, was in fine form. He intoned prayers for the Royal Family, at which Jasper visibly bristled, only to relax a little when he realised that the Rector was not mealy-mouthed when condemning what he and many others saw as the profligate lives of those who lived in and around the Court. He explained that the comet God had sent the previous December was meant to serve as a caution and yet the people and their leaders had not taken heed. The comet was a solemn one, faint and slow moving, so its meaning would not be missed. Hadn't their own apothecary, Mister Smith, sitting here, seen it with his own

72

eyes, and told them how it went? Next, he launched into a blistering sermon reminding his congregation that plagues, like fires, famines and floods, were sent by God as punishment for the sins of the nation. He referred to a passage about the whore of Babylon, Revelation 18.8, in the course of his terrifying diatribe: *'Therefore shall her plagues come in one day, death, and mourning, and famine; and she shall be utterly burned with fire: for strong is the Lord God who judgeth her.'* He left the congregation both terrified and determined to do better, his task well done. The church bells would peel throughout the day to remind parishioners of the fast day, and the most devout would be back at noon and then again for evensong. Most, though, would feel that by attending a full service on a Wednesday morning they had paid their dues and were free to go about their day – albeit in a very quiet way, since the shops and alehouses would be closed.

After the family had returned home, Jasper and Lucie turned their attention to the plague preparations they had discussed the previous day. So far, Tupingham was mercifully free of the pest, but they were rightly worried. One recipe in the book Simon had brought home caught Lucie's eye. It was an electuary for "women with child, children and such as cannot take bitter things". She told Jasper she was wondering whether all her teeming women and those with young children should be taking this medicine as a preventative. Jasper agreed it would be prudent to make up a stock of it at least, and read the recipe aloud, making a mental note of what ingredients he had to hand and what he would need to order in:

Take Conserve of Red-Roses, Conserve of Wood-Sorrel, of each two ounces, Conserves of Borage, of Sage-flowers, of each six drams, Bole-Armoniack, shavings of Harts-horn, Sorrel-seeds, of each two drams, yellow or white

73

Saunders half a dram, Saffron one scruple, Syrupe
of Wood-Sorrel, enough to make it a moist Electuary;
mix them well, take so much as a Chestnut at a
time, once or twice a day, as you shall find cause.

He had most of the necessary ingredients at hand, so could,
with well-chosen substitutions, make a version of the recipe
straight away. These little balls of medicine would be easy
enough to wrap in brown paper and store in batches, so he
and Ned set to work. It was hard working while fasting, but
somehow the tension between their bodies' needs and the
demands of their task helped the pair remain intent on the
purpose they were mixing their cures. They also prepared
some bouquets of dried herbs that people could burn to
fumigate their homes, one of the popular recommended
preventatives. Jasper knew, from past infestations, that once
plague got anywhere near Tupingham there would be a high
demand for fumigations.

Tucked into the back of the medical book was a six-page
pamphlet Simon must have bought alongside it: *Directions
for the Prevention and Cure of the Plague fitted for the Poorer
Sort.* Jasper flicked through it and considered the advice to
abstain from boiled herbs such as cauliflower, cabbage,
coleworts, spinach and beet. He was sceptical about this,
since the latest thinking was that the plague was a disease
bred in the earth and breathed in as a poisonous gas in the
air. The pamphlet also contained behavioural advice, such as
avoiding alehouses and other abstinence, which Jasper did
agree was proper in times of public crises like the one they
were living through.

Lucie had allowed Martha to go home with the Joneses,
her kin on Warley Lane, after church. She would be of help
there. Those living hand-to-mouth in the weaving
community could not afford the luxury of spending a day off
in contemplation and would want to do some work. Indeed,
one wag from the farming community had muttered, as the

74

Rector chid the congregation about famine coming from God, that if they were forced to waste a perfect summer day around Lammastide on prayer, and it rained after and spoiled the harvest, then a famine would indeed be caused by God and his representative on earth, the King. If she were a betting woman, Lucie would be willing to wager that Martha's small bonus would find its way to helping the Joneses and probably buying a new apron for the Mallet girl, the tanner's disabled daughter, in whom Martha took an interest. The midwife decided to spend her afternoon in her garden. The herbs, flowers and shrubs which grew there supplied many of the needs of the apothecary shop, and she had become quite expert over the years. Lucie spent a few minutes looking over the bountiful plot, lost in memories of past summers, and how the garden had evolved under her attention.

Outside of the birthing chamber, it was in her garden that Lucie felt at her most spiritual. God had created plants to cure every ailment: of that she was sure; the garden deepened her faith at every turn. She had such a lovely, quiet, and productive couple of hours weeding, watering, and cultivating that she almost felt guilty that her afternoon had been so pleasurable when she was meant to be praying specifically for relief of those poor souls afflicted with the pest.

A sudden clatter as Henry accidently kicked a pail broke Lucie's reverie. Lucie paid him a few pennies a week and he made sure the garden was in good order, no matter how busy she became with her mothers. That afternoon they had worked in such companionable silence she had almost forgotten he was there.

As she returned to the kitchen with some of the garden produce, Simon appeared and took the basket from her. She didn't ask how he had spent his afternoon, but back in the country shirt and breeches he had worn for helping on the land this past few days, he looked like her boy again, and so very much healthier than when newly arrived from the city. Taking the opportunity to chat to Simon on his own, she raised the subject of her windfall from the King and how she was resolved to spend it on an overhaul of the shop front. Simon agreed that this was a superb scheme. More than that, he said that if she waited until the harvest was gathered in, he would seek a journeyman painter through the guild of painters and stainers. He would obtain a quotation for painting the woodwork for her, and take charge of refashioning the sign himself. He'd always loved to see pictures, as well as making them, and had often sketched in the margins of his school books, to the master's chagrin. Since he had been home, Lucie had seen him doodling in the wax tablet he carried in his pocket. The tablet was very finely bound with engraved leather and the attached writing implement he used to mark the wax was almost certainly silver. When she had complimented him on the fine object, Simon had muttered something about it being handed down from a friend he'd made in London, and she had decided it better to let the matter drop.

She was sure that his artistic nature would mean he would find an expert sign-writer and produce something beautiful. The fly in the ointment was that Jasper must never know the money used to titivate his shop was the King's coins, but they'd cross that bridge when they came to it. Jasper had not mentioned the money since his outburst yesterday, and Lucie knew from experience that he was quick to anger, especially where the monarchy was concerned, but that he was unlikely to carry out his threat to make her return the money. His rage usually died away as quickly as it rose.

Chapter Eight

'This day I laid the wife of Joseph Bennet of twins.'

The harvest had mostly been gathered in and the nights were drawing in earlier and earlier. Simon appeared to be in a low mood when he called in to see his mother.

'What is on your mind, son?'

'Nothing, really, mother,' he replied, looking a little ashamed of himself. 'I'm just a bit mopish about missing this year's waygoose feast.'

'This year's what?' asked Lucie, wondering if her ears were playing tricks on her.

Simon explained that in the printing trade, around St Bartholomew's Day, there was always festivity and feasting in the open air, as the master would treat his apprentices to a party. He hadn't the least notion of where the name came from, but the event was an important marker in a publisher's year, signalling the end of summer and the start of working by candlelight in the print house. After completing his apprenticeship and then several years as a journeyman printer, this was to be only the second year that Simon would have jointly hosted the waygoose celebrations, as one of the owners of the business. After a month at home, he was missing his London life sorely. It wasn't the same, but Lucie suggested they hold their own waygoose in the garden.

'There's no need, mother, truly. I only wish I was back at home in London,' Simon said.

Without being aware, Lucie clutched her hands to her chest. She remembered happier times, when the Three Doves bustled with children's laughter and tears in equal measure. The children played with their football in the street out the front, with Hannah matching the boys kick-for-kick. They'd all been prone to teasing Simon for being a home-bird who much preferred sitting by the hearth with his pen to playing long outside. Home then meant her, but as hard as it was, she knew Simon's heart was now in London. There, he was surrounded by people with similar interests and he had the theatre, which he adored, on his doorstep.

'Well, perhaps we could do something together anyway?'

They resolved to take their dinner sitting on the banks of the river. Martha and Mary were occupied in the garden, stitching the linen drawstring pouches that the apothecary used for supplying remedies and applying treatments. There was no point inviting Jasper along since he would be off to his coffeehouse after dinner, and would stay for a couple of hours as usual. Jasper disapproved of alehouses, but had become very taken with his afternoons in Hearne's coffeehouse, drinking dishes of coffee or hot chocolate in the company of other townsmen. They read the news sheets, shared gossip, and put the world to rights. Jasper found it very convivial, not least because coffeehouses were only frequented by men, although of course women served and cleaned them. As an apothecary who was married to a midwife, Lucie knew Jasper often felt surrounded by women's business, so a penny a day most days to take a dish of coffee and enjoy the company of like-minded men was good value, for her as well as him. These fellows prated on all day about world affairs, with the King's sea war with the Dutch and the financial toll this was having on the nation as a familiar topic, on a par with the latest news of the Great Contagion. Despite this, Jasper never invited Simon to join him, much to Lucie's chagrin.

Just as the pair were packing bread, cheese, and a pigeon pie into a basket, Ned ran into the kitchen to say that the wife of Joseph Bennet was at her time and needed the midwife.

'Oh son, I'm sorry,' Lucie said, marking her son's Adam's apple rise and fall as he masked his disappointment. His mother being called away whenever he or his siblings were trying to have her attention had been a regular feature of Simon's childhood. She knew her children had resented it then, sometimes wailing when they were very small, but now, a grown man, Simon understood his mother had both a calling and an obligation. A dutiful son, he returned the pigeon pie to the cupboard as she hurried away.

———————⊷●◆●⊶———————

By the time Lucie and Mary arrived, Barbara Bennet's labour was well underway. Her pangs were close together and her breathing shallow. Since the birth had been anticipated for this week, Ned had delivered the birthing chair to the Bennets' several days ago, and so with Barbara seated in it, Mary oiled her hand and examined the labouring woman. She found the womb wide open and ready for the birth. Something didn't feel quite right, though, so she asked if Lucie could also touch her. Barbara winced at the idea of a second examination. She was standing up now, supported by her women, legs wide apart and groaning with pain. Lucie tried to persuade her to go on the bed so that an examination could be more effective, but she was adamant that she needed to be upright. Lucie would have been happier if Barbara lay on the bed but she didn't believe it was the midwife's place to compel women to a particular place against their inclinations, unless it was a matter of life and death.

Nevertheless, Lucie successfully coaxed Barbara back onto the chair, where she soon let out a long moan.

'They don't call it a groaning chair for nought, do they, my dear?' Lucie smiled sympathetically while she waited for the pang to end so she could perform her examination. This suggested that the baby's head was lodged on the mother's pubic bone. It took Lucie a good half an hour to move the child into a better position to be born. As Lucie knelt on the floor in front of her patient, her knees became sore and she felt every one of her fifty-seven years. Her arm felt like it might break with the effort of manipulating the child. Once it had been freed, the mother's pains ramped up. Not long afterwards, she was delivered of a live but weak baby son. Mary was on hand to take the baby, and one of the women helped Lucie stagger to her feet, to stretch her legs before she delivered the afterbirth. There was no ribaldry and mirth about this baby's chord like there had been at the birth of Anne Jones's lusty son, since all the women present could see this young man faced a struggle if he was to thrive.

After taking a swig from her cup of small beer to refresh herself, Lucie got back in position, crouched in front Goodwife Bennet. Reaching back into the womb to try and locate the after-burden, Lucie was surprised to find another sack of water, something that she had encountered often enough not to shock her, but not something she had anticipated this time, since Barbara's belly had not appeared especially large. She broke the second sack with her nails, and as the waters flowed forth, she announced to the company that they needed to prepare for a second child. A great excitement filled the room, but Barbara, mid howl, was too consumed by her pains to properly understand this news. Exploring further, Lucie could feel that this baby was coming arm first.

'Oh, Barbara, listen my dear, you have another child, and it's ready to be born!' she told the bewildered mother, all the while looking directly into her eyes to help her focus.

Barbara's pang subsided and she cried, 'No, no I can't do it again. No, I am going abroad presently.' Lucie's eyes twinkled with amusement at this bold statement. Goodwife Bennet, although attempting to rise, was most certainly not stepping outside, but was going to deliver the twin she held in her womb. She was used to women making extravagant pronouncements on the point of delivery. It was a reaction to the pain the body was racked with.

'It is fortunate you are standing,' Lucie continued. 'We need to get you on the bed as soon as possible.'

Barbara was apparently about to object, but seemed to register from the look on Lucie's face that this was now an instruction, not a request. Her women helped her to move across the room and get her into position lying on her bed. Waters and other humours ran down her legs as she walked. Lucie oiled her hand and arm once more, and then attempted to thrust the second baby's arm back inside its mother's womb so it could be born more safely. Barbara screamed in pain at this operation, which was so vigorous that the whole of her belly visibly shuddered, but within a few minutes, her second son was born alive.

To make sure both lots of afterbirth came out cleanly, Lucie decided to give Barbara a draught of some special powders from her bag, prepared by Jasper. The ingredients included dittany of Crete, penny royal, round birthwort, cinnamon and saffron. Lucie mixed them into wine. As an extra precaution, she applied henbane to the vulva. A few minutes later, she reached into the womb and helped ease out both afterbirths.

'What do we need to do now, Mary?' she asked.

'Remove the henbane straight away, Mistress Smith, lest it keep working and draw forth the matrix itself next,' her deputy replied.

After Barbara's ordeal, it took some time to get her settled and tucked up carefully in bed. The babies had both responded to Mary's careful tending and were also swaddled and sleeping next to one another in the wicker crib.

'Someone had better go and find Joseph and let him know he's become a father twice over,' said Lucie. 'We've had so many boys born this season! I wonder if there's something in the air.'

Taking their leave, the midwives walked back across town, the last of the daylight fading as they walked. But they were back at the Three Doves by nine o'clock and ready for some supper.

'Still here, son?' Lucie said when she saw Simon sitting at the kitchen table.

'Yes, I've been working in the garden a bit and chatting to old Henry. I *tried* to converse with father, and I supped with Martha.'

Martha had made mutton stew: 'I thought since there was a chill in the air of an evening now, I'd make something warming. You can have a dish of the sauce now to dip some bread in, we'll leave it over the low fire overnight and it will be perfect for dinner at noon tomorrow.'

'And we'll have that pigeon pie now,' declared Lucie, smiling at Simon. 'If you've spared us a slice each, of course. 'Twould be a shame to waste a good waygoose treat!'

They fell on their suppers hungrily, and drank the ale Martha had poured them too. As they ate, Simon said, 'Mother, I have a confession to make. This afternoon, I thought to sit at your desk to write a letter I owe a friend in London, but I'm afraid it still remains undone, as instead I've been reading through your journals.'

'They are not for men's eyes, Simon. The secrets of the birthing room are women's business, not men's.'

'That's the thing, mother. The journals got me thinking. I know you use them to help you teach. But think how many more midwives would learn from you if we made them fit for printing. I've published several guides to women's health, but nothing like this, and you'd be writing from life, not other books. Think about it, mother: you'd be the first English woman to write a midwifery guide. It could make your fortune!'

'No, Simon,' Lucie said firmly. 'I don't think so. I choose a private life. My records are just that. Notes for me and my deputies.' She sat stiffly upright, upset by her son's breach of propriety.

'But, mother, pray think on it. Your notes and some of father's receipts, where necessary – particularly the ones you call on most. What a help that would be. Think of the lives you'd save!'

'That's enough now, Simon. Mary and I have had a long day's work, delivering twins. Father's already in bed, I suppose.'

'Yes, he went up half an hour or so ago. To avoid sitting with me, I'll warrant.'

'Simon,' chided Lucie, reaching up to give him a peck on the cheek. 'Goodnight, son. I'll see you tomorrow. Martha, pray make sure Ned's in his bed and the door is locked before you come up, will you? Mary, come, 'tis time you and I followed the master's example and took to bed. We'll consider what lessons we are to learn from this birth in the morning, when the light's better for writing.'

Martha turned to Simon after the midwife was safely out of the room.

'Young Ned's out,' she whispered. 'He'll be drinking with the other apprentices. The master thinks he's in the back room of the shop, but he sneaked out an hour or so ago. I saw him on my way to the privy.'

'Boys will be boys, and 'prentices are the worst. I know, I was one,' said Simon, with a rueful smile. 'Lock the door after me, anyway,' he recommended. 'A night in the garden will concentrate his mind wonderfully.'

Martha and Simon exchanged a quick hug as he prepared to leave for the inn. The boy had been barely out of skirts when Martha came to work in the household. It was comical to see him as a business man and a master printer, and Lucie wasn't the only one who missed him when he was away.

As Simon stepped over the threshold he bumped into Joseph Bennet, who looked worried.

'Can you call Mistress Smith for me? My wife has a slight fever and the women are troubled – and so am I,' confessed Joseph.

From the kitchen, Martha called out that she would go and fetch the mistress straight away.

'I understand your wife bore twin sons, Joseph. Pray give her my congratulations.' Simon waited with Joseph for his mother to come down; he remembered the other man being a couple of years his senior at school.

'Yes, we're still all in a maze. We're just beginning to grow accustomed to it.'

Lucie appeared, wrapped in her cloak over her nightdress.

'Come on, Goodman Bennet, we'll go and see your wife. I expect she is well enough: sometimes if a woman's humours have corruption in them, labour will stir it all up, and then it makes her feverish, being already weakened after the delivery.'

At the Bennets' house, she found Barbara was tired and a little hot to the touch.

'I thought so,' Lucie said. 'She's cacochymical, so we'll give her some purging medicines tonight and a cooling clyster tomorrow.'

'Forgive me, Mistress Smith' said Joseph, 'but I don't know terms of physick. What is cacky. . . cockymac. . . .?'

Barbara's mother came to the rescue: 'It's a hard word they like to use, Joe. I've heard it often enough, though I don't reckon I could say it. It just means the pangs have mixed her humours, and she needs something to cool the fever and then something to clean out the back part to rid the crudities from her stomach. Am I right, Mistress Smith?'

'Quite so. Well, Goodman Bennet, if you'll come back to the Three Doves with me, I'll give you the medicines and tomorrow I'll come back to administer the clyster.'

Lucie took the opportunity to take a quick look at the babies. Both boys looked well enough, if rather small and pale, and she hoped they'd thrive. All the same, it might be worth asking Dr Archer to come and baptise them presently, as a precaution. What with the mother having a fever, she feared some of the corruption might have passed to the children in the womb.

The medicine was waiting for Lucie and Joe when they reached the Three Doves. Jasper had followed his wife downstairs, heard the conversation in the kitchen, and deduced what Lucie would require. He had duly prepared a decoction of chicory water and violets, boiled into a sweet syrup. Lucie reflected, not for the first time, that Jasper, despite his choleric disposition, was the perfect husband for a midwife.

'Give your wife a couple of spoonfuls of this tonight and again in the morning, and we'll see how she gets on,' he advised.

When day broke, because of her disturbed night, Lucie had dispatched Mary to go and administer the enema. She'd told Mary she was aching all over too after all that crouching. Mary found the mother somewhat improved, but the second twin was now ailing. Mary determined from his rasping breath that the child was likely troubled with phlegm. She advised his grandmother to lay him only on one side or the other – for lying on his back might choke him. To remove the excess phlegm the child was going to need a suppository of Castile soap, which was gentler than normal soap, as it was made with olive oil and not animal fats and lye. She carried these in her midwife's bag, only requesting some fresh butter from the grandmother to make it pass into the boy's body more gently. She then gave the child a spoonful of syrup of violets and advised that each time the child was undressed to be changed over the next few days, he be given a spoonful of this medicine, and have his belly stroked downwards to force down the phlegm.

As Mary was settling the child, Dr Archer arrived to baptise the twins. Barbara and Joseph had settled on Benjamin and Bartholomew for their names, in honour of the day they were born, and Mary was delighted to be asked for the first time to stand as one of the twins' godmothers. She left in good spirits, knowing she'd done her best for the family of the Bennets, and that the children were welcomed into the family of the church. Lucie would demand a full account of her actions when she got back to the Three Doves, but there was now little more they could do, and whether or not the mother and children made a full recovery, was in God's hands.

Chapter Nine

It was a quiet afternoon in the back of the Three Doves. A stifling, late-August day had left few people in town, and Lucie and Ned were in the shop, while the master was at Hearne's coffee shop catching up with all the news.

Mary was in the kitchen, grateful for once of the cool of the north facing, often-gloomy room. She was reading through some notes from a volume of Lucie's journal, when a case from seven years ago, long before she'd begun her apprenticeship, caught her attention.

'This day I arrived too late to lay the wife of John Mallet. The child already delivered, but much injured, though like to do well.'

The entry read:

> I arrived at the house of the tanner's wife outside the town wall. It was then eleven o'clock at night, and very bad weather. I was soaked to the bone. Before I got there, the child had been born, but since the women told me all was well, I took the time to dry myself in front of the fire before going upstairs to attend her.
>
> When I got to see the child – a maid – I saw all was far from well. The baby was missing an eye and the whole face was much injured. Her lip was torn and her jaw swollen. I gave the child some warm sugared water on a spoon and rested it upon the tongue, and she sucked it down. I asked the

women how this happened, and they replied that the mother had fallen downstairs a few days before she came to be in travail and must have hurt the child then.

I could tell that the child must have presented face up because of a mark on its forehead. The injury must have happened because of the carelessness of the woman who had delivered her before I arrived, and who held her so harshly she put the child's eye out. There was no helping now, the damage was done, poor mite.

Having attended the mother and satisfied there was no more to be done, I returned home, but sent proper dressings for the child's face. God willing she lives and does well despite her poor start.

Mary recalled seeing a little girl playing with her hoop on the edge of the village, who had only one eye. The girl had a mass of golden ringlets which tumbled out of her cap and framed her face beautifully. She had often wondered what had happened, but never imagined it was the result of a birth injury. She picked up the journal and went into the shop.

'Mistress Smith, can you tell me about the tanner's girl born with her eye plucked out?'

'Oh yes, little Cissy Mallet. Such a sweet thing. Martha raised her here by hand for over a year, you know,' replied the midwife.

'Really?' Mary was shocked. 'Did the mother refuse to rear her?'

'Not as such, but they had no notion of how to care for her. She couldn't suckle and needed spoon feeding at all hours of the day and night. Her wounds took many weeks to heal and needed more careful tending than anyone in that household could provide, so we took her in and Martha became fond of her. I didn't have much to do at all. Once she was waddling about and eating her meat freely, her father demanded she return home. Martha was heartbroken, truth be told. She wouldn't say so, but I think a piece of her was hoping the child could stay with us always.'

'Who was it who hurt her so terribly?' Mary asked.

'Well, the women packed together and no-one would tell me anything, but I believe it was the grandmother, the mother's mother. She is dead now but was a woman much given to hard liquor and was in her cups when I arrived. Truly, I think she was so rough because she was drunk.'

'Such a fearful thing to happen! Life is hard enough in any case without rough handling setting a poor maid back at the very start.'

'Cissy doesn't let it hold her back, and she is such a bonny girl, don't you think, Martha?' Lucie addressed the maid, who had just returned from an errand at that moment.

'Not just bonny but towardly, too. Mistress Robbins tells me she's first in her class at school and knows all her letters,' Martha placed her shopping basket on the table. 'She can write her name on her slate neatly, too. The school mistress is thinking of keeping her on past seven to help the younger ones with their letters.'

'Martha's hiding her light under a bushel. The fact is the child does well because Martha has looked after her ever since she fostered her,' said Lucie. 'She still makes the child's clothes herself, don't you? And don't you pay Mistress Robbins for her schooling?'

'It's my pleasure.' Martha shot Lucie a stern look which made it clear she did not care for her business being discussed. 'The tanner would never pay for a girl's schooling, but raised no objection to me doing so, even if he considers it a waste. Cissy's a good girl, and quick-witted, and goodness knows she's as close to a child of my own as I'll ever know. But I don't single her out; no-one can accuse me of that. I knit and sew for cousin Jones's brood as I can, but I don't trumpet it abroad to the whole parish.' With that she swept out.

Martha was not one to wear her heart on her sleeve, and, as close as she and Mary were as bed companions and friends, she had never confided her feelings for Cissy, and didn't care for being talked about like this.

It was true, too, that she helped her Jones cousins out with more than just sewing clothes for the children. In the evenings, with her work for the Smiths complete, she had been going to their house to watch the children while their mother caught up with the piecework from which she and Sam made their living. Martha's family were weavers, and she too had been brought up to the sound of the loom and was adept at carding wool and spinning yarn. Many of the weavers, spinners, and combers in Warley Lane were distant kin or friends of Martha's immediate family, of whom she was the only one left. The upheaval of the wars and the death of the man she had been betrothed to – who was also in the trade before he took up soldiering – saw her decide to become a domestic servant rather than continue exercising the skills she'd been raised with. Her betrothed had been an infantryman at the Battle of Naseby under Phillip Skippon. He'd served Skippon at the Battle of Turnham Green right at the start of the wars, for he lost no time in joining up. She'd learned later that while his last battle was a victory for parliament, one of Prince Rupert's men had shot her Oliver.

While her ability to help her cousins financially was limited, once the children were asleep, Martha would put in a couple of hours' hard work at the loom or with the wool to help the family out as best she could. Even a snatched hour added a welcome few pennies to the family's pay. She'd found her skills had come back to her quite quickly. It was tiring, and if the Smiths knew her work with the Joneses went beyond babysitting, they would not be happy, but Martha enjoyed being amongst the weavers more than she thought she ever would again after Oliver died.

'Ned, mind the counter a moment, I need to speak to Martha,' Mistress Smith shouted into the store room where the lad was counting the stock. 'You stay here too, Mary, but give me the journal and I'll see it is returned to the trunk.'

Martha was busy scrubbing the large kitchen table with sand when Lucie came through. The vigorousness of her action showed her distress.

'Martha, what's wrong? Looking after the child like that is a good work, isn't it? Something to be commended, not ashamed of.'

'I'm not ashamed, but it's not something I care to have everyone talking of,' Martha said. 'I've no wish to be pitied as an old spinster who can't have her own children so takes it on herself to tend another's child.'

Lucie folded her arms. 'Come now. No one thinks that, I'm sure. Everyone knows you lost your promised husband in the late wars, but you're young enough yet. You could still entertain hopes to have a family, if a man you could look to marry crossed your path. Couldn't you?'

Martha let out a hollow laugh.

'No chance of that. I am two and forty!'

She'd not allow herself to believe that her friendship with the widowed weaver who lived hard by the Joneses could ever go past companionship. And even if they did offer one another some bodily solace, it was only because they were both equally lonely. The intimacy she enjoyed with Anthony Higgs had given her private delight, and she had reassured her lover that she was past the time of life when children might come along, for she knew the widower wanted no more family.

'You're in your sixth climacteric year at this age,' announced Lucie, after some swift mental arithmetic. 'All the seven-year changes are difficult for the body, and this is worse than many. But women breed into their late forties. It's not common but anything is possible, by God's grace.'

'Oh, Mistress Smith,' replied Martha, 'I'm no Sarah, to be sent a son in old age!'

Like many other Scripture passages, the story of Abraham and his wife was subject to multifarious interpretations.

'Sarah was ninety years old,' Lucie pointed out, 'but you're not half that age, so you wouldn't need a miracle.'

'But I would,' wailed Martha. 'I have flashings, and my courses are leaving me. I scarce have one in four months now, and we all know without flowers there can be no fruit. That's one of your own sayings. And anyway no children came when I lay with Oliver after our betrothal. It is not something that was meant for me.' Martha finished scrubbing the table and moved on to scour a pewter cooking pot with the same sand.

'I had no notion, Martha. I am sorry; though you are a little young for this change of condition yet. Though it can arrive any time after a woman turns forty, the end of this decade is more usual. I know you'd hoped to marry and have children one day. I wish you'd told me. The master could help with some remedies for the symptoms.' Lucie sighed. 'There were so many young lives changed for the worse because of the wars. And for what? The King is back as if nothing happened.'

Most of Tupingham had been firmly on the side of Parliament in the civil wars and was disquieted by the restoration of the Stuarts under Charles I's son. Only Lord Calstone, up at the Manor, had profited considerably from this event. Not only had all his sequestered lands and property been returned to him, but the new King had elevated him to the nobility by giving him a barony, knighted his son Robert at his coronation, and given his enthusiastic blessing to the marriage of Sir Robert and a younger daughter of his cousin.

'Martha,' Lucie wanted to forget about the wars and their consequences, 'you've lived with us for so long now, you know we think of you as kin, you'll always have a place under my roof, you do know that.'

'I do, and I thank you. Now,' Martha said, 'that's enough being maudlin! Why don't I make us a dish of hot chocolate each, and one for Mary? And we can have it with that cake the Bromfields left for us a few days ago.'

The grateful farmer had called into the Three Doves to pay his bill, with news of his wife's total recovery. He said his wife had wanted them to have the fruitcake that she had baked herself. He'd also left some white meats from his dairy herd and a ham that he had preserved himself. One of the benefits of being a midwife was that grateful parents or godparents of new-borns often sent gifts as they were able. Even the gruff tanner had sent a piece of soft calf skin for Lucie to have made into a new pair of gloves. They always say those that have the least are the most generous, and for all their restored status, no-one on the Calstone estate had made any gifts to the midwife or her deputy. On the contrary, her bill for the delivery was yet unpaid. Perhaps his Lordship thought the letter and gift from the King absolved him of a duty to pay, or more likely he paid the London physician handsomely, and regarded the country midwife's modest bill as someone else's responsibility. Lucie had wondered what Sir Robert and Lady Eleanor would think if they knew this. Perhaps they wouldn't care either; perhaps, despite her instinctive liking for them, the apples had not fallen far from the tree.

Chapter Ten

It was the second week of September. Lucie and Mary were walking back from All Hallows Church after the funeral of Bartholomew Bennet, who had survived for only three weeks. While his brother Ben grew and thrived, the second twin was too phlegmatic to live. The nearest physician was in Grantby, the small city the best part of a day's ride away, even if the family could have afforded his services, and the infant had received the best care available in the midwives' careful attentions and the apothecary's skill. Little Bartholomew's grandmother and Mary his godmother had stood in for his mother, who was still lying in during her woman's month. She had been adamant that she would walk to the church but had been successfully dissuaded when she fainted while dressing. Lucie was minded to send for the chirurgeon to come and let blood in Barbara's ankle to try and speed her recovery.

As they got home, the mood in the Three Doves was sombre. This was a godly household who saw death as part of His plan, but it was still hard to comprehend at times. Fulfilling their duties as midwives, Mary and Lucie had carefully laid out the tiny body and wrapped him in cerecloth for his interment. They viewed this task as an honour, since it was the last office they could offer the child, now gathered back in by the Lord, but it was always a time to consider whether a different treatment might have produced a different outcome. It was the reason Lucie kept her notes so meticulously up to date, and quizzed Mary about each case as a lesson the day following a birth.

It was not just local events that were on people's minds: news had reached Tupingham, through a letter to Simon with the last two *Weekly Bills* enclosed, that in the last week of August over six thousand Londoners had succumbed to the plague. Simon's correspondent claimed that locals were convinced the figure was nearer ten thousand, partly because deaths of members of non-conformist congregations were not entered into the parish records, and also because parish clerks were less than eager to admit the severity of the visitation in their neighbourhood. The second Bill, from the following week, was just as bleak. People would ask one another in the street how many were dying in the country as a whole, as the contagion was processing up and down the land. It was almost unimaginable, because while the plague broke out every generation, the numbers on these bills were unlike anything anyone had seen before. Jasper could just about remember the outbreak back in 1625 when he was an apprentice, but knew nothing like this.

Simon's correspondent wrote that death was the only topic of conversation, and that everyone looked weary, and wary of one another. It also brought the news that Dr Burnett, a physician of Jasper's acquaintance, had died. This was a shock, as Burnett's man had died of the plague some weeks before and Burnett's house had been recently reopened after the long days of quarantine were up. Physicians and other healers were getting a bad name for fleeing the city – with most of those who could afford to leaving, but the ones who stayed appeared to be paying the highest price. Jasper declared that they needed to pray harder that it stay away from Tupingham. He wasn't greatly afeared for himself particularly, as he had lived through it as a youth, therefore considered himself less disposed to contract this contagion than others, but he had seen firsthand the destruction and sorrow the pest wrought.

Customers came and went all morning, and the plague was

on everyone's lips. It seemed Simon was not the only one receiving intelligence on the topic and rumours spread fast in the small town. One worried mother brought in a child with belly-ache, and said it almost seemed too petty to make a pother about it when those poor souls in other parts of the kingdom were dropping like flies.

'Nonsense, Goodwife Brook,' replied Jasper. 'Keeping well is one of the best defences you'd have, should the pest arrive. To have any chance of surviving it, your boy needs his health.'

Jasper announced that the child had worms in his belly, gnawing at his entrails. The boy was three years old and so Jasper sold his mother a jalap for 6d which would purge them from the boy's body.

After lunch a messenger from Grantby, the nearest city, arrived to say that the periodic assizes had been held there the day before, with Lord Calstone in attendance as a local dignitary. A young woman by the name of Sarah Turnbull had been convicted of felony and burglary. Since she was a repeat offender, who had already been branded on the hand with the mark of a thief, the judge had sentenced her to be hanged. Turnbull was now pleading the belly and hoping to have her sentence suspended. A jury of matrons in the city had examined the prisoner but couldn't agree whether she was pregnant or not, and so the court had sent for Mistress Smith to come and give the deciding opinion, which they hoped would settle the matter. Calstone's coach was put at her service – in fact, it already awaited her at the Boar – and a night's accommodation at an inn in the city was to be provided, plus a fee. Grantby was a good couple of hours' journey past Calstone Manor, if the roads were good, so Lucie would be a long way from home.

'What do you think, Jasper, should I go?' she asked her husband.

'I am not sure you are free to choose, wife. This looks mighty like a summons,' he replied. 'But you'll not get that promised fee if Calstone has a hand in the business.'

'It says the Mayor and burgesses of the city will pay, so I'm sure we'll be reimbursed. Should I take Mary with me?'

'No, take Martha as your companion. If any of your women come to their time, it's better that Mary remain in Tupingham, to deliver them.'

'That's true enough, though her spirits are very low after the death of poor little Bartholomew Bennet, and his mother's lingering sickness. Perhaps you should remind her that she did nothing amiss. Oh, you should know, I sent to the chirurgeon to bleed Goodwife Bennet to help her recovery, so don't give her anything while I am away without considering that she has just been bled.'

Martha and Lucie were soon in the coach, hoping to reach the city by nightfall, and Lucie had an appointment to examine the prisoner first thing in the morning. Jasper made each of the women promise to carry one of his scented pomanders at all times, to protect them from the noisome city smells which carried disease. There was no hint of the plague in Grantby but he was not willing to take any chances with their welfare.

The inn they had been lodged in was clean enough and not too rowdy. Supper was provided for them in their room, and the women settled down for the night. Martha reported feeling quite sickly and off her meat, and they put it down to the journey and being thrown around in the coach on the uneven roads. Lucie said it was quite understandable, since this was a new experience for Martha, and quite unlike travelling in an open wagon.

In the morning they were up early and had a while to wait before the appointed time for Lucie to attend Sarah Turnbull, who was under lock and key in the gaol. Martha's nausea still lingered a little. Taking the opportunity that presented itself, they bought a still-warm cake each from a street vendor to break their fast with. They also bought a horn cup each of ass's milk from the dairymaid who walked up and down with her beast ready to milk it on demand. Lucie suggested that if this breakfast did not subdue her nausea, perhaps Martha should consider being bled herself. There was bound to be a chirurgeon near at hand. After they had eaten, they browsed the shops. There was indeed a barber-surgeon's shop, marked by a pole painted spirally with red and white stripes, but the screeches coming out of the open-fronted room from some poor creature having a tooth pulled, meant the women walked briskly on. Lucie ordered a length of woollen cloth in a comely deep green to have a new winter skirt made, and some fine linen for a new shirt for her husband. She examined some pieces of Nottingham lace for sale on a stall near the fabric shop, but nothing caught her eye. She then indulged in an entirely new form of luxury, as some of the newfangled tiny porcelain dishes which were meant for drinking tea, the new China drink the Queen was supposedly very fond of, caught her eye. Simon had tried some in a coffeehouse before he left London and said it was very refreshing, so she was keen to try it. She decided to buy a couple of ounces of black tea leaves and two dishes. If they hated it, she was sure Jasper would make good use of the leaves in the Three Doves, for this herb was reputedly an excellent remedy for headaches.

Like Tupingham, most of the shops in Grantby were open at the front, and rather than entering them, customers stood at a counter formed by the lower shutter under a canopy formed by the upper shutter. Some, though, were enclosed with a glass shop window like the Three Doves, meaning customers had to go inside and at least had a measure of privacy in their consultations. The difference was that the city had several streets filled with shops, whereas their home town only had one high street, a market square, and a coaching inn with a couple of alehouses in addition. The main road in Tupingham was also quite wide, so that carts and carriages could make deliveries and travel along the cobbles unhindered. In the city, the shops faced one another, and the upper storeys were jettied, overhanging the lower ones so far that people on the first floor could lean out and chat to one another without shouting. The road was paved with stones, with a drainage channel running down the middle filled with piss, dung, waste water and other detritus like food peelings. Particularly noisome was the waste dumped outside the butcher's premises, presently being picked over by roaming dogs; while passing this scene both women drew heavily on their scented pomanders.

The smell was even worse than normal in Grantby since there had been no rain for a while. People, horses, asses, dogs and cats vied for space in the narrow streets that formed a tangled cluster around the comparative calm of the Cathedral Close. If the city authorities engaged rakers and scavengers at all, as Lucie supposed they must, then it was difficult to discern what labour they got in exchange for the fee, for the streets were piled high with all manner of waste, and filth ran down the open gutter in the middle of the road. Both Martha and Lucie agreed that while the city was diverting to visit now and again, they really couldn't imagine living there.

Street vendors called out, advertising their goods. Some faces were familiar as they also attended the market in Tupingham, and the women greeted those traders with cheery waves or nods. News sheets were on sale in every street for a penny. Lucie bought the current day's, which was full of the story of the verdicts and sentences at the assizes. This gave them some further details of the case against Sarah Turnbull. It stated that on the Lord's day, with two men, she had broken into a merchant's house, knowing the family to be away, and had bound and gagged the maid-servant so she couldn't raise the alarm. The trio had made away with money and plate worth seventy pounds.The evidence was damning for they'd had been caught with the stolen property in their possession just a few days later.The news sheet noted that she was pleading the belly in response to the death sentence which had been passed upon her. Apparently, the jury of matrons called to examine the prisoner had been split as to whether she was pregnant or not, with two in favour and two against.

The gaol was indistinguishable from other buildings in Meer Street, since it had been a vintner's before the present constable had taken over the lease. He and his wife occupied rooms at the front of the property, with the rest converted to hold debtors and those awaiting trial or their sentences to be carried out. Without knowing for certain it was the right address, Lucie knocked on the door and the women were admitted straight away. A rat scurried across Lucie's foot as she crossed the threshold, and she shuddered. Martha was asked to wait in the constable's quarters, since she didn't have permission to visit the prisoner. Lucie was led down a dank corridor: she now understood why the disease that carried off numerous prisoners was known as "gaol damp", and if she had found the smell on the city street offensive, it was nothing compared with the stench in the gaol. The pomander made little impact on the assault on her senses, and she wondered how the constable and his wife could bear to live with this foul odour, not to mention the noise. Prisoners shouted appeals for coins from the midwife and banged on their cell doors for attention. Men, women, and even two children were crammed into the two rooms that served as the accommodation for the eighteen residents.

'You'll find the convict in there,' the officer told Lucie, showing her into a small office next to the two rooms. 'I'll wait outside.'

Inside, Sarah Turnbull was in an angry humour, pacing the small room in an agitated state.

'Come to stare at me like I'm a lion in the Tower, have you? I had plenty of your sort yesterday, an' I don't see why I have suffer it again. I don't know who you are, but I *am* with child, and you'll see that as soon as you touch my belly. Why do you stand there like a statue? The likes of me not good enough for you to talk to?'

'You haven't let me speak a word, my dear. My name is

Mistress Smith. I have been midwifing since before you were born and there's not much I haven't seen. If you are with child, as you say, it won't take but a moment for me to know you speak the truth.'

'Don't you "my dear" me! You're all the same – itching to see me neck stretched!'

With that, she spat in Lucie's face. Green, soot-specked phlegm ran down Lucie's cheek. Luckily, for all her reaching out, the prisoner couldn't get hold of Lucie, for her leg irons held her back.

'How dare you!' shouted the midwife, feeling around in her pocket for a napkin. The constable entered the cell with his officers. They grabbed Turnbull's arms and he told the woman she had forfeited her right to have a private examination. She must now suffer to be examined with the three men in the room.

Lucie stepped nearer to the prisoner. She went to lift the woman's skirts, and found them stained with dried blood, shit, and piss. The smell was unbearable: the prisoner had not washed in a good while, and the dried blood suggested she had had her courses quite recently. Glancing at the woman's secrets, Lucie could tell by the sores and running that she was also infected with a virulent case of the French disease. She couldn't allow any extraneous considerations to cloud her professional judgement in the matter, but could see that, even as she struggled against the guards' hold, Sarah was puffing her belly out artificially. Little wonder, really, since it was quite literally a matter of life and death.

'When did you last have your courses, Sarah?' Lucie asked.

'I don't know,' the prisoner replied. 'The likes of me don't keep a reckoning, do we? But it must have been a long time ago for I am surely big-bellied and quickened last week.'

One of the guards raised his eyebrow; he was a youngish man, still new enough in the job to be mortified by holding a woman prisoner like this while she was intimately examined.

Lucie caught his look and explained.

'You can't hang a woman carrying a quickened child – that would be murdering an innocent – for quickening is proof of a living child, the mother feels its first movements in her belly.'

All the while, Lucie was touching the prisoner's belly; then she loosened Sarah's leather stays so she could palpate her dugs. The prisoner twisted and thrashed against her captors, trying to break free from their hold, making the examination difficult.

'Get away, you wrinkled hag!'

Lucie was assailed by the rank savour coming from the younger woman's almost toothless mouth. The criminal's front top tooth had a smooth round hole worn in it, from, Lucie supposed, a clay pipe stem, apparently permanently lodged there when she was free. She hit on an idea.

'Perhaps if you could calm yourself, my dear, I could ask the officer to supply you with a pipe of tobacco when I take my leave?' The prisoner looked suspicious but did stop resisting so fiercely, although the tension in her whole body did not lessen.

After a few minutes, Lucie concluded her examination. She backed away from the prisoner before delivering her findings.

'In this case, we have no fear of killing a baby, for this young woman is not with child. You have my word as a midwife. Her womb is quite empty.'

'You're quite sure?' asked the constable. 'I need not remind you that your judgement has serious consequences.'

'Indeed you do not,' replied Lucie. 'I am a God-fearing woman and sworn to carry out my duties as a professed midwife to the best of my ability. I am not in any doubt.'

Sarah Turnbull began screaming and screeching, desperately trying to free her arms to lash out at the midwife.

'You lying bitch! You are content to send me and my child to the gallows! You evil, evil witch,' she spat out.

'Sarah, no matter what you say or what sentence has been passed on you, I cannot say what is not true. I think you know you are not quick with child.'

103

Sarah strained and thrashed against the guards and her irons, with all the strength of a cornered animal, as the governor ushered the midwife out of the cell. As they made their way back through the gaol to the constable's quarters, he apologised over and over again for the prisoner's behaviour.

'I assure you, Mistress Smith, I run an orderly gaol. The prisoner will be severely punished for her behaviour today.'

Lucie was shaken. She had not been attacked like that before in the course of her duty, and it wasn't something she cared to repeat. She had no qualms about her opinion, or the fact that it would lead to Sarah Turnbull's imminent death. Hanging for serious crimes was a fact of life, and it would have been a sin to lie to save a life fraudulently, but she nevertheless reminded the constable that any further consequence for a woman due to die in days was neither necessary nor just. In the constable's kitchen, Lucie was given a bowl of warm water, a sliver of soap and a clean linen towel.

She thanked the constable's wife for her consideration, but refused her offer of refreshments. She was keen to remove herself and Martha from this awful place, but before leaving she handed a few pennies to the constable's wife, requesting some pipes of tobacco and some ale be sent to Sarah Turnbull. She knew she'd need to ask Jasper for a cleansing inhalation when she got home to get rid of the terrible stench in her nostrils. Gathering their bags and the parcels of shopping, Lucie and Martha stepped back onto the street. Lucie took a deep gulp of air; Grantby air might not be very fresh but it was an improvement on what she had lately been breathing.

On the opposite side of the road, watching the gaol door, a woman waved and called out excitedly when she saw the pair. Both Lucie and Martha squealed with joy at seeing Alice Wallis. Dodging the carts and people in their way, they dashed over the road to greet her.

'You're a sight for sore eyes, Alice! It's been such a long

time since we saw you. Tell me, how do you come to be here? Were you waiting for us?'

Alice explained that she had recently moved back to the area and had begun practising as a midwife in Grantby. She had been on the jury who examined Sarah the first time.

'And what was your verdict, my dear?' Lucie asked.

'Oh, there was no possibility of her being pregnant: she had the blood of recent courses on her shift! Two others on the jury – older respectable women but not midwives thankfully – were taken in by her, and they said they'd have to send for a midwife from Tupingham, so I came down to see if it was true. And here you are, and with Martha too! A double treat. I heard Lord Calstone requested you personally,' Alice replied.

'So I believe. He was entirely less cordial when we met last, at the lying in of his daughter-in-law. A slip of a girl, but she did her duty and bore him a grandson. I'm pleased you saw that the prisoner was not with child, or I'd fear my tutoring had been wasted on you,' Lucie said with a smile.

Alice and Martha laughed at Lucie's teasing.

'You delivered the Calstone heir? I thought the likes of them had their own ways and didn't call on country midwives.' Alice showed affectionate pride in her instructor.

'That's a true word! Would you believe my lord engaged a physician from London to "supervise the delivery"? From that man's talk, you'd conclude he'd read every book ever written on the birth of mankind, but I could see he'd never delivered a woman in his life. He was smart enough not to object when Lady Calstone urged her husband to send for me and Mary Thorne – she's my latest deputy – to do the work while he got the credit. But enough of this, pray tell me your news. Doesn't she look well, Martha?'

Alice Wallis, or Shore, as she was then, had been an apprentice of Lucie's towards the tail end of the war years. After she finished her apprenticeship she worked alongside Lucie in Tupingham for a number of years, before she married a cloth merchant and moved away.

105

'It must be full ten years since we saw you last. Have you and Mister Wallis any children?' Martha asked.

'Oh yes, we've had four in the last ten years, two of each,' replied Alice.

'Four, just like me, and of the like kind too,' said Lucie wistfully.

Martha took her mistress's arm and gave it a squeeze. 'A livelier bunch you could not have imagined when I first joined your family, Mistress. I miss those days too,' she said sadly.

'My Sarah would be of an age with the wretched creature who shares her name inside those walls,' Lucie said.

'Aye, well that'd be all they'd have in common. Our Sarah was a modest, fair maid. Towardly too,' Martha said with pride in her voice at the memory of the bright girl taken too young. There had only been Simon in the household when Alice moved in, and he had gone off to begin his apprenticeship before her marriage. Lucie asked Alice to tell them all about her brood, and they chatted amiably for a few minutes, ignoring the tuts from busy people unhappy that the women were blocking the path.

'Od's fish, lad, have a care!' Martha called after an impatient blue-capped apprentice who'd shoved her in his haste to get by. Then she turned back to remind Lucie that they should be returning to the inn.

'The coach will be waiting for us,' she said. 'Alice, say you'll come and visit. We'd be delighted to receive you, and meet your children. What a treat that would be, wouldn't it Mistress Smith?'

'I tell you what, I've applied for my midwife's licence at long last, and my application will be heard by the Bishop of Grantby in the next few months. My husband means to make a supper for our friends afterwards.' She turned to Lucie. 'I meant to write to you at the Three Doves, to ask if you would be willing to write me a testimonial, but if you and Martha could make us a visit, you could testify in person and meet my little family.'

'That would be lovely, Alice,' said Lucie, gathering up her parcels. 'If we can, we shall. Pray write and tell me as soon as you know when the date is set, and I'll see if I can speak for you. I should like to, very much. But there's no knowing what work my mothers will make for me, of course. It might be best if I send a written testament in advance, in any case. Then the Bishop's clerk may read it beforehand, even if I am called away, or the winter roads do not permit such a journey.' The conversation was interrupted just then as a large dog ran between the women, almost knocking Martha over, causing her to step backwards into the muck of the road. After checking she was unhurt, Lucie continued.

'As I was saying, I have it all at my fingers' ends, Alice, never fear. All the notes on births you assisted me with are in my journals, as well as all the cases you took charge of after your training was ended.'

Alice looked grateful, but a little apologetic, appearing suddenly unable to meet the midwife's gaze. Then she said, 'I suppose you wonder why I waited so long before getting my licence? It was partly the wars and the years after, of course, when the licensing stopped altogether. But when the King came back I never troubled myself about it, because I didn't work often, just now and again, and it seemed I was forever teeming or nursing myself. But now I'm working hard again, it feels right to be qualified for my office, and I hope the Bishop agrees.'

After some further prompting by Martha about the late hour, the women parted, with expressions of regret that they could not converse longer. As they walked back to the inn to get in the coach, Lucie admonished Martha for the oath she had sworn at the rough apprentice. Her maid apologised and said it wasn't like her, but she was feeling unwell still and forgot herself. Lucie agreed to let that be an end to it and returned to more pleasant conversation. They both agreed that Alice Wallis coming to see them had made the whole trip worthwhile. Lucie had always felt it wrong that the licensing of midwives had fallen into abeyance and was pleased to see it resume. Alice must have been practising for about sixteen years, and only now would she become officially authorised. That was one consolation for the King's Restoration, she supposed.

Chapter Eleven

At eight at night, and already dark – since September was progressing apace – Martha answered a knock on the door. Oliver Hill stood before her, wearing riding boots and spurs that jingled as he shifted anxiously from foot to foot. A groom stood behind him, holding the heads of their two horses.

'My wife has started her travail, but she wants three months of her reckoning, and we're afraid she'll miscarry,' he told Martha in a breathless voice.

'Pray wait here, sir, and I'll call my mistress,' Martha replied.

Lucie, Jasper, Mary and Simon were sitting at the kitchen table talking. One of Simon's friends, who had stayed in London, had sent him a letter enclosing the latest *Bill of Mortality*. The figures for pest victims were half of what they were at their peak in August, but still terrifyingly high and certainly not enough of a drop to convince Simon it was safe to return home. The letter also reported that Thomas O'Dowde, the chemical physician who had defied the plague to stay in London, had himself succumbed to the disease at the beginning of August. His wife Jane had died just nine days later. His daughter Mary, married to the merchant Edward Stanthwaite, had now taken over her father's medical practice. O'Dowde and his wife must have died before Dr Burnett, whose death had been reported in the last letter Simon received; it seemed the plague was still killing indiscriminately, and there was no knowing, from one day to another, where it would strike next. Or evidently even where it had struck already.

Jasper commented on O'Dowde's claim to have been able to prevent or cure the plague.

'Obviously his pills weren't as effective as he boasted.'

'Well, the letter says Mary is telling everyone that her father was so attentive to his patients' care that he forgot to treat himself with his pills,' replied Simon.

'Sounds odd, and doesn't explain how his wife died a week later. Surely when he knew he'd contracted the contagion he'd have urged her to take the pills.'

Simon agreed, but explained that, according to the letter, Mary was telling people that the plague had killed him after he'd developed a craving for musk-melons.

'Everyone knows melons are notorious for their cold and wet properties,' said Jasper, shaking his head. 'Unless you counter that by taking them with old cheese, then they need to be left to the young and hot to eat. I bet he had a rare belly-ache after gorging on them.'

'That's just what the letter says,' Simon showed it to his father. 'Mary said his over-eating left her father's body open to the pest, obviously she'd not want to give an answer that proved the truth of the old medicine.'

'Well for all he rejected the evident truths of Galen's humours, he made himself phlegmatic and it's no wonder he became ill. He could not have supplied a better proof of the folly of his chemical fancies,' Jasper remarked. He'd always held a low opinion of O'Dowde, an Irishman who thought himself above the station of apothecary, the honourable craft for which he'd trained.

'I expect he left a swingeing sum in his will. He'd have feathered his nest in the King's service. Does the letter say?'

'It says he left several hundred pounds, but no will. It seems there was some controversy because Mary's merchant husband has already had a great deal of her family's money and lost it in various schemes. But now O'Dowde has died intestate and Mary is suing for probate as his only surviving kin,' Simon summarised the best piece of gossip in the letter.

'What a calamity!' Jasper spoke with relish. 'It seems O'Dowde believed those secret chemical drugs of his would make him immortal.'

The conversation came to an abrupt close as Martha called for Lucie, who went to the shop door to talk to Mister Hill. She asked after his wife's symptoms and agreed that they sounded worrying, and then called to Mary to take up their midwifery bundles and come with her. The Hills were minor gentry and lived in a somewhat larger house than most, just off the main road through Tupingham. With some farm land and a private income, the Hills were often seen around the town engaging the services of the locals; Oliver Hill himself was an alderman and sat on the parish boards.

'Do you wish my wife to ride, Mister Hill?' Jasper asked, having followed his wife through to the shop to pay his regards to his fellow town councillor. 'I can fetch her horse from the blacksmith's.'

'I'm obliged to you, Mister Smith. And if your wife's woman cares to ride also, she can mount behind me. Otherwise my man can walk with her to my house.'

It was agreed that both women should ride, Lucie on her accustomed side-saddle and Mary clinging around Mister Hill's waist for dear life. It was unusual for a gentleman to come out himself to summon help like this, so Lucie knew things were unlikely to be good with his wife.

On arrival, Lucie gave Eliza Hill a thorough examination but could see no obvious sign of labour. She found her to be very melancholic and almost delirious when the spasms struck. It was clear that the young woman was in deep discomfort. Lucie asked her when she had last gone to stool, and she learned it was several days ago. But Eliza said she wasn't concerned about that as she had eaten but little since, having lost her appetite recently. Lucie touched Eliza's belly again and felt a hearty kick from the baby, so was reassured on one matter, at least.

'In my opinion, the pains are caused by costiveness, not labour,' Lucie told her and the gathered women. 'I think a clyster will set you to rights within the hour.'

Eliza began to object, asking how she could be costive when she had eaten so little, but with gentle coaxing, eventually deferred to the more experienced woman. Lucie proceeded to mix the enema and bade Mary to usher Eliza onto the bed that she might administer it behind the curtains with a measure of privacy.

'Now we wait,' Lucie told Eliza. 'We'll soon see if I am right or not.'

'Should you not be giving her some physick to prevent a miscarriage?' Oliver Hill's mother asked.

Lucie explained that she was sure it was not Eliza's time and that she had every confidence this treatment would work. The women sat and chatted convivially, sipping from cups of warmed wine as they waited for something to happen. They did not have long to wait, for just ten minutes after the enema was given, Eliza sat on the pot and with a loud grunt evacuated such a large quantity that it surprised them all. After showing the contents to Lucie, who noted the hardness of the stools which confirmed her diagnosis, the maid dashed out of the room to empty the pot, and was only just back in time, when after a few minutes' rest, Eliza rose again and went to stool a second time, passing an altogether more soft motion.

After this she declared herself quite exhausted, and doubtless aided by the soothing warm wine, she fell into the soundest of sleeps. Confident the problem was now resolved, Lucie explained to Mary that although clysters were useful to speed labour when women were at their time, it was equally true that women nowhere near their time were often costive, and, if left untreated, this would be bad for the pregnancy.

They had been at the house scarcely an hour, and it was now only just after ten. Mister Hill resolved that Mary should ride behind his man on the journey home. Lucie and Mary agreed to call back the next morning. Arriving home by a quarter to eleven, they met Martha at the door – she had just returned from her evening at the Jones household. Simon and Jasper were still in conversation, much to Lucie's surprise. Having found common ground in the discussion of plague-ridden London, the men had almost enjoyed each other's company while the women were out. Simon rose to leave as his mother and Mary came in. Pulling on his cloak, he asked his mother if she had had a chance to consider his suggestion that she should write a handbook or guide to midwifery for publication.

'There's nothing to consider,' she told him. 'I've no wish to make or meddle with such a business.'

Jasper rose from his seat at the table. 'What's all this?'

'I think Mother should write a book, to instruct other midwives by sharing her experiences,' said Simon. 'I thought she could use the cases in her journals and put in the receipts you both use most commonly. I'd oversee the printing and take the greatest care with it. We could have some excellent woodcuts made – I'd pay for them myself.' Simon picked at a whitlow on his thumb while he spoke, making it look even angrier. The colour now matched that which was rising on his neck from speaking up to his father. 'I promise you it would be in great request – the first such guide by a real English midwife.'

'No. I absolutely forbid you to go on with it,' his father answered. 'Your mother is not writing for the presses, and I am staggered to think you would even dream of making a parade of her experience just to help you make a profit.' He almost snarled at the idea. 'And stop picking at your thumb. A fine mess you have made of it. I'll have to prepare you a poultice from cow dung in the morning to draw out the swelling.'

Although the conviviality experienced between the men over the last few hours had clearly evaporated, Lucie was

113

somewhat calmed by Jasper's care for their son's health.

'Thank you Father, I would be grateful. It is rather sore, I freely admit.' Simon seemed to misjudge his father's concern as a sign he was softening and tried another way to win Jasper around to his own view. 'It's not uncommon for women to write printed books nowadays, sir. You should drop your old-fashioned notions and think of the good such a book could do.' He offered a warm smile which he appeared to think would charm the older man. 'My mother has trained – what is it? Four, no, five deputies, and they are all doing good work, just as Mary is sure to do – but with her cases written down and for sale in a book that's not too costly, just think how many people she'd be teaching.'

Jasper did seem to soften, but only slightly.

'Quite the rhetorician, aren't you my son? I can tell you've thought it over thoroughly. But my answer is still no. My wife will not be writing for the public. Her journals are her private records and it's not meet for them to be opened to prying eyes.'

Lucie shifted on the spot, if her son had any sense at all he'd drop the matter now. She wished he could tell her opinion by the intensity with which she stared at him, but her son was careful not to meet his mother's gaze. He was clearly not ready to let the matter rest, and his next strategy was to invoke the words of the Bible.

'Father, Paul's Epistle to Titus is that it is the elder women's duty to "instruct the young women". Pray think on it, at least.'

'And Paul also tells Titus to stop the mouths of "disobedient and vain talkers",' responded Jasper, not to be outdone in Bible knowledge by his own son. He let out a deep sigh, 'Enough of this! Your mother more than fulfils her Christian duty, as well you know, and I won't have you preaching to me in my own house.'

The irony that in standing up to his father like this, Simon was displaying more of the older man's temperament than either man realised was not lost on Lucie. On impulse she tried to break the tension by offering the men a noggin of perry each. 'I am going to take one,' she said, trying to sound much brighter than she felt. Jasper accepted the cup.

Simon only shook his head in response, and continued his petition. 'But think of all the women and children who die needlessly for want of a trained midwife. All the harm done by ignorant and brutish hand women who don't know what they are about. It's true, isn't it, mother? What's the name of that woman who lives like a witch in the countryside, whose messes you are sometimes called to remedy?'

'Mother Henshaw you mean? You might well call it right, but these women wouldn't read the book in any case. Most of them can't read. Now, no more of this,' she said firmly, walking across the kitchen to return the flagon of perry to its shelf near the hearth. 'Your father has spoken and we must obey him.' Standing on tiptoes, she reached up to give her son a farewell kiss on the cheek.

As Simon took his leave, Lucie said, 'I am sorry for that, Jasper. Simon knows a son's duty better than to argue with his own father like that. I am sure when he comes around in the morning for his poultice, he'll remember his duty and seek your forgiveness.'

Jasper smiled, remarking that Simon seemed to have inherited an unfortunate love of prating from his mother. The tension flooded from Lucie's body. With relief, she allowed Jasper to guide her to the stairs with his candle.

Chapter Twelve

Lucie and Mary had squeezed into a cramped room in Warley Lane, having been called to Anne Allen, wife to a comber. She was now heavily pregnant and bleeding just as heavily. The family had sent for the midwife, assuming that this meant the baby was on its way.

The two roomed cottage was home to a couple and their two children. The comber, John Allen, worked in the room next to them, preparing fleeces to be spun into woollen yarn. Fibres and dust hung in the air and had settled on all the surfaces. Lucie asked Anne, over the woman's moans, when she thought she would be at her full reckoning. Panting heavily, Anne replied that she still had a month to go. Lucie was immediately concerned, and ordered her patient to lie down on the bed. From the state of Anne's skirts and the sheets and clouts it was clear she was bleeding heavily and in great danger. Lucie advised Mary to examine Anne's belly, and watched her grease her hand to carry out the internal check. She saw her deputy's brow furrow as she performed the examination. At length she withdrew her now blood-drenched hand.

'There are no signs at all she is at her time, Mistress Smith,' Mary announced in a puzzled tone.

Lucie considered this for a moment, but resolved not to re-examine Anne, trusting in Mary's skills. She drew on her years of experience to make sure to steady her breathing before she spoke to Anne. 'How long have you been having your flowers, Goodwife Allen?'

The woman, curled over on the bed, hugging her belly. She replied that she had been bleeding off and on for a month, but it had become worse that day. Gritting her teeth, she reported having been in pain for the last twelve hours, which is why she had concluded that the baby was coming.

The midwife turned away as she thought a while, then, moving back towards Anne, announced that the most likely explanation for these symptoms was that the pregnant mother was suffering from an extremely violent craving.

'You are longing for something. Can you think what it might be? I've known women long for all manner of things, including stuff not fit to be eaten – like the one who wanted to bite her husband's buttock! – so there's nothing you can tell me that'd shock me.'

'Mistress Smith, we're a poor family. What would be the use of folk like me having longings?' Anne said in a strained voice.

'Until we get to the bottom of this we'll not be able to get you well.' The midwife spoke firmly. 'And you're in peril of your lives, both you and the child, so tell us what it is you've an inclination for. No matter the price, if it can be had, we'll do all we can to save your longing.'

After a pause, Anne confessed that she had desired a simple peasecod: she had recently seen a lad holding one up in the autumn sunshine, and felt a longing to bite through such crispness and relish the sweet fresh peas within, but then her pains came on, and she forgot about the desire. Recalling the strength of her desire for that humble plant, Anne let out a gasp. Surely all this trouble could not be due to that, could it? The midwife confirmed that it could indeed; Lucie knew very well that unfulfilled cravings were extremely dangerous to teeming women.

'But this one is easy enough to satisfy, thank goodness,' she continued. Knowing what was ailing Anne, Lucie felt her sense of foreboding lift a little.

'I have late peas yet growing in my garden. Mary, will you run home and gather some for us? We'll give you some to eat now, and make pease pottage with the rest, so you shall have store of it for the next few days. If you're still craving when it runs out,' she told Anne, 'we'll get you more.'

Lucie stayed with Anne for the hour it took Mary to make the round trip. Martha, who was used to encountering poverty in the parish, had given Mary a tied muslin cloth filled with steeped oats so that Lucie could quickly get a nourishing pottage prepared. As fortunate as the occupants were in their rich and varied diet, there was never a day when the apothecary kitchen didn't have some basic pottage on the go, stuffed with whatever herbs, plants, and vegetables were in season. Martha had also pressed on Mary one of the penny loaves she'd bought to serve with the family's meal, and a square of best butter. In addition, knowing this family was not likely to be provided with spare linen, Mary had also brought some sheets back with her. Lucie had washed Anne, bathed her secrets and got her all cleaned up while she awaited Mary's return. Now Mary was back to help, she could change the bed sheets and put Anne into a clean shift. She had placed a pair of double-folded clouts between Anne's legs to absorb the flow, and left a set of clouts beside the bed so Anne might keep on top of her flow. The midwives often lent bed linen to poorer families for women to deliver on. No wonder there was always laundry on the bushes in the garden at the back of the Three Doves.

Mary told Anne that they would take her dirty sheets and clothing home to wash and save her a job. In reality, it was because the linen was going to take some cleaning and repairing, and Martha was second to none in her skills at reviving linen that was probably only really fit for cutting up into clouts. By the time Anne was comfortably tucked up in her clean bed, having munched on some lovely crisp pea pods, Lucie had rustled up a quick pea soup, which she offered with a hunk of bread. The two children, who had been sent to Goodwife Jones's cottage while their mother was with the midwives, were now home and fed with brewis, which Mary had prepared by breaking up the rest of the bread and mushing it into the soup. They weren't exactly starved but were used to sparse fare, living often on milk thickened with flour, and pottage flavoured with whatever plants Anne had foraged from the nearby hedgerows – unless their father had had an especially good week and they could afford something more substantial.

The workers' cottages in Warley Lane didn't have gardens and were dark and cramped together. Most of the money they earned was needed for rent, and they were always on the back foot when it came to their bills. The row had clubbed together and had a rather sorry looking pig out in the communal yard, who also lived on poor rations since the people in the row were not likely to have much by way of left-overs, but when he was slaughtered, which would be soon, the score and more families living in the ten or so houses would at least have a taste of pork during the long winter months.

The revival in Anne's spirits was quite remarkable to behold. Her bleeding appeared to have stopped and she was looking much cheerier in herself. She even made a weak joke that some would think it a longing for peasecods that had got her in this predicament in the first place. Lucie pretended to be shocked, but then gave Anne a warm smile and met her gaze with those blue eyes that inspired women to trust the older woman instinctively, and she was relieved to see evidence of Anne's reviving spirits. It was well known that peas were a windy plant, so a good provoker of lust in those that needed a little help. How they grew on the plant, all plump and stiff, was the way the Lord had made the properties of this plant clear. Since cheer both indicated and encouraged recovery, Lucie was now confident Anne had every chance of going to her full time.

'We'll keep an eye on you, but look after yourself. Rest

today and I think you'll be up and about your usual work tomorrow,' Lucie said, taking her leave.

As the midwives walked back to the Three Doves, Mary asked Lucie all about what she had witnessed. It was unlike any case she'd seen in her training.

'I've seen it a few times before, Mary. A woman's longings must always be heeded, for it's dangerous both to her and the child to pay no mind to them – as we have just seen,' Lucie said. 'The mother's imagination has prodigious powers over the unborn. Remember how if a mother sees a hare on the path in front of her it could cause the baby to have a hare-lip? There was one woman I heard of who'd looked on an Ethiopian merchant while she was big-bellied, and afterwards gave birth to a dark-skinned child, even though she and her husband were fair-haired and fair-complexioned.'

'Is there any remedy for things like this?' Mary asked.

'They say if a woman who has been frighted by a hare rips her husband's shirt in the manner of a hare-lip, then this will save the child from being marked, but I know not if it works. As for the other things that the imagination can cause, I don't think there is a cure.'

'I'm glad you told me, Mistress Smith. If I had acted after my own devices, I'd have tried to open the womb, break the coats and hurry the baby out. Wouldn't that have worked?'

'No, Mary, it would not. I've known several cases where mothers were destroyed by midwives and ignorant women carrying out forced deliveries when a woman has pains a little before her time. That's why today's case is so important for me to write up and keep in mind, for just like Anne there, many women are inclined to hide their longings through shame or poverty. In her case the cost was not great, so she risked her health needlessly, I fear. And, of course, the cure we wrought is there for all to see.'

'I have to be honest, Mistress Smith, and say that I'm not sure I'd have believed this, if I hadn't seen it with my own eyes.'

They completed their journey in companionable silence, reflecting on the events of the morning and planning how each of them would help this family until the delivery. Lucie vowed to have a root around in her spare linen chest and see if there were some clouts and other linens she could spare for the Allens. She'd also alert the townswomen and see if they could offer any spare crockery, for she'd noted that the children were sharing one cracked a bowl for their soup, and the family would soon be one more in number.

As they turned into High Street, the midwives saw Mister and Mistress Pardoe walking down the street together.

'Ah well met, Mistress Smith!' cried William Pardoe. As the midwife acknowledged him and Isabelle, he went on, 'My wife thinks we'll have need of your services in the next few months.'

'That is good news, indeed,' the midwife replied. Isabelle had not followed her advice to attend her neighbours' births, but clearly Lucie's reassurances had helped her. 'Are you certain, Isabelle?'

'I am not yet quickened, Mistress Smith, but I have not had *those* since we spoke in June and it is now October, so I am hopeful,' she replied with a blush.

Lucie ran through a list of other symptoms of potential pregnancy: sickness, loathing her food, strange longings, sour belchings, sore dugs, and so forth, as Isabelle squirmed at answering such questions in her husband's presence.

'When we lived in the city, we sent a jar of my wife's water to the local physician, who used it to confirm her pregnancy. Should we send some to you?' William Pardoe asked.

'No, indeed,' replied Lucie. 'Piss can reveal some matters, but those who pretend to ascertain pregnancy with it are quacks and charlatans. Even though it is still a profitable trade and I grant you they make a good show: tasting, smelling, and staring at piss as if it will reveal a secret. You'd have done as well to save your money. It puts me in mind of the day the shoemaker's wife brought a bottle of her husband's water to the Three Doves. She said her husband was too busy to come himself and hoped that my husband would be able to judge his case and send a proper remedy from seeing the piss. Instead, Mister Smith poured it away, filled the bottle with some of his own, and gave it to the poor woman, telling her to bid her husband make him a pair of shoes, using his piss to measure his feet by. Word soon got round not to try that with Mister Smith if you seek his counsel.' While Isabelle looked grave, Mister Pardoe and Mary tried unsuccessfully to conceal their mirth. Lucie continued, 'The secrets of the belly will be known soon enough, one way or another. So, if you have any qualms you know where to find Mary and me. My husband can advise on any physick that might help and I'll be sure to attend you when your time comes.'

Back at the Three Doves, Simon was in the kitchen chatting to Martha. Lucie was delighted to see him, for he'd been but an infrequent visitor since the harsh words with his father a couple of weeks before. Lucie gave all the dirty linen to Martha, with a rueful smile.

'I'm sorry to bring in more work for you, Martha, but the comber's wife was in a very sorry state when we arrived. It was lucky they sent for us when they did.'

Martha swept the pile out the back door into a bucket of cold water and salt, ready for boiling up later in the day. While she was out of the room, Simon coughed slightly, as if steeling himself.

'Mother,' he said. 'I think it's time for me to return to London. I fear that if I stay away much longer I'll have no business to get back to, and the numbers in the latest *Bills* show the plague is abated somewhat.'

Lucie could feel the blood drain from her face as a cold, prickling sensation ran down her body. Her belly began its increasingly familiar griping. She eased herself into Jasper's armchair by the hearth.

'Oh son, pray reconsider. I couldn't bear to lose you, my

only child!'

'I know, Mother, but I feel the time has come. And here's some better news: I've found an artisan painter who can repaint the front of the shop for you. He's a good workman and much in request. He commands 3d per yard square per layer and will need to lay three coats, in oils, because the window frames, timbers and door are exposed to the weather. He'll also need the cost of his colours and oils, and four nights' lodging in the town; from my description he reckons it will take him five days.'

'That seems a fair price. We could hire him for the week your father goes on his annual trip to London.'

Simon said he could see the wisdom of this plan. Each year, Jasper went to London to buy new supplies and converse with fellow members of the Worshipful Society of Apothecaries.

'It's his custom to go just before Christmastide, as you know,' continued Lucie, 'so if it could be done then, the shop front would be a splendid early New Year's gift for your father.'

The Society's home in Apothecaries' Hall was in Black Friars Lane, and Jasper normally lodged nearby at The Dolphin on Fleet Street during his trip. His membership of the Society was dormant, since being in the provinces meant he'd get little value from his quarterage fees, but this was a good way to keep up with the current practices of his craft. Simon cracked his usual joke about seeing if his father would care to see a play at the indoor playhouse at Lincoln's Inn Fields. Of course, this all depended on whether the playhouses had been allowed to reopen. For him, he said, London would be a much duller place if not. His father's puritanical streak meant he would never set foot in a playhouse anyway, so Simon's jest was purely theoretical.

'What about the sign? Did you ask if he could do that, too?' Lucie asked.

'No,' said Simon, 'but I've already placed the order for that.

There's a sign maker in Grantby. I went to see him a couple of weeks ago and struck a bargain for one. It should be more or less complete by now. I thought that since the sign up at the moment is quite rotten, it would be better to begin again, rather than repaint it. I'll bring it to you before I leave, and you can hide it in the scullery or somewhere until the rest of the work is done. Won't it make the most splendid final flourish, Mother?'

Lucie was all in a maze at this news. *Fancy Simon going to all that effort, and organising all this, despite the troubles he'd had with his father since he returned.*

'You're a good son, Simon. This has warmed my heart, I'm sure. I can hardly wait to see the new sign for myself.' She clasped her hands in front of her chest, seeing that Simon's face too was lit up at her joy. Gazing at her son, a sudden thought caused Lucie's face to drop.

'Like I say, I am truly touched, Simon. I can't wait to see it. But if you've done it in hopes of changing your father's mind about the book, it will have been a wasted effort, just so you know.'

'Mother, I know my father too well for that. We publish dozens of books a year and it was only an idea, after all. It was a very good one, and it's a shame it's not going to happen, but what will be, will be. I certainly wasn't depending on him changing his mind.'

'I'm glad to hear it, son. Now give your old mother a hug, and we'll be ready for dinner. It smells delicious. You'll stay, of course?' She relished the comfort and familiar smells of her son's strong body in her arms. Lucie only reached his chest these days.

'Yes, mother. I'm always delighted to eat our Martha's cookery.' Simon pulled away. 'Oh, I forgot to tell you a letter arrived while you were out.'

Lucie opened it. The letter was from Mister Wallis in Grantby. Alice's licensing application was to be heard at Grantby Cathedral on the twenty-seventh of November, and they hoped Mistress Smith would be able to attend, and that she would still be happy to speak in respect of Alice's competence. Martha was also very welcome if she could be spared from the Three Doves.

While they dined, Lucie and Mary told the family the story of their morning at the Allens'. Lucie caught Simon and Jasper sharing a rueful smile that seemed to say they had heard enough of women's business over lunch. *Oh, let this be a sign that they are going to be on better terms now*, she thought. Ned was taking no notice of the chatter, busy spooning meat into his mouth at speed, before helping himself to more. Lucie took the opportunity to ask Martha to look in on Anne when she went to see the Joneses, and to report back. She asked Jasper if he would be content for her to return to Grantby for the licensing and he gave his blessing. He added that she should take Martha with her, and give the Wallises his greetings, too.

Striking while the iron was hot, Lucie left Martha to clear the table and went upstairs to her desk where she took out a quill and ink and prepared to write back to Mister Wallis, to tell him she would be honoured to attend. She had already written out a detailed supporting statement, giving the names, dates, and outcomes of a dozen births Alice had attended, along with details of which of the women were yet living and could be called upon if required. This was in her desk and ready to enclose within the letter, so the Wallises could present it to the Bishop's clerk in advance of the hearing. If she made haste, perhaps Jasper would be willing to drop the documents into the postmaster's office on his way to Hearn's.

Chapter Thirteen

'Thir day I laid the wife of William Robbinr.'

On the third Saturday of October, Lucie and Mary were called to the wife of Alderman Robbins. He and his wife Suzanne lived in one of the larger residences in Tupingham, just in front of the town green. Suzanne ran a school for children up to the age of seven in a room at the front of the house. Although this was the couple's first child, the birth went smoothly. Suzanne was well supported by her women, who at the midwife's command had spread a sheet under Suzanne's bottom as she lay on her bed and lifted her slightly to help the womb open. As she found bearing down difficult, Lucie advised her to hold her breath for as long as possible between pains to encourage the child into the air, and this seemed to work, for her healthy man-child was born soon after. The alderman was delighted with the lusty son his wife had produced at her first pregnancy and said it was a sign of hope for many more. Lucie was amazed that she'd delivered yet another boy, how odd that almost all the births were of boys this year, but she was sure nature would even things back out with time.

Such was Alderman Robbins' delight, in fact, that although Suzanne would be upstairs in bed, he planned to hold a big gossiping party at noon on Monday, straight after the christening, to reward the women who had attended his wife and toast the birth with some of his council friends. Suzanne had a new lying-in bed gown to wear when people called into her chamber to see her. The gossiping was the talk of the town the next day, as people chattered excitedly about who was and who wasn't invited. Lucie couldn't help but think that if some of the food being prepared for the party was sent to Warley Lane it would do much more good. As the Bible made clear, it was part of God's plan that some people should be poor, but she was sometimes troubled by the differences between those who had nothing, despite all their hard work, and those who had too much.

Lucie and Mary changed clothes for the party, their morning chores complete. Lucie told Mary that this birth would be another good one for her licensing report, that they should add it to her list as soon as possible, and that although it was good manners for the midwives to attend the gossiping they wouldn't stay too long. She went upstairs and took out the new green suit she had had made with the fabric purchased in Grantby. The seamstress had used her utmost skill and the material had worked up beautifully. There was a hint of winter's nip in the air, so Lucie chose her quilted petticoats to wear underneath, for the first time this autumn.

Remarkably, Jasper had decided to accept the invitation too, because it came from one of his fellow aldermen. Simon was also going, since he was travelling back to London on Tuesday's coach, so this occasion would serve as a small farewell for him. The thought of his leaving caused a ball of disquiet to form in Lucie's stomach. She was used to him living away, but knowing he was travelling back into the contagion made her intensely fearful. The secret foreboding which had been growing in her throughout 1665 was heightening all the while, and she had made several urgent dashes to the privy since hearing the news.

Ned was to remain at the Three Doves minding the shop. He could serve remedies that required no mixing and take messages; any enquires for the midwife could be referred to Martha, whose vast experience would enable her to judge whether to run and fetch her mistress or to take a message.

The Smith family walked together from All Hallows where Lucie and Mary had stood in for Mistress Robbins at the Christening. The gossiping party was a merry affair, the wine plentiful, the food superb, and Lucie was pleased she was there and with both the men who meant so much to her. One of William Robbins's cousins, Nathaniel Woolrich, was attending and presented ten shillings to Lucie and five to Mary. He had just stood godfather to newborn Jeremy, so made presents to the midwives as tradition demanded. Mister Woolrich then asked if he might have a word with the midwife in private. They stepped out into the schoolroom, which was empty while Suzanna was indisposed.

'I wanted to, ah, discourse with you, Mistress Smith, on a subject of some difficulty,' he said, clearly finding it hard to choose the right words.

'Well, there's not much I haven't heard, so pray proceed.'

The fashionably dressed young man, who Lucie guessed was in his mid-thirties, began by explaining that he had been married to his wife for some eight years, but they had not yet got any children. He asked if she could give him any advice. Lucie replied that this was a very tricky matter. The cause might be found in either the husband or the wife, or it could simply be that they were ill-matched. She asked the man if all was well with his yard and its standing faculties, and was greeted by him puffing out his chest with a look of horror on his face. He drew in a deep breath, as though he was about to speak harshly, Lucie quickly cut him off, remarking sharply, 'I am sorry, but you came to me with this matter, not the other way round, sir.' She added in a more gentle tone, 'And if you did have weaknesses, we have remedies, so it is better to be honest.'

The younger man's chest visibly deflated, and he nodded meekly. Lucie asked him if he thought his wife was in good health and if she had her courses regularly, as they were the flowers without which no fruit ever followed. Satisfied on that score, she told Mister Woolrich that she could give a list of suggestions from her long experience, if he pleased. She offered to write them out and send them to him later. However, the man immediately drew out a little leather-bound book of waxed pages from his breeches pocket, and untied its silver stylus, ready to take notes there and then. Lucie saw that this table-book was well-used, but not nearly as ornate as the one Simon carried.

'I think I'd best sit down to inscribe your instructions, Mistress Smith, if you don't mind me sitting before you?'

'Not at all,' replied the midwife, and began her list, counting the points on her fingers as she went:

1. *The best season to conceive of a child is straight after your wife's monthly course is stayed.*

Lucie added, 'You must ask her to impart this to you, although I am sure you know, since she withdraws from you during her time,' before continuing,

2. *Do not hug your wife too hard or too frequently.*

3. *Eat no late suppers. Undigested meat or drink sitting in your stomach hinders the concoction of seed.*

Lucie paused while the gentleman's pen caught up with her words.

4. *Drink the juice of sage. Change your regular drink from beer to mum-ale, which is thickened with wheat so is more nourishing, and put sugar to it.*

5. *Keep her belly warm but her back cool. She can use warm toast for this purpose.*

6. *Provide yourself with drawers of light Holland stuff, to cool your privities.*

At this the younger man's pen stayed a moment, and Lucie noticed how he bristled at any advice pertaining to his contribution to the matter, whilst cheerfully writing out the tips for his wife's part. She glanced at his tablet to make sure his notes were true, and told him she had but two more recommendations.

> 7. *Let not your wife's stays be laced too straitly, nor have her laced at night.*

'Have a care to ensure your good wife informs her woman of this point. It is important she does not let herself be tightly laced in this season,' the midwife added, as the man's pen scratched furiously across the wax.

> 8. *Raise the foot of your bed so your heels be higher than your head.*

After dotting the final sentence, the gentleman ran back through his notes to make sure he had omitted nothing.

'Do you have a view as to whether the best time for, ah, enjoyment is at morn or night, Mistress Smith?' he asked.

'No, you must do it when you both most desire,' said Lucie. 'That is the surest way. Make sure to cherish your wife with caresses and endearments, and plenty of amorous tickling to increase her desire for you, for then the womb will reach down to seize the seed and is more likely to retain it.'

'Goodness me, that's quite a list,' he replied, and then hesitated a moment before adding, 'Um. I hate to ask, but I can rely on your discretion?'

'Naturally,' Lucie said. 'There is one thing more. A test to find out which of you is ... infirm.' She would not say "at fault" as others did, for in her experience, barren couples were simply unfortunate. 'There's no need to do anything until you have tried the methods I have just stated, but if they don't bring you joy, then you could try it.'

Lucie went on to describe what he should do:

> *Take a handful of barley and steep part of it in the man's urine and part in the woman's for a whole day and night. Then take the grains out, dry them,*

131

and plant them in two small pots, filled with good earth. Every morning for the space of seven days, let the grains in each pot be watered with urine from the person in whose water they were first steeped. The party whose seed is first to grow is the most likely to have children. If both pots grow, then neither of you has any infirmity and you will have children in time: patience will supply your want. If it comes about that one pot never grows, then that party has an infirmity and must consult a midwife or physician. If neither pot grows, then your marriage is barren and you will never be fruitful.

'What nature wants, art can hardly make perfect, I am afraid,' she concluded.

Lucie shifted her posture slightly, now the formal part of the interview was over, and she prepared to rejoin the party. As she moved she felt the bones in her hips creak. Mister Woolrich seemed pleased with their discourse, and thanked the midwife heartily, before asking, 'how much do I owe you for this consultation?'

'I require no fee,' replied Lucie with a smile. 'You have just given me the ten shillings in respect of your new godson, which was very kind, and more than enough. May you receive God's blessings in your endeavours in this matter, sir.'

As she prepared to leave the gossiping, she saw Jasper deep in conversation with his cronies from the council. She made a signal that she and Mary would soon be taking their leave, and decided she would just look in on the new mother and her child first.

'Oh, Mistress Smith,' Suzanne began at once. 'I'm so pleased you are here! I have been thinking. I really don't want to nurse my son myself. I want to get back to my schoolroom as soon as I am churched, and nursing an infant would hinder that.'

Lucie was saddened to hear this; she had long held that the practice of mothers who were able to nurse but chose to employ others to do what she considered their duty, to be a remedy in want of a remedy. Nevertheless, it was not for her to judge so she endeavoured to maintain a light tone as she advised Mistress Robbins.

'Why don't you nurse for the first few weeks while you are lying in? It will speed your recovery, and help your son.'

'I suppose so,' said Suzanne, without sounding convinced. She put Lucie in mind of the very young mother she had delivered at the Manor five months before. Lady Eleanor hadn't taken the least interest in her son, but Mistress Robbins did not have the excuse of being green and immature, and had been delighted in her big belly. Perhaps she had a touch of the mulligrubs. Many women felt a little melancholy in the days after their travail. She would send Mary back with some warming medicaments later that day in case Suzanne was indeed a little melancholic.

'Try it for a few days,' Lucie advised brightly, while feeling for the woman's pulse. 'That's good. Your pulse is beating just right.' She patted Suzanne's hand. 'Start nursing tomorrow, for that's when your milk should come in. You may send for me and I can help you latch him onto the breast if you please. If it really does not suit you, I know a poor woman who will likely welcome the chance to earn some extra money nursing your boy.' She was thinking of Anne Jones and her needy family. Taking in the Robbins baby for a few months would help them out; the child would also be near enough for his mother and father to look in upon him regularly.

The Three Doves was already lit up, with candlelight twinkling through the crossed panes of glass, when Lucie arrived home. It was mid-afternoon but the nights were drawing in rapidly and it was a dull day to boot. The glow also highlighted the worn paint of the frames, further confirming the expedience of booking the craftsman, who'd be coming in just a few weeks' time. A quick peak in the window revealed that Ned was chatting to a couple of customers, so rather than interrupt, Lucie took the ginnel straight through to the kitchen where she found Martha busy with her smoothing iron, in the semi darkness. She removed her cloak and hung it on a hook on the door, before bending into the fire to light a taper.

'I don't know how you work in this light, Martha. I can hardly see.' She lit up a row of candles on the mantle. Martha insisted the light from the fire was enough to iron by and carried on with her work.

'Would Goodwife Jones be willing to stand as a wet-nurse for the Robbins' baby, if they need one, do you think?' Lucie asked her. 'The family would get more money by it, and if she were better fed, her own child would be receiving better milk. And she has a boy child, too, which is perfect. As you know, it's always best for a nurse's child to be the same sex as her nurseling.'

Martha agreed to ask her cousin when she next visited her. She put the cooling-down iron back on its ledge over the fire, and picked up the second one from the fire, resuming her task of pressing sheets. Lucie took the opportunity to rest in her armchair, watching Martha while she worked. It had been a busy afternoon.

'You know, Martha,' said Lucie at length, 'I think you must be right about you being at the change of life. If you don't mind me saying, your waist is quite thickened, and you have always been so slender. That happened to me at this time, and as all can see, I am grown quite stout in my old age.'

There was no response. Lucie knew Martha had heard her because the maid bit her lower lip. Lucie's fear that she had offended her seemed to be answered when Martha slammed the iron on the sheets a bit harder than necessary. *There I go, prating away thoughtlessly*, she chided herself. Perhaps it was best if they both feigned the belief that she hadn't spoken.

Lucie was just making a show of using the arms of her chair to help her back onto to her feet, when she turned at the sound of the door latch. Simon came in seconds later, with a big parcel in his arms.

'Father's still chatting at the gossiping, so I thought this was the time to bring the sign round for you to hide somewhere,' he said. 'Before I left, I asked Alderman Robbins's housekeeper if the remainder food could be taken to the poor of Warley Lane. That was fitting, wasn't it?'

Lucie smiled at her son. Sometimes she felt he could read her mind. The sign was wrapped in hessian and tied with string. Lucie and Martha helped him unwrap it. The women were amazed at the talent of the painter. He had kept to the original design, easily recognised by passers-by, but the new doves were pristine, and the sign glowed with fresh, gay colours. Added detail appeared in the form of lettering. At the top was the name of the apothecary: *J. Smith, Licensed Druggist.* Under the image of the three doves the wording read, *Also Mistress L. Smith, Licensed Midwife.* The image was replicated on the reverse.

'Oh, Simon, it's perfect!' Lucie clasped her hands together. 'Isn't a sight to behold, Martha? How smart it will look. It must have cost a pretty penny. I'm not sure I can wait until Christmastide to show your father.'

'You must, Mother. Hanging it before a slovenly shop front would destroy half its beauty,' he replied reasonably. 'The cost will serve as a token of thanks for advancing me the funds to set myself up in the print house and booksellers.'

Rewrapping the parcel, he asked his mother where he should put it. The board was large and heavy, an ell tall by half an ell wide. Lucie said it would have to go under her bed, as there was nowhere else they could hide it.

'No,' said Martha, 'put it under the bed where I sleep with Mary. The master might take a look under yours if he reaches for the pot in the night and it's not to hand.'

Mary had arrived home shortly after Simon, having had a couple of errands to run after the party. She nodded her assent. She too thought the sign was splendid and offered to help Simon carry it up the two pairs of stairs to her attic room.

'I can manage well enough, but thank you Mistress Thorne,' he declared with theatrical bow, complete with arm flourish. The women laughed and Lucie shook her head, smiling at her son's silly capering. The tension between Lucie and Martha appeared to be forgotten for now. On his arrival back downstairs, Simon mentioned to the women that he was returning to the Boar Inn to pack, ready for the stage-coach early the following morning.

Lucie's gut griped. She begged to be excused while she made for the privy yet again. She took her time outside to regain control of her passions, so she might appear calm when she returned to the kitchen. As she washed her hands in the scullery she called through to her son to elicit his faithful promise that he would call in before he left, to take his leave of her and his father properly.

Chapter Fourteen

Simon kept his word and called at the Three Doves very early the next morning. He was wearing his London garb, but thankfully without the confounded periwig which both Lucie and Jasper hated. His natural hair had grown back while he'd been in Tupingham, and he looked much better. Lucie already sensed the distance growing between her and her son nevertheless, marked by how different he seemed in his city fashions. She didn't doubt his first stop back in London would be to the barbers to have his lovely hair shorn to be replaced by the false hair after the King's fashion. Jasper greeted him with a hearty handshake, clasping his son's upper arm with his other hand. The men looked into one another's eyes with undeniable fondness. Lucie's heart swelled and she half suspected there was an unspoken accord between them to demonstrate to her that they parted with affection not enmity. When Jasper broke their hold he picked up a protective pomander from the counter and handed it to Simon. The heady scents of lavender, rose, cloves, and myrrh filled the shop and brought back memories of Lucie's recent trip to Grantby.

'Carry this with you when you go abroad, son. I've made up another as a plague-cake to be worn under your shirt next your skin. The sweet scent will give you some measure of protection from the bad air and noisome stinks in the city. These filthy savours are on every corner, and they spread the contagion. Be sure to carry a branch of rosemary too, whenever you can. It will help keep you safe.'

Simon's eyes filled with water at this thoughtfulness. Lucie was so tempted to reveal the secret of the new shop sign to show Jasper his son was just as thoughtful, but all would be revealed in due course.

'Thank you, Father. I'll be sure to follow your advice.'

'See you do,' responded Jasper a little gruffly. It seemed to Lucie that her husband too was struggling to maintain his composure. 'Also, when you return to your lodging, make sure you air it thoroughly. You will need to light a charcoal fire in a stone pan. Don't put it in the chimney, but in the centre of the room. Are you marking my words, Simon? Do this at least once a week until the danger is past. And here's something to put in the hearth: whenever you ask for a fire to be laid, add a little of this mixture to the flames.' He handed his son a package wrapped in paper. The smell of frankincense, juniper, dried rosemary, and bay leaves emanated from it. 'You can also make a fume from rosemary steeped in strong vinegar.'

Lucie pitched in with her own advice: 'If your apprentices can't afford such measures, Simon, and they can't come by the ingredients your father can supply, then tell them that warm bread and a boiled onion in each room will also do much to draw in the poisons. Your father and I will hold you in our prayers and trust you will do the like for us.'

'Thank you, Mother. And Father, thank you too! I am blessed indeed with such kind and loving parents.' He tucked the pomander and other items into his satchel, next to the victuals he'd bought to make a dinner of during the first day of the coach journey. 'Mind you both take care too. And look after one another. Father, pray inform me if you decide to make your customary trip to Apothecaries' Hall, and perhaps we'll dine together one evening. It's but a short walk from Blackfriars to St Paul's, as you know. I'd be pleased to show you the changes we've made to the print house and the bookshop out in front too, if you'd like to come and see them.'

As Simon took his leave, Ned burst into the shop, announcing that the Calstone coach was in the street outside. They had been so absorbed in their leave-taking that they had not noticed it through the window. Lucie saw what looked like a brief expression of concern pass over Simon's face before he appeared to check himself. A liveried servant followed hastily behind the apprentice into the shop, and handed a letter to Mistress Smith. He then bowed and turned to leave.

'Let's hope this is in settlement of their account,' Jasper commented, a little more loudly than he usually spoke, as if he hoped the retreating servant would hear him. Lucie tucked the letter in her pocket. There would be time enough for reading that when she had seen her son off.

With a last hug for his mother and another for Martha, Simon finally made his way out of the shop. The door banged behind him.

'You're a kind father, preparing all those measures to keep our son safe in the city,' Lucie said to her husband, sniffing hard. She drew her napkin from her sleeve and wiped her eyes and nose. She felt empty now Simon had gone, and moved closer to Jasper, who took her in his arms.

'Yes, well, he needs to have a care, doesn't he? I can only do so much,' he said to the top her head.

Jasper had confessed to her years ago that the thing he would never be able to admit to anyone else was that when he looked on his son's pockmarked, but still handsome face, what he saw was a visible mark of God's displeasure. No matter how hard he had prayed and served the Lord, the remedies Jasper mixed in God's name had not been blessed with the power to save all his brood, only this one son. Lucie knew he would never, ever resolve the guilt arising from his conviction that he had not been in favour with the Lord when it most mattered. As part of his faith, Jasper regularly examined all aspects of his life to search for signs he was in the number of God's elect, whose earthly trials would finally be revealed as signs of God's favour, and who were predestined for eternal life in Heaven. The catastrophe in his family made it apparent that he could not assume this was so for him. All four of their children had had the horrendous disease at the same time – Simon less severely – and despite all their best efforts, the other three had perished. It was only their deep faith and their trust in the Lord's plan that stopped the couple from falling into despair at their loss.

There had not been any more children after that, and as the years passed and their hopes faded, it became hard for Jasper not to see this as further punishment for his sins. The couple had prayed together on the matter long and earnestly, especially in the years immediately after their tragedy. Crucially, in all their conversations on the matter, Jasper had insisted that he saw this as his failing alone, her cheerful frankness, he said, was a sign of grace.

At around ten of the clock, Martha came through from the kitchen to see if they required something to eat or drink. Seeing her reminded Lucie of the letter in her pocket. The seal was strong and she had to find Jasper's penknife to get into it. Inside was an invitation from Lady Calstone to take tea with her the next afternoon.

I haven't even tried the China tea I bought a few weeks ago in Grantby and now I'm being invited to take tea with her ladyship, Lucie thought. *What's all this about?*

The note didn't require an answer. Its tone rather assumed that an invitation from her ladyship was a command. Lucie decided that she would indeed go to the Manor the next day. It would be another airing for her new green suit of clothes if nothing else, something to look forward to, and a trip out would perhaps help to ease her inner ache at the renewed loss of Simon from their home.

Outside on the street, Simon had been beckoned over to the Calstone coach. Seated inside was his friend, Sir Robert, who said, 'Quick, get in.'

'What's the news with you, Robbie?' Simon clambered up. The coachman had already relieved him of his trunk and was tying it to the roof with Sir Robert's belongings. His friend ushered Simon into the seat on the far side of the coach, that he might stay by the door.

'I heard you were leaving for London, so I invented a reason for returning to the city on business. Cecilia didn't question me, and the old man lingers about the court, and isn't here to stop me. So I thought I'd kidnap you before you got on the stage-coach – that we might travel together. A scheme of dazzling ingenuity, even if I say so myself!' As he spoke, he drew the leather curtain across the window so they would not be stared at by the townsfolk.

'Cecilia? You mean your mother, Lady Calstone?'

'She's no mother of mine. My natural mother died when she was brought to bed of me.' The coach lurched into motion, bumping over the cobbles. 'Cecilia's the old man's second wife. I call her Mother to keep the peace. But she feels like a stranger to me. I was sent to grow up with my wife's family when I was still a babe in petticoats, you know. Od's blood but it still feels queer saying "my wife". My first memories of the Manor here are of visits to the old man. Lord Northerton was more of a father than Calstone ever was.'

Simon was still in a maze that he was in the Calstone coach. While his friend babbled away, he lifted his satchel strap from across his chest. He placed the bag on the floor. The coach was not large and the two men were of necessity sitting very close to one another. Simon felt hot. Robbie, as his friends called him, continued chattering away.

'It was a strange family, now I think of it. The Countess acted more like an older sister than a mother to me, and Nell was like my little sister. We were happy in our way, but then Lord Northerton and the old man agreed that Nell and I

141

should marry – Od's wounds, Simon, when you think about it, there's little wonder my love for my wife is more brotherly than anything else! It's all confoundedly odd, though I pity the poor girl being married to a wastrel like me.'

Simon wished his friend would not blaspheme so freely, but that was just one of the many differences between them.

They sat pressed together in silence for a moment, as the coach rocked from side to side. Robbie declared brightly, 'No matter! The latest Lady C is in charge while father is away, even though I am in my majority and she should by rights defer to me, but she is occupied with the children, and my wife and son – so is too busy to mind what I am about.' He lifted a corner of the curtain with his index finger, to check on their progress. They had left the town behind and were now on the dirt road through the countryside, and so he opened the curtain fully and allowed light into the coach.

Simon coughed. 'Speaking of your wife,' he said. 'How goes Lady Eleanor and the infant Charles?'

'Well enough, I think. She's a sweet girl, but I haven't seen much of her since the birth, just at the supper table from time to time – although she pays more attention to that confounded lap-dog of hers than she does to the company. The nursery maids assure me the child thrives; I looked in on him most days and he is enchanting.'

Simon shifted in his seat, looking straight at his friend. 'This scheme is madness, Robbie! What if anyone is suspicious about why you collected me in the coach?'

'Why would they? No-one saw you get in.'

'What if the servants at the Boar spread the news that I didn't take my place on the stage-coach?'

'Don't be a coxcomb,' said the younger man. 'No-one listens to servant gossip.' He was now searching a wicker hamper he'd pulled out from beneath his seat. Simon shook his head at the offer of a biscuit.

Robbie chewed on the fresh jumbal, before pausing to lean over and kiss Simon, his free hand moving towards his

142

lover's breeches. 'I'd rather eat you than this, if I had my way,' he said. Simon's yard rose in response and he groaned, his passion coupled with guilt. It would kill his parents to know of his taste for the attractions of young men. To compound the offence, he had taken for a lover a Royalist, whose family's values were everything his father hated.

'Stop, Robbie! Not now, not here.'

'Od's wounds, man, we've not had a chance to be alone for an age!' He seemed not to remember their recent trips to Grantby: with some careful planning, Simon's commissioning of the Three Doves sign and its collection a few weeks later had enabled the men to spend two delightful nights together.

At the coaching inn, Simon and Sir Robert would not be disturbed. No-one would question their arrangement, since travellers normally bedded together, but because of Sir Robert's rank the two of them took extra care not to attract undue attention lest it led to extortion, or worse, Lord Calstone finding out.

'Do you remember when we first met?' Simon asked Robbie as he climbed into the bed. It had been the previous summer. The pair cuddled up and reminisced about their first few encounters, how they'd become acquainted through the playhouse set, and only later discovered their families lived near one another.

'You could have knocked me down with a feather when I learned you were from Tupingham,' said Robbie. 'Who would have guessed that?'

When they arrived in London early the next evening both men were shocked at the sight that greeted them. People with the plague and plaisters on their sores begged on the street, many houses were still shut up with a cross on the door, and an eerie air hung about the city. Sir Robert dropped Simon off near his print house in a side road near St Paul's Cathedral, and carried on to the Calstones' London house near Covent Garden, just over a mile away. Simon held his pomander close to his nose as he stepped into the street. The print house was still standing and had not been plundered, which seemed a mercy, given the poverty all around. The interior was covered in dust and the presses would need some attention before they ran again, after nearly twelve weeks of idleness. His gaze alighted on the crates of books, packed in haste before they left, and memories of that time came flooding back. For a moment he wondered if his decision to return was the right one.

The Millers also lived in rooms above the shop. They had arrived back in London a day or two earlier, meaning the living quarters were much more welcoming when Simon clumsily entered the room, having caught his satchel-strap on the door handle. John Miller and his wife were sitting near a cheery fire. John immediately rose to greet him.

'I hope we have been wise to come back, Simon,' he said, patting the younger man soundly on the back. 'It is good to see you, all the same!'

'I confess I had precisely the same thought downstairs, John.'

Ruth Miller smiled and rose to pour Simon a cup of ale. 'I expect you're shattered after two days on that stage-coach. The seats are so hard, aren't they? And they cram you in with sour-smelling strangers to get as much money from each trip as they can.' Simon thanked her. He declared his journey had been unusually pleasant, but that he was pleased to be home.

The Millers had left their children with relatives in the north of the country where the air was cleaner, so the household was quieter and duller than Simon was used to. He was good with children and loved dandling the little ones, or playing a game with the older ones before bed time. The thought of the youngsters put him briefly in mind of his mother and he hoped she was not too distressed by his departure. The best thing would have been if she'd been called to a birthing immediately after he left and that would have taken him from her thoughts for a while at least.

'Not found yourself a wife then, Simon, while you were

home?' Ruth Miller smiled. 'We thought that your days might have been so dull without the diversions of city life, you might have gone hunting for a sweetheart.'

'No, sadly not, Ruth,' he replied. 'There was plenty to occupy me at home, though.'

He accepted with relish one of the flour scones Ruth had just finished cooking on the griddle over the hearth, and told them about how he had designed and commissioned a new sign for the Three Doves. He mentioned his mother's plans to have the front window frames, door and timbers repainted; about the letter his mother had received from the King for her services to the Calstones; and about the quarrel with his father at Simon's suggestion that his mother wrote a book. John agreed it would have been a marvellous thing to have secured such a unique edition, but understood that without her husband's permission, his mother could never even begin it.

'What of the apprentices?' Simon asked. 'Have you been able to find them and recall them to work?'

John sighed, 'I'm sorry, Simon. I should have told you before, but I didn't know how. We've lost all four to the plague.' He paused for a moment while Simon took a deep breath. 'With the city so devastated, we shall have a hard time finding enough hands to work in the print house.'

Groaning, Simon banged his fist on the table, suppressing the profanity that was on the tip of his tongue. The print house had been a close business, how could he have moped about something as irrelevant as not holding a waygoose feast when his employees were, unbeknown to him, dying? Such a horrible death, too! The youngest had been only fourteen and had only just begun his indenture.

'God be thanked, the journeyman Stephen was spared, he will get the presses running if anyone can,' John said. 'Ruth will open the bookshop when we have cleaned and fumigated it, but without most of our men, I fear we're in a sad quandary. We have both run through our savings and funds are low.

Well, at least, mine are.'

'Mine too. I lodged at the inn in Tupingham. I thought it would serve no good purpose to lodge at my father's and irritate him daily.'

Simon heard footsteps in the corridor and the door opened. He turned as the Millers' housemaid came into the room.

'Oh, Kate, my dearest Kate, you're a sight for sore eyes!' He half-rose from his chair by the fire, slopping his ale on his sleeve but he cared not. 'I just heard the terrible news about the lads and I didn't dare ask after you. Thank God you have been spared!' Impulsively, he took her in his arms and spun her round, hugging her close.

'Ha, you don't get rid of me that easily, Mister Smith! I'll have you know, I've slept in your bed these last two nights, so it is well aired for you,' she said in her broad London accent.

'I'm most grateful to you for that service, Kate. It has been a smooth journey, but I'm still ready for an early night. I'll just have a bit of supper if you have any for me, and then I'll turn in.' He planned to follow his father's instructions to fumigate his quarters thoroughly.

Chapcer Fifceen

'Thir day I laid the lace wife of John Allen, comber.'

Lucie didn't have much time to mope about Simon leaving, for the very next day, as soon as they had finished dinner, she and Mary were called to Goodwife Allen. It was her time for sure now, as her waters had gone. Martha came along to Warley Lane with them, carrying bundles of linen. She would act as one of Anne Allen's gossips and help out with any children of the cottages. Anne Jones and Jane Croft were also there to support their friend, and there were two sleeping babies in the crib, one new-born and one about four months old.

Anne Jones explained to Lucie that the older children and Jane's baby Matthew were all with her upstairs neighbour, Widow Rose.

'Who have we still got with us?' Lucie asked, peering into the cradle.

'That's my boy, Toby,' Anne Jones said, 'and the little one is Jeremy Robbins, the schoolmistress's son. He's to lodge with me until he's a year old. He's only been with me since yesterday, and he seems content. But the pair of them keep me so busy! Toby still takes the breast every two hours, and as for little Jerry, he only stops sucking when he's asleep, and not always then.' She fussed with the coverings over the two babies, lying top-to-tail in the wooden crib. Jeremy Robbins

147

looked so tiny next to Toby Jones; he was not yet a week old. 'Still, the money I'll earn will be a great relief to us, and Master Robbins has promised to supply extra diet for us all, so we'll fare better than we have for a long time, as long as my milk holds out.'

Lucie was surprised Suzanne Robbins had put the mite out to nurse without asking further advice from her, but it was probable she had learned from Martha that Goodwife Jones was a willing wet-nurse and would give the child a good home. She had clearly not followed Lucie's plea to at least attempt nursing him, having sent him to a nurse at just three days old.

Completing her preparations for the birth ahead, which included offering up a prayer for guidance as she did at every birthing, Lucie turned to see that over on the bed Anne Allen was not doing well at all. She had lost a great deal of blood throughout the pregnancy and now she was bleeding again. Her waters had broken that morning, which meant Lucie would have to lubricate the vagina with grease, since the waters normally helped the baby slide out. Anne's pains were coming every couple of minutes, but Mary's examination showed that the womb wasn't yet open. She asked Lucie to repeat the examination.

Lucie greased her hand with almond oil and thrust it inside Anne to discover that the neck of the womb was almost completely shut, but she was still bleeding heavily. Lucie went to her bag for her eagle-stone to speed the delivery by opening the womb. She had not used it since that day Mother Henshaw had destroyed Jenny Bromfield's unborn daughter with her stubborn refusal to seek timely aid, and had gone near to destroying Jenny, too.

Lucie did not place much trust in this remedy in today's circumstances. The tang of blood filled the air and Anne was strangely quiet. Lucie experienced a familiar foreboding in her guts, which had begun to fret again. Jane Croft had been busy bringing in water from the stream that ran at the end of the row of cottages, and heating it on the fire, and Lucie scrubbed her own hands vigorously in the warm water with Castile soap. As she washed, she felt a calmness take over her, and was grateful that her gripings eased. When she looked back on this day, she would need to know, for her own peace of mind, that she had used every resource at her disposal. She began her work. Feeling for Anne's pulse, she found it was fast, a sign of fever, and of blood loss. She prepared a decoction of feverfew in wine. Mary trickled it into Anne's mouth from a spoon drop-by-drop, with great patience. Meanwhile Lucie took a pot of wax, added a few drops of spermaceti oil, and took the mixture over to the hearth to melt it. She asked Jane to pour it over a piece of linen when it was ready and this would go on Anne's belly to strengthen it, and lessen the pain she was in.

'This special *parmacety* I used will give her the strength of the whale it comes from,' Lucie told the women, using the common pronunciation of the medication.

While she waited for the draught to take effect, Lucie led the women in prayer, starting with one that a wise man might have written especially for midwives: 'O Lord God, have mercy upon all women great with child; be pleased to give them a joyful and a safe deliverance: and let thy grace preserve the fruit of their wombs, and conduct them to the holy sacrament of baptism.' She had a strong feeling that the most important thing she might achieve today would be bringing the child out in time to save its immortal soul. After a quarter hour had passed, Anne remained only half awake, her friends pressed cool cloths against her forehead while the midwives checked her progress again. The womb was contracting forcefully. The tightenings could be seen through the thin cloth of Anne's shift. The neck of the womb was opening but would admit only a couple of fingers. Lucie feared that the after-burden had become detached from the side of the womb. The chances of Anne Allen giving birth to a live child were now as slender as her own hope of survival. The women in the room weren't aware of the full extent of the mother's peril, but couldn't help but be alert to the number of muck-wet bloodied clouts piling up beside the bed. Lucie turned to address Anne Jones.

'It's time to take those babes to a more wholesome air. Since you have a newborn to tend, can you take them home? You've already given us more help than we could ask, and there are enough of us left here to look after Goodwife Allen.'

Lucie didn't want innocent babies in the room where death's shadow was already falling. But it was still important to keep up Anne Allen's spirits and strength, if only to give her child a chance of being born alive, so Jane tried to spoon feed her some of the chicken broth Martha had brought for the women while they awaited the birth. Gossips normally made sure the midwife was replete with any refreshments, but with food being sparse in this lane, Martha had discreetly brought the pot of soup and a couple of loaves inside the linen bundle she carried. The tiny amount Anne was able to swallow soon came back. Lucie took Mary to one side and asked her to send one of the cottagers in the utmost haste for Mister Collins, the chirurgeon, and another for Dr Archer. Anne was becoming light-headed and delirious. Porringers were filling with her blood and the room was full of its distinctive, metallic odour.

Anne Jones came rushing back in. She said her husband Sam had agreed to mind the babies, and would fetch her to feed and change them whenever they cried. As news of Anne Allen's danger spread down the row of cottages, the men had stopped work and were milling around in the back yard. The midwife tried yet again to open the womb, that the baby might be delivered. She, too, was covered in blood and her arm was cramping badly in response to the sustained efforts she was making in such a confined space. Withdrawing her hand, she winced at the blood lodged down her fingernails. She stretched out her fingers, which tingled sharply. She felt a corresponding dizziness in her head. *Stay calm*, she admonished herself.

The chirurgeon arrived within twenty minutes, red in the face, having run all the way. Lucie had had no more luck getting the womb open in the minutes they waited. He ordered all the women but Lucie and Mary from the room, and set to work, rolling up his sleeves while reminding Mary to hold Anne's mouth wide open to give the child the best chance of getting air. Both women knew the real battle here was to deliver the child alive, if only for a few moments. Mister Collins promptly declared it a hopeless case. As he withdrew his blooded hand from Anne he said he could feel that the after-burden had indeed come away from its moorings, but he couldn't find any way of delivering this baby unless he cut the mother's belly, which he would not do while she lived.

Lucie asked him to step aside. She knelt next to the bed, her bones creaking as she lowered herself into place. She indicated to Mary and Mister Collins that they should pull Anne, one leg each, to the edge of the bed. As they moved her a great flux of blood gushed onto the bed and the three exchanged the briefest of knowing glances. Once again Lucie felt inside the womb for the child. Thrusting her hand in deep, she could feel the weakest of heartbeats on the child's chest. It is a good thing Anne is not fully conscious, Lucie thought, how excruciating this operation would otherwise be for her. Finally, she got hold of the child's legs, pulled it into position, and brought its body out feet first into the world, by strength alone. She held the body, which she'd wrapped in a warm sheet, while the chirurgeon made a swift, deep cut to Anne's privities so the head could be born without delay; there was no occasion for delicacy now. It was a boy, just about living, but limp and leaden of hue. It was clear he wouldn't survive long. In cases like this the midwife was obliged to baptise the child immediately. She left the chirurgeon and Mary to try to remove the placenta. Glancing over her shoulder she saw that when it appeared, it was ragged and incomplete. If Anne had been bleeding from a

151

single vein, Mister Collins might have been able to cauterise it with a hot iron, but Lucie knew that the sight before him was evidence of a state of devastation within the body beyond the power of any surgeon to remedy. There was no real hope, but as Anne was alive they had to keep on trying. He and Mary fought to stanch her bleeding, stuffing cloth after cloth inside her and pressing down hard on her abdomen, but even as they did so, Anne's shallow breathing became more and more laboured.

Meanwhile, Lucie baptised the baby, welcoming him into the family of Christ by using water from one of the buckets soaking the cloths to mark a cross on his forehead. It was far from perfect but wouldn't do further harm, since the child was fading by the second. She took great care to use the right words: 'Creature of God, I baptize thee in the Name of the Father, and of the Son, and of the Holy Ghost. Amen.' The name might strike some hearers as strange, but she knew of other midwives using it in desperate haste, and she had no time to find out Goodman Allen's chosen name for his son. The main thing was that she had secured his soul. She had the Prayer Book's warrant for that. She knew the words by heart: *It is certain by God's word, that children which are baptised, dying before they commit actual sin, are undoubtedly saved.*

She passed the baby to Mary and turned her attention to Anne.

'We are losing her,' Lucie whispered to Mister Collins.

'Yes,' he hissed back. 'But have you ever known a woman presenting like this to survive? Because I haven't.'

While Mary held the babe she also mopped Anne's brow and offered reassuring words, letting her have a moment to feel the child's tiny face on hers. Once again Lucie marvelled at the empathy and grace her young deputy displayed. The midwife and chirurgeon tried every trick known to them to save Anne. They stuffed napkins and cloths inside her womb and raised her middle, but still the blood flowed. They were

152

not winning the battle. Lucie glanced up at Mary, who shook her head to let the midwife know the child had slipped away.

'We must ask her husband to come in and say his farewells,' the chirurgeon said, when Lucie passed on this news. 'Goodwife Allen will follow her son presently.'

They made the bed as tidy as possible, covering it with a clean top sheet, and placed the infant in his mother's arms, where he looked as if he were sleeping. Mary had swaddled him with the same tenderness she had shown Jenny Bromfield's babe, months earlier. John Allen came in presently, holding his two children's hands. It was only near four in the afternoon but already the sky was darkening, as if in sympathy with their grief. Lucie, Mary, and the chirurgeon stepped outside to allow them to say goodbye in private. Lucie, looking back, saw John take up his wife's limp hand and lay it on the heads of each child in turn, so that they might receive her last blessing. After a few minutes, Anne's friends re-entered the bedroom so that they could say their goodbyes too. Anne was long past the point of knowing who was there, but they wanted her to go to her death knowing her friends would look after her children.

In the yard, Martha was talking to Anthony Higgs. She understood it must be a painful afternoon for him, bringing back memories of his own wife, who had died in similar circumstances a few years before. In that case the baby had survived, and Anthony had found himself a widower, with two small children to care for. On impulse, or so it felt to her, he took hold of Martha and pulled her into a corner, under the eaves.

'Martha, this day has reminded me that life is but short,' he said in a hoarse voice. 'Who can tell what the future holds, or how long we are granted on earth?'

153

'Where is this leading to, Anthony?' Martha found herself bursting into tears. She instinctively, but only fleetingly, touched her belly as she pulled away from the weaver.

'Marry me,' he said bluntly. 'Marry me. Martha, I love you, and surely you don't want to be a servant forever? Come and live with me, be a mother to my children, and you can work once more in the trade you were raised in.'

Martha's tears turned into full sobs. This was too much to absorb. Opposing thoughts crossed her mind at one and the same time. *Could I? What if I said yes? No, no, you know you can't, not if Anthony knew the truth.* Her sobs gave way to whimpering. After a few moments she took in a deep breath and composed herself. She grabbed Anthony's large hands in her own.

'Anthony, I don't know what to say. I had no notion you were thinking this way; I thought you just wanted a friend.'

'You lay with me,' he reminded her. 'Many times. There's plenty who'd take that as a promise of betrothal.'

'I know, and I am not ashamed of lying with you. As you say, life is short, and the late wars and all the strife in the land have taught us to take comfort where we can.'

'So will you be my wife?' he said.

'I'm in a maze. I don't know. I'm much older than you for one thing. And there are other matters to consider. Let me sleep upon it, with Anne lying so close to death, I can't think to any purpose.'

Anthony said a terse 'as you wish,' and went to stand with the men.

Martha watched her lover stomp into the distance. Tears ran freely down her face, and she made no attempt to find her napkin. It was like being rooted to the spot.

Eventually Lucie noticed her maid standing alone and walked over to her, offering her a drink from her own ale. 'It's a terrible business isn't it?' she said.

'Pardon?' For an awful moment, Martha thought her employer had overheard what had just passed between her and Anthony. 'Oh, I'm sorry. Poor Anne Allen. Yes, it is terrible. My heart feels like to break.'

'To what did you think I referred?' Lucie gave her a quizzical look. 'And what were you and Goodman Higgs talking about? You both looked as if your minds were very agitated.'

'I'm sorry; I was momentarily lost in sadness. Of course I knew you meant Anne. What else? It's true, though, that the terrible things that happened today have brought back Goodman Higgs's own grief. Remember, his wife died in childbed four years ago.' She avoided her mistress's eye.

Lucie pulled her shawl more closely around her shoulders, and Martha noticed, even in the low light, that her shirt was covered in Anne's blood. She could see Lucie was worn out. It was now properly dusk and the temperature was dropping rapidly. We should go back indoors, before the mistress catches a chill, she thought. She took Lucie's arm to guide her back towards the cottages. Lucie was just making her reply. 'The poor man. I had quite forgotten he was a widower; he had his children before he came to Tuping...' Then she stopped speaking. They both saw through the dimness that John Allen was coming out of his cottage. He shook his head, and burst into tears. His whole body heaved with the sobs. Anne had gone.

With a leaden feeling inside her, Lucie returned to the cottage. She and Mary would lay Anne out and prepare her for burial. At least she would be buried with her son, so she wouldn't be alone. Lucie was weary to her very bones. The birth had taken a physical toll on her as she had used all her strength to draw the unfortunate child forth. She'd need to ask Jasper to help her bind her aching arms in cerecloth for the night to give them some ease, and perhaps she'd rub some oil of earthworms into her sore knees before she got into bed tonight. In addition to the physical symptoms, she was flooded with sorrow that she hadn't been able to prevent this. She kept thinking back to just a few short weeks before when all poor Anne needed was a few peasecods, and they had been merry as Mary fetched them for her. How pleased they'd felt to have affected such a swift cure.

Soon Dr Archer arrived in Warley Lane to pray for the soul of Anne and her son. He said he was deeply sorry not to have got there in time to baptise the child or pray for Goodwife Allen as her soul departed, but he had been away from the rectory when sent for, and had set out the instant he received the message. Jasper was with him. The news had begun to filter through the town; Jasper had brought some of the preparations used to clean and prepare the corpse, and waited to walk his wife and her deputy home after their sad task was completed. He'd also brought a clutch of tobacco pipes from the Three Doves for the mourners. He didn't care for the herb himself, and Lucie thought it a touching gesture. Jasper gave her a squeeze on the arm as she went into the partitioned area of the room that served for the Allen's bed chamber. In just over an hour their work was done, and they left Anne looking pale but peaceful.

Lucie had assumed that Martha would want to stay with the Joneses, but to her surprise she said no, she would return home with them to the Three Doves. The sack full of sheets, clouts and midwives' clothes must be attended to straightaway if they were to come clean.

Dr Archer planned to sit with the bodies all evening, along with John. Anne and her child would be buried the next day.

The Smiths, Mary, and their housemaid formed a sombre party walking back through town. Lucie and Mary were filthy with the blood they had failed to stanch as it ran from Anne. They wrapped their cloaks close around them. When they got to the alehouse, Jasper called in to ask that some hot food for supper be sent to the Three Doves, since no one had been in to cook all afternoon. While nobody had any appetite, they all knew the importance of maintaining their strength.

As they waited for the meal, Jasper banked up the fire that Ned had let die down while they were out, and poured out some noggins of perry from the flagon on the shelf for each of them. Martha made her excuses and went into the laundry to begin to soak the enormous quantity of linen she had left there. Jasper took a lighted candle and stepped into the shop while his wife and Mary removed their day dresses and shirts so they could wash themselves in front of the fire. Their dresses would have to be hung to dry and brushed clean, and the aprons, shirts, and sleeves boiled. Lucie and Mary would have to sup in their padded petticoats and underskirts, and their night-dresses and jackets that Ned had been sent upstairs to fetch. Lucie had a wardrobe of three dresses plus her new green suit, but Mary only owned the one winter and one summer dress, so would have to wear her summer one until her thicker dress was ready again.

When a dish of sausages atop a bed of boiled cabbage from the Black Bull arrived, Mary served it, and they ate in reflective silence. While Martha cleared the table, Jasper read to the family from his Bible, choosing the comforting verses in Ecclesiastes 3 which reminded them that for everyone there was *a time to weep, and a time to laugh; a time to mourn, and a time to dance*, and that this is all part of the Lord's plan. He then led them in prayers, not just for Goodwife Allen and her child, but for those left in Warley Lane, for this would be a sad loss to the whole neighbourhood. Martha sobbed openly, as if her heart were breaking. It seemed odd to Lucie that she should be so strongly moved, but the afternoon's events had left them all weary and mournful, and perhaps that accounted for her desolate mood.

When they were all tucked up in bed, the curtains drawn tightly around them, Jasper took his wife in his arms and made love to her with the slow, sure, comforting familiarity of a lifetime spent together. The weight of his body made her feel safe, secure, and loved. In return she put her arms around his back and hugged him tightly. Passion wasn't the defining feature of their coupling tonight; rather, an instinctive need to connect at a deep spiritual level. *So then they are no more twain, but one flesh*, the familiar gospel drifted through Lucie's mind. Afterwards, they lay cuddled into one another, and Lucie whispered to her husband that she was blessed to have him.

'Not so blessed as I, wife. It is I who am the lucky one.'

Lucie lay awake for a long time, recalling the events of the afternoon and her earlier dealings with Anne Allen over and over, racking her brains to think of something she could have done to save her. She pictured those two children, now motherless. However, she knew in her heart that she had done everything in her power: she had called the chirurgeon in a timely fashion, had laid out the deceased with the utmost respect and dignity, and discharged her duties to the absolute best of her oath as a midwife. Days like that were thankfully rare, but that made them no easier to live with. As she was dropping off, she remembered Simon's leaving, and a knot rose in her stomach afresh at the thought of the danger he might have travelled into. She was once again grateful to Jasper for the careful preparations he had made to keep Simon safe, and her tension lessened. She rolled over and snuggled up to her sleeping husband, as sleep finally took her.

Chapter Sixteen

Goodwife Allen's funeral service took place the next morning. She had been wrapped in a flannel winding sheet, as the law demanded, covered in late-blooming wild flowers. The sheet was knotted at the top and bottom. Her babe was wrapped in cerecloth and placed in his mother's arms inside the sheet.

The ancient stone church looked sombre against the bare trees and grey sky as the mourners followed the cart bearing the bodies to the church yard. When they arrived the church bells pealed six times to mark the passing of a woman, and then after a pause, chimed once for every year of Anne's short life. The bell was then rung three more times to mark the death of the infant. The service was attended by many men of the parish, all acutely aware that there but for God's mercy might go any of them or their loved ones. Lucie Smith and Mary Thorne, attending in their capacity as midwives, were representatives of the other women of Tupingham, for women seldom attended funeral services. Those who had wanted to had said their farewells and made their peace with Anne as she lay in her bed the previous night and on this morning.

Dr Archer delivered a moving sermon, reminding the congregation that all of them were in the midst of death even as they lived, and Anne and her child were lowered into their grave in the flannel sheet.

Afterwards, Samuel and Anne Jones received the mourners in their home, since John Allen, penniless and dazed with grief, could not be expected to offer any hospitality. Parish relief met the cost of funerals of the poor, sparing John one worry at least, and it provided biscuits and wine for the mourners afterwards. Alderman Robbins was in the company. His wife could not attend since she was five days past delivery herself and so still in bed. Even had she been able to do so, Suzanne Robbins would not have been able to attend the funeral, since it was not yet time to attend her thanksgiving after childbirth, and without being cleansed by her churching service she was not able to enter the holy building. Lucie found the alderman taking the opportunity to cuddle his son, whom he had not seen since he was removed to his wet-nurse's home. The midwife enquired about Suzanne's health, and heard with relief that the newly lain woman looked to recovering from her melancholic humour.

After a decent interval, Martha, Mary, and Lucie left the mourners and went into the Allens' house. They had taken delivery of a new straw mattress, clean bedding had been brought in and the room had been made fresh once again. The women of Warley Lane had dragged the spoiled straw mattress into the yard and burned it while the funeral was taking place, not an unusual occurrence in itself, as births often meant straw mattresses were not fit to keep and had to be changed. Even ladies of quality went "into the straw" for their deliveries, rather than ruin an expensive feather bed. Nevertheless, mattresses were rarely as blood soaked as this one.

The wicker cradle that John had lovingly crafted when Anne was expecting their first child – and which had been airing by the fire ready to receive its anticipated occupant – was discreetly taken to another of the cottages for storing, so that John didn't have to look upon it when he returned. The rushes on the floor had also been burned and the floor mopped with hot water and lye, even though that normally only happened once a year, in spring. The women had laid new rushes and then lit a fume in the room to clear any remaining bad air, and ensure the home was fit for John and

160

his two children to return to. On the table they left the produce the townspeople had brought to the Three Doves that morning. Bread, butter, meat, cheese, a pot of pickled vegetables, an apple pie, and a flagon of small beer would keep the grieving family nourished over the next few days.

The older children had taken the younger ones into the street at the front of the cottages to play with hoops and balls, and distract them a while. It was now mid-afternoon, meaning the whole sad episode was over and done with only a day and a few hours since Goodwife Allen's labour began. Weary and weepy, the three women went to bid farewell to the Jones family before returning to the Three Doves.

Goodman Allen approached Lucie. 'Make sure to send me your bill, Mistress Smith,' he said. 'Despite the sad event, I'll pay for all, but it will have to be a piece at a time.'

'John, there is no charge. I won't hear of it,' Lucie swallowed hard. She only charged the poor a fraction of her normal fee in any case. 'Alderman Robbins has already given me money to pay the chirurgeon. So pray think no more on it.'

When they arrived back at the Three Doves, Jasper told them the boy from the alehouse, who'd called to collect the pot from the previous night's meal, said a decent sum had been raised to help tide Goodman Allen over. The loss of even a few days' work would cost him dear. The boy had lingered as if expecting the apothecary to contribute a donation, but Jasper said he knew Lucie would not have taken a fee for her services, and considered that to be more than enough. Defensively, he pointed out that he already contributed to the parish's poor relief funds.

The women took the weight off their feet in front of the kitchen hearth and supped from cups of spiced wine to revive their spirits. Then Ned came in to inform Mistress Smith that a liveried servant from Calstone Manor was in the shop, requesting an interview with her. As she rose to go through to greet the messenger, her tired brain suddenly confronted her with a memory that startled her so much she almost dropped her cup: she'd been commanded to go to the Manor the previous afternoon to take tea with Lady Calstone. The day before yesterday, when Simon had left and the invitation arrived, felt like a lifetime away. There was nothing to be done about it anyway, and the midwife's oath specifically forbade a midwife from leaving a poorer woman to visit wealthy one – not that Lucie ever would have done such a thing.

'I have a letter, Mistress Smith, and my lady bids me to return with your answer,' the servant said. Lucie peeled back the wax seal and read the contents:

> *My dearest Mistress Smith,*
>
> *I was disappointed you did not respond to my last Letter, and that you did not come to the Manor to visit me at the appointed time. I am minded to think that you were called away on Business rather than that you were indisposed towards me.*
>
> *However, my Lord's Household Steward tells me that my Lord refuses to settle your bill for the three days you spent at the laying of my Daughter-in-law, considering that paying his Physician is the beginning and end of his liabilities, and that you should petition Dr Thomas for your due Proportion of his Fee. I am sure the Steward must be mistaken, and so, to avoid further Mistakes, if you call on me at the Manor as soon as your Business will allow, you will receive what you are owed and a little more for your trouble.*
>
> *Pray tell my Servant when we might expect you.*
> *Your Friend and Servant,*
> *C. Calstone*

Lucie considered the letter, then said to the servant, 'Excuse us a moment. I need to converse with my husband in private.

Tell Ned if there's anything you require in the meantime, and he will supply it.'

In the kitchen, Lucie showed Jasper the letter.

'Well she gives you no choice, does she? If we wish to receive your due reimbursement you must dance attendance on her. These people,' he said with exasperation. 'You'll have to go; there's no help for it. Do you wish me to accompany you?'

'No, pray ask the servant to tell her ladyship that I will go tomorrow. If I leave after breakfast I can be there by noon. Will you ask Ned to let the blacksmith know I shall require the horse first thing in the morning? It's getting dark now and I'm bone weary. I'm not a young woman any more, and I can't go galloping up and down the country on a whim.'

———————•◦•◦•———————

The next morning, Lucie rose and put on her green suit of clothes. She took some pottage and small beer for breakfast and then made her way to the blacksmith's to collect her horse. It was nigh on November and the morning was dark with cold. Heavy rain beat down.

I must be quite mad, thought Lucie. I'll probably catch my death out in this weather, and to what purpose? Any decent person would have sent the money without making such ado of it, or insisting on a personal interview, with China tea.

William Wadeston, the blacksmith, had the horse ready, and invited Lucie inside to greet his family while he walked it round to the street.

'Are you sure about going out in this weather, Mistress Smith? Is a woman at her time? If not, I'd advise you not to stir till the rain abates. The roads will be muddy and dangerous.'

Lucie explained that she had an appointment at the Manor and, having failed to keep the first one because of Goodwife Allen's sudden death, was obliged to go.

163

'I'll be fine, William. You know it takes more than a drop of rain to stop me.' She spoke with a cheeriness that concealed her misgivings.

The blacksmith, however, was right. The roads were awash with mud, and around three miles into the journey the mare slipped into a ditch, and Lucie fell off. No harm was done other than some bruising, but with no one to help her remount, she had no choice but to complete the journey on foot. The walk was long and difficult, and Lucie's boots were soaked and likely ruined. By the time the Manor finally came in sight, the pain she was suffering from the fall and from walking – or rather slipping and sliding – had started to take their toll. She walked straight up to the front door and rang the bell. She'd been invited as a guest, and devil take anyone who expected her to trudge round the back in this weather. The servant who answered the bell did his best to hide his surprise – and, truth be told, amusement – at the boldness of this bedraggled old woman in coming to the front door as if she naturally belonged there, but once she told him her name he knew she was an expected guest. He called a boy to take the horse to the stables and reassured Lucie that it would be well tended to by his Lordship's grooms. He then said he'd ring for her Ladyship's waiting maid to show Lucie up to her rooms.

'No,' said Lucie, now completely mistress of the situation. 'Pray show me to the kitchen so that I may wash some of this mud off me and get dry.'

Under her cloak her dress wasn't too wet, save for the hem, but her stockings were ruined. A kitchen maid found a towel for her to dry her hair and face. The cloak was hung in front of the fire so that it would be dried before she left. Luckily, she'd had the foresight to put a spare cap in her bag, so after combing and re-tying her hair, she popped the clean, dry cap on and felt more like herself. The cook sent one of the kitchen maids to fetch a dry pair of stockings and slippers from her own room, since everyone knew that getting your feet wet like that could lead to serious illness. She also insisted that Lucie had a warm drink and a biscuit to revive her spirits. At length, she was ready for her meeting with the lady of the house.

Cecilia, Lady Calstone, had her youngest daughter with her. The child was banging a silver rattle and wearing a dress almost as ornate as her mother's. Lady Eleanor was also in the room, with her baby, who was sitting up in a nurse-maid's lap. He too had an expensive toy in his hand: a coral teething ring with a silver handle. Lady Eleanor was still no more of a mother than she had been the last time Lucie saw her. She fussed and delighted in Dash, her small spaniel, and seemed oblivious to the presence of her son. After the greetings were out of the way, Lady Calstone signalled for both children to be taken back to the nursery, and suggested Lady Eleanor might prefer to take her leave too.

'Thank you for coming, Mistress Smith,' Cecilia began, once the room had been cleared. 'I wish to consult with you upon a matter requiring the utmost discretion. But first, here is your payment. I am very sorry for the delay, and have paid you from my own funds rather than cause any debate with my Lord, so your discretion would be appreciated.' She handed Lucie a heavy purse. 'I trust that is sufficient?'

The purse had five pounds in it, which was far too much, and Lucie protested. Lady Calstone, however, would not be dissuaded.

'I expect that useless physician billed us for far more, and he didn't do anything, so please take it and enjoy it.'

When Lucie had tucked the purse securely into the pocket that hung inside her petticoat, Lady Calstone got to the real reason for summoning her.

'I'm suffering terribly with the *whites*. I was the same a few years ago, and I went to the spa at Bath to take the waters and had some other medication, and I was cured, but it's not convenient to make such a trip at present.'

'I see,' replied Lucie. 'What are your symptoms?'

165

Lady Calstone gave a list: soreness and a heavy discharge from her secrets, severe lower back pain, and lethargy. Lucie asked for permission to examine her, and the two women went through to her bedchamber in the next room. Lying on the bed, Lady Calstone lifted her skirts and the midwife saw a very similar set of symptoms to those she had seen in Grantby gaol. Acrimonious humours flowed from her vagina; the area was inflamed and had the beginnings of sores developing. Lady Calstone had a virulent attack of the clap.

'May I ask when the last time was that you and his Lordship lay together?' the midwife asked.

Lady Calstone brushed down her skirts and sat up. 'It has not been customary with us since I fell pregnant with my youngest child more than three years ago. He did come to my bed once while he was home for Lady Eleanor's delivery. But he was rather full of drink from celebrating his grandson's birth, and so it was nothing to speak of.'

The examination complete, Lucie left Lady Calstone to rise and tidy her petticoats. She reflected how sad it was that the so-called *French disease* was rife in the country, but she was in no doubt that this was what ailed Lady Calstone. It seemed that his Lordship's high living with his actresses and courtesans had consequences for his wife. Lucie did not contradict her patient's belief she had the whites, for surely no good would come of telling her the true diagnosis, and said that she would send some medication and directions for its use when she got back to the Three Doves. The apothecary used a treatment made from fine shavings of guaiacum, a special wood which was imported from the Caribbean. This meant the treatment was expensive – clearly not a difficulty for this patient – but the case would need some careful handling, nevertheless. This disease was thought easy enough to cure in its early stages, but a longer-standing and recurring case, like this seemed to be, was very tricky. Lady Calstone could not receive the mercurial cures, which were more effective, because then

166

everyone would know the true nature of her condition. For the time being, Lucie was able to leave some soothing ointment with Lady Calstone to ease the present burning, but would have to get the full treatment from home. Lady Calstone insisted on having the coach prepared to transport Lucie back to Tupingham, despite its only having got back that morning from taking Sir Robert (and, unbeknownst to either woman, Simon) to London. One of the grooms would ride Lucie's mare, and Lucie could send the treatments back with the coachmen.

As Lucie set off, she realised with a wry smile that while she had taken refreshment in the kitchen, she had not been offered a dish of China tea, and since she had not yet found time to try the supplies she and Martha had brought back from Grantby, maybe she was destined never to taste this new-fangled drink.

Chapter Seventeen

It was a dark mid-November night when Mary awoke and became sensible that her bed-mate was no longer there. Usually this would not have troubled her, as most people had a period of wakefulness between their two main sleeps of the night. But Martha usually slept soundly, being the first of the family up in the morning, making sure the fires were set and water drawn before the others had risen. However, it was too early even for Martha to be up and about. Perhaps she was ill, and Mary could mix her a draft to ease what ailed her. After all, Martha was entitled to receive some care once in a while, since she was always tending to everyone else.

Wrapping a blanket close around her, for the nights were truly chilly now autumn was giving way to winter, Mary gingerly descended the two pairs of stairs to the ground floor. She had to feel her way carefully in the pitch black, lest she stumble and wake the Smiths. Ned was sleeping soundly in the kitchen on the truckle bed he pulled out every night from the corner of the store room. It consisted of a narrow wooden frame with short legs and ropes criss-crossed across it, and his bundle of bedding was unfurled upon it every evening. Each morning Ned was meant to roll the sheets and thin mattress into a tight roll to be stored atop the press in the kitchen. More often than not, Martha attended to his bedding bundle while he sleepily dragged the bed to its daytime position.

Ned smelt a little of liquor, so must have sneaked out again

169

that evening. Mary didn't know how he dared risk the wrath of the master if he was found out, but Ned was becoming increasingly wilful.

She found Martha in the store-room through the shop, in front of the master's receipt book. She was holding a single candle over the page. Strangely, the candles in the pewter sconces on the wall which would have helped her see properly remained unlit.

'Martha?' Mary asked gently, 'Is everything well? Is there something that ails you?'

Martha slammed the book shut.

'No, well, yes, but nothing out of the common way.'

'Can I help?' asked Mary. 'Why did you want to look out a recipe rather than just ask Mister Smith?'

'Well, it's a woman's problem. My courses have been sparse this past while and my womb is congested with humours, making me swell and feel so tired.'

'But couldn't Mistress Smith advise you on this matter? Women seek her out all the time for just such . . . '

Mary's voice faded as Martha brushed past her, walking back out of the shop.'Perhaps I just didn't want to bother the Mistress,' began Martha, in an angry hiss. 'Goodness me, I don't need to answer to you. I was doing nothing wrong, and I'll remind you I am twice your age and have been in this household near as long as you've been alive, so you've no right to question me.'

'Martha, I'm sorry I have angered you. I'm sure I meant no harm. And if you change your mind, I shall be glad to listen to you. I know I am young, but I have learnt a good deal about women's ills and their remedies, these past years.'

'I don't want your advice and I'll thank you to keep this to yourself, Mary,' replied Martha. 'Now I'm going to have a cup of small beer to help me get back to sleep, do you want one fetching back to our bedchamber with mine?'

Mary nodded, 'Yes, please. And, Martha, I'm truly sorry if I intruded. Let's not fall out.'

As Martha climbed into their bed and passed Mary her beer, Mary said, 'I don't want to anger you again, but I've been thinking. Is it possible you're so tired and your courses have been sparse because you've over-laboured yourself, working here all day and helping your Jones kin with their children in the evenings? You are always busy, after all.'

'Maybe that's it,' replied Martha. 'You get off to sleep now.'

A couple of hours later, still in the pitch dark, Martha shook Mary awake.

'I'm afraid Mary, sore afraid.'

'About your womb being congested? We've more remedies for that than I can count.'

Martha hesitated. Mary wished she could look into Martha's face, the better to read what was on her friend's mind, but she could not even make out her hand in front of her face in the absolute darkness of their chamber.

'I fear it's far worse than that ... I truly thought my breeding days were over ... but ... Mary, I fear I am with child.'

'What!' Mary pushed herself into a sitting position. 'How? You can't be.'

'You're not much of a midwife if you don't know how,' Martha joked weakly.

'Well, yes. But ... Look, I think you had better tell me why you think you're with child and start at the beginning.' There must be something else that ailed Martha.

After taking a sip from her cup, and a deep breath, Martha began telling Mary how, while she had been spending her evenings back amongst her weaving kin, she had struck up a friendship with the widower Anthony Higgs. The man she had been talking to in the yard on the day Goodwife Allen died, Mary remembered. She'd thought there was something strangely intimate about their exchange, although she hadn't heard what they'd said. His two children were being raised communally with everyone helping out, Martha told her, and sometimes he spent his evenings at the Joneses' home.

171

Martha had found this friendship kindling into love and desire. At length, she had yielded to Anthony's advances, reassuring him that he needn't fear her falling with child, for her fruitful season was past.

'Oh, Mary. What am I to do? What a fool I have been!'

Despite the chill, Mary felt the palms of her hands, gripping the coverlet, to be sweating. 'What does this Anthony say? He'll marry you, of course.'

She was too experienced in midwifery to be shocked at a child being conceived out of wedlock. She knew that fully a third of brides were in the family way at the altar, but normally their grooms had at least agreed to marry them before they coupled: indeed, most had already been formally betrothed.

'Oh would it were that simple. I – I can't tell him!' Martha began laughing in a distracted way. 'He has enough ado to keep the children he has already, and I promised him all was safe. When we were in Grantby, the Mistress and me, remember I told you about that dog pushing me into the road? I hoped maybe that fright might ... well you know. The stupid thing is,' she said, sniffing now, 'he asked me to marry him on the day Anne Allen died but I couldn't give him an answer because of this.'

'You must tell him,' Mary was firm in her response. 'He ploughed the field and he has to take the consequences. You're neither of you in the first flush of youth, and he knew what he was about. But, Martha, I need to know something ... you weren't looking through the receipt book to destroy the child, were you?'

Martha hesitated a moment too long.

'You were, weren't you?' Mary clasped her hand over her mouth.

'Hush! You'll wake the master and mistress,' Martha whispered urgently. Mary was tempted to remind Martha that but a few short minutes ago *she* had been the one laughing unnaturally.

'Martha,' Mary struggled to contain her shock. 'That'd be murder, as well you know.'

'Not if it's just a congested womb it wouldn't, and we don't yet know it isn't.'

'I think you do know,' Mary replied quietly.

'Well,' Martha sounded defiant. 'I wouldn't be the first. I've seen women traipse in and out of the Three Doves over the years with all sorts of tales about stopped courses, congested wombs, and corrupted humours, who were really trying to make sure they wouldn't bear yet another child.'

'Be that as it may, you're not the woman to want to destroy anything, Martha. You've wanted to be a mother all your life.'

'Yes, but not like this! Not in shame. And while it would be a fearful sin to make an unborn mite pay the price of my shame, it's the only way I can see out of this trouble. But in truth, the book showed me nothing.'

Mary remembered her own explorations into Jasper Smith's receipt book, often by the light of a flickering candle, and how difficult it was to read his crabbed writing, and his strange language – composed of unintelligible abbreviations, symbols, and long words – so strange to her she could not tell rightly what language they belonged to.

'It is a strange volume isn't it? I confess to being unable to make head or tail on't. I can help the children read the words in their horn books,' Martha said, 'But I know very few beyond that. I was never going to make out any recipes properly, much less act on them.'

'I'll help you find a way through this. You're not on your own now, Martha,' said Mary, with a deep compassion, while feeling for her companion's hand and squeezing it.

'If I am to have the baby, I will have to keep it quiet until near my time, to save as much as I can, and then go away. I can pass myself off as a widow somewhere. Goodness knows there is no shortage of those and no-one will question it, if I go far enough away.'

'Martha, no!' Martha had been in the household years, so this suggestion was beyond Mary's comprehension. 'This is almost as mad as your first plan. And what of your little Cissy? What would happen to her?'

'Perhaps she could come with me . . . '

'Now, this is too much. You know the tanner would not allow that. Stop now. I'll say nothing, while we think what to do. How far gone do you think you might be?'

'I've not had my flowers since – maybe June.' Slowly, Martha lifted her shift and pushed down the blankets so Mary might see her growing belly in the dawning light.

'About four, five months, maybe,' Mary said expertly. 'Let me touch you. Have you quickened?'

Martha shook her head. 'I am not sure what that would feel like, but I think not. No, definitely not.'

There was no doubt in Mary's mind. She felt turmoil swirling within her, knowing she would have to tell the mistress. She also knew that if the master found out, he would throw Martha out of the house before she had finished the story. Logically, telling Anthony was the only thing to do. The right thing, too. But persuading Martha was going to be a battle.

Their conversation was brought to an end as the women could hear stirrings from the floor below. The Smiths were rising ready for the day. Martha needed to get downstairs and set the fire to start some pottage, and rouse Ned, so no-one would suspect anything was amiss.

———————————

The day progressed in an unremarkable fashion. Lucie had asked Mary if she had heard a strange noise in the night, which sounded almost like laughing, and Mary – thinking fast on her feet – had replied that Martha had a nightmare and shouted out. The first frosts had hit and a steady stream of people poured into the Three Doves seeking help with coughs, colds, and a case of chilblains. A letter from Simon with the latest Bill of Mortality enclosed said that plague was on the rise again, taking three hundred and ninety-nine souls more than the previous month. Fully three quarters of those that had died last month were victims of the pest. If only Simon would come home, like he had in summer.

The shop reopened after dinner, and Anne Jones walked in carrying little Toby, who was now just over five months old.

'What do you lack, Goodwife Jones?' asked Jasper.

'Pray, might I might have a quick word with Mistress Smith?'

Jasper signalled to Ned to go and fetch the midwife. Mary, coming through the doorway, noticed that Ned was keeping his head down and doing his best to conceal his hangover from the master, who would not be impressed if he knew the boy had been sneaking out drinking with other apprentices at night.

'Mistress Smith says you are to go through to the kitchen, if you please, Goodwife Jones,' said Ned on his return to the shop.

Sitting in front of the fire, Lucie had been knitting some stockings for Simon, and looked up fondly at Anne as she came through with Toby on her hip.

'How are you, Anne, and above all, how is this little man? Mary,' she said as her deputy followed Anne back into the room. 'Will you look at him? He's clearly thriving, even if he does look a little flushed in the face today.'

'Oh, we're well, Mistress Smith. Cousin Martha has been such a friend to us since his birth, helping to watch the children so that I can attend to my other work, especially now I have Jerry to tend to, too.'

Lucie felt an odd undercurrent as she noticed how Martha caught Anne's eye, and seemed to shake her head, almost as if in warning. Anne hesitated slightly, and then continued.

'Mistress Smith, it was Martha who said I should look in and show you Toby. He is having terrible pains from his teeth.'

175

'Right. Teeth are nothing but trouble from the minute they start coming through to the moment they come out!'

'All of my other children were miserable when they were breeding teeth but Toby seems to be in more pain than any.'

'Let's have a look, young man,' said Lucie, rising to take the baby from his mother. As Anne passed the well-wrapped bundle over, he caught sight of Martha across the kitchen and struggled to free his arms from his blanket and wave them frantically in her direction, to the delight of the whole room.

'Breeding of teeth can indeed be a dangerous time for some children,' Lucie explained, feeling in the child's mouth. 'That all seems fine. I can feel his fore teeth, they are almost through. Then will come the eye-teeth and the grinders last of all. The pain is because the teeth are sharp in the gums and can make them inflamed, and cause fevers, and even convulsions in some. Scourings are normal when the eye-teeth come out, so watch for some messy clouts when they start.'

'Yes, his cheeks are very red and his sleep very broken, Mistress Smith.'

'Watching is common, I'm afraid ... and, of course, if he wakes all the time, so will the rest of you. I'll wager you're wearied out. Does he feed well?'

'Oh yes, he takes my dugs well and likes some pap, too. What do you recommend to help him?'

'The gums are thick, and that's why the teeth hurt as they try to break through. You could rub fresh butter or honey on them. And try giving him a candle made of virgin wax to chew on – Mister Smith can sell you one in the shop. If that doesn't help then the juice from quinces often will, and they should be easy enough to get hold of in this season, being recently harvested, but if they are not to be had, I'd suggest you boil up the brains of a hare and anoint his gums with that.'

'Thank you, Mistress Smith; your advice is always so easy to understand. Martha, would you be able to bring a wax candle next time you come over and I'll give you the money?

We've missed you these past few days.'

Before Martha could say more, Mary rushed in to answer for her.

'Here, let me show you out through the shop, and we'll take a candle: you can give Martha the money later. I am sure she'll be over again soon.' When Mary had seen Anne out and returned to the kitchen, Lucie rounded on the conspiratorial pair.

'What's to do?' she asked. 'You shooed her out of door before I could ask after Jeremy Robbins and how her charge kept.'

'Martha's a little over-laboured, aren't you?' Mary turned to the maid. 'I told Mistress Smith about your nightmare last night Martha, and how you shouted out.' She spoke in what seemed to Lucie to be an exaggerated tone. 'A cordial would likely do her good, perhaps we should ask the master for one? But I advised her to stay in the last few days and rest of an evening. That's all, isn't it, Martha?'

'Yes, that's right. I have been just a little weary,' Martha said after a moment's pause. 'I'll be myself soon, I'm sure, and I'll walk down to Warley Lane tonight and look in on my family.'

'Hmm,' grumbled Lucie, glancing suspiciously between the two of them.

Mary followed Martha into the yard where the washing was on the bushes, drying in the weak sun.

'You didn't tell me you'd stopped going around to the Joneses. Is this to avoid Goodman Higgs?'

'Obviously! What else was I to do? I must break off from Anthony. To be forever calling in doesn't help, does it?'

'So what have you been doing? It's lucky the mistress believed you'd been early abed and didn't question us further.'

'I've just wandered along the river bank. I thought of throwing myself in more than once.'

Mary's mouth fell wide open in shock. Self murder, or even thinking to do such a thing was an unpardonable sin.

'That's it. No more,' she snapped. 'We shall tell Mistress Smith and Goodman Higgs. No one need know how I found out and what you were doing in the shop last night, but this cannot continue.'

Martha grabbed the younger woman's arm, stopping her from going in.

'Very well. Pray just give me a day or two longer to do this in my own time.'

She picked up the washing basket to gather in the laundry for ironing.

Chapter Eighteen

The first customer of the day was the mother of six-year-old Nicholas Walker. She called in with him on the way to Suzanne Robbins's school, where he was a pupil. The boy was much troubled with repeated bouts of hiccoughs, or *huckets*, as his mother called them.

'Do you think the cause is too much repletion?' Jasper asked.

Goodwife Walker looked back at him uncertainly.

'I mean, does he eat too much, or too fast, maybe?'

The mother wasn't sure, so Jasper advised her to observe the boy and if she concluded this was the likely cause then the cure was to oil a feather, stick it down the child's throat and make him sick.

'The other likely cause is a cold stomach,' Jasper said. 'And for that you should anoint the belly with oil I can mix that should effect a cure.' The oil Jasper had in mind was made with camomile, wormwood, mastic and quinces.

The boy's mother agreed to take some of the oil, since the weather was so cold it stood to reason the boy would have a cold stomach, so Jasper sent Ned out to the back room to mix a small jarful.

When he came back, Ned announced that he'd just remembered that Mistress Dill at the Black Bull alehouse wanted a quick word with Mistress Smith when she had the time to call. It wasn't urgent, though.

'When was this message delivered?' asked Jasper.

'Oh, um, I saw their cellar boy in the street early on and he told me. I just forgot to mention it when I came back in,' Ned replied.

'Well, you'd better go and inform the mistress, then, hadn't you?'

———————◆◆◆———————

Lucie and Mary took a walk down the road to the Black Bull, taking in the crisp morning air. Lucie still suffered much discomfort from her fall from the horse, more than two weeks ago. It had been made worse by being thrown around in the Calstones' coach all the way home. The coachmen had been cross at being sent straight back out when they had just returned from London and Lucie's comfort had paid the price. On their arrival at the alehouse, Peggy, pipe on the go as ever, was pleased to see them and offered them a small beer each.

'I wanted to ask you about Harry, my latest boy. Do you think he has squint eye?' she asked, thrusting the baby towards Lucie.

Lucie turned the child around and took a look but thought him too young yet to make a diagnosis.

'When he is in his cradle, where do you have the candle placed?'

Peggy wasn't sure, as young Lucy was taking most care of the child after dark while her mother ran the alehouse. When Peggy took over again at bedtime, the child slept in his crib beside his mother's side of the bed, so she could more easily nurse him, but they did not leave a candle burning in the room where they slept. Lucy said the candle was on the table behind the crib in the evenings.

'Ah,' said Lucie, 'in that case, there's your answer. You need to put it on one side for a while and then the other, or have bright pictures on one side and the candle on the other. The baby must be accustomed to turn his head, so as to use both eyes equally. But don't let him stare directly at the candle, lest his eyes become distorted.'

'That's fine then, we'll do that, won't we, Luce?' Peggy said to her daughter. 'There was one other thing. I don't like to turn away trade, but thought you should know that apprentice of your husband's is in here most nights, drinking and carousing with the other apprentices. They get quite boisterous sometimes and I've had to rebuke them.' Peggy went on to describe how just the other night Ned and his crew had been scuffling and tussling, kicking up the sawdust on the floor, and causing chaos. Matters came to a head when one of the apprentices tossed another in the air and he landed on the corner table. This table was the spot taken every day by Stephen, Bill, and Old Tom, who all carried scars from the wars. One was in want of some fingers as a result of his musket misfiring, another was left with a limp after having surgery to remove bullets from his thigh on the battlefield at Worcester. Old Tom was different in that his mind had been fuddled by things he had seen and heard on the field of battle and he was often deeply melancholic, muttering incoherent phrases over and over, and sometimes flying into a rage, before becoming silent again for days at a time. These men were always found in their spot in the alehouse making their penny's worth of ale last as long as possible. The townspeople were protective of them and Peggy often refilled their tankards from her jug without fuss when she was wiping down the tables.

Lucie puffed out her chest, putting her hands on her hips. This was the first she'd heard of the matter, and she promised it would be resolved. The women took their leave and walked to the postmaster's office to check for mail. On the way, Lucie told Mary that she believed the consultation about the baby's squint was a ruse to get them there, so that Peggy could report Ned's misconduct. At the postmaster's office there was a letter for Lucie from Simon. She tore it open immediately, only to find disappointing news about the

181

painter he had engaged. Apparently, there had been a miscommunication and the painter had thought himself engaged to do work indoors, for it would be far too cold in December to work with paints outside. Simon apologised for the confusion but said he had retained the craftsman to do the work in spring if his mother still wanted him. The plague news was much better than it had been in the summer months, but the infestation was still rife in the capital.

Lucie was disheartened, and Mary tried to raise her spirits by reminding her that they still had the lovely new sign and they could arrange for it to be put up when the master went away and so he'd still get his surprise. They walked back to the Three Doves and determined to carry on sorting out the linen press and taking stock of what needed replacing to see them through the long winter of regular deliveries.

Whenever they had spare time, when the garden was too cold to work on, the women would sit and stitch little nightdresses or crib sheets or caps for the babies they delivered. It was something they all enjoyed: Mary was especially skilled with her knitting needles and made some beautiful blankets. Lucie's eyes were not as sharp as they once were and she could no longer do much sewing by candle light, so had only a brief time in the day in which to sew. She decided then to make a new nightgown for Jasper, for him to take on his trip to London the next month. In the light of Simon's news, however, she hoped her husband would reconsider his plans.

Martha had finished all her chores, and, rather than sit and sew in the afternoon, she declared that she would go to the Joneses and look in on Toby to see how his teeth did, and if the candle had helped. Lucie told Martha about the Calstone baby's silver and coral teething toy, and they chatted about the stark contrasts in the world that the two boys would grow up to inhabit. Mary said she had a mind to keep Martha company – with Mistress Smith's permission – so that she could see if there was anything she could do to help the Allen children. Mistress Smith gave her a couple of hours' leave, but warned her not to get too attached to the family, for she would see plenty more in poverty and grief if her desire for a midwife's occupation were to be fulfilled. When the two women had left the kitchen, Jasper asked Lucie to tend the shop for him in order that he might deal with his apprentice.

As soon as the pair were in the kitchen alone, Jasper boxed his apprentice's ears soundly. There was precious little difference in size between the two – Ned, at nineteen, was as tall and broad as the apothecary – but the younger man knew better than to resist the blows, even though in all probability he could block his master's fist with his forearm. Doing so would, of course, end his apprenticeship and see him sent home to his mother in Deptford in disgrace. When he was finished, Jasper gruffly ordered the younger man to sit on the bench at the table while he pulled a small, unbound book from his pocket.

'This is a book from my own shelves. It took some finding, Ned. I picked it up back in '36 as a young married man, because it's the funeral sermon of an apothecary given to earthly pleasure rather than piety. I think there are lessons herein you'd do well to consider, my lad.' He opened the browning copy of *The Young-Man's Warning-Peece*, found the places he had marked, and read aloud, *'The Ale-house must bee your Chappell, Kitchin, Work-house: the first draught is your prayer, the next your breakfast, and the last your work."* Sounds familiar, eh? This young man, William Rogers, was an apothecary like me and like you mean to be, who did not turn back from the path of unrighteousness until it was almost too late.' The anger had left Jasper's voice and he sounded sorrowful. 'On his very death bed this Rogers admitted, *"I have been a fearefull drunkard, powring in one draught after another"*.' Jasper looked up from the book and studied Ned to make sure he was paying him full attention, before continuing: *'"One draught after another till one draught*

183

could not keep down another: and now I would be glad if I could take the least of God's creatures which I have abused. I have neglected my Patients, who have put their lives into my hands, and how many soules have I thus murthered? I have wilfully neglected Gods house, service, and worship, and now, though I have purposed, God strikes me thus; before the day of my promise comes; because I am unworthy to come among God's people againe."'

Jasper paused to let the words of a penitent sink in. 'Do you see, my lad, if you practise our ancient and sacred profession when taken in drink, you not only risk doing much harm, but might be guilty of the worst crime of all: taking a patient's life through wrongly-dispensing or worse?' With that, Jasper rose and handed the book to Ned, instructing him to study it and prepare to be questioned on it in due course.

———————————

Martha was furious with Mary for tagging along with her to the cottages and putting pressure on her. They trudged to Warley Lane in a tense silence. Once there they went their separate ways, Mary into the comber's house to talk to him while he went about his work and Martha to the Joneses, to chat against the background noise of the loom which was ever in motion during the day. Anne was feeding Jeremy, her nurseling, while her own son was sitting propped up in his crib playing with a wooden top his sisters must have given him: the whip, fortunately, was not in the crib with him.

Anne expressed pleasure at her cousin's visit. But she began asking uncomfortable questions. She had evidently decided to tackle the prickly topic of what was the matter with Martha, and why she had been so distant recently. Had they offended her? Anne asked.

Martha sighed and shifted on her chair. Since Mary was now in her confidence, she decided she should tell Anne

184

what the problem was, too. Her cousin's wife would give good counsel.

'The thing is, Anne,' she started, and then paused. She tried again, blurting it out. 'Anthony asked me to marry him on the day poor Anne Allen died.'

'But surely that is good news! When is the wedding? His young uns will be lucky to have a step-dame like you.' Excitement shone in Anne's eyes. 'We would be neighbours to boot. Why didn't you tell me before?'

Martha dropped her chin. Her hands went to her belly without her noticing the action.

'I haven't said yes. I can't marry him. There is something he doesn't know.'

Anne's face clouded with concern.

'What is it, cousin? Are you ill?'

'No, not ill ... I'm with child. Mary confirmed my suspicions this morning.' Martha bit down hard on her bottom lip, the glisten of tears appearing in her eyes.

Anne paused while she absorbed this. 'I, um, well I remember you thought you were likely barren when you were betrothed to Oliver and never caught. This is a shock, but I'd say that makes all the more reason to marry him, and quickly before you start showing properly.'

Martha stood up. She was too restless to sit long. 'That's just where my trouble lies. I told him I was past all that when I agreed to lie with him. Like you say, I didn't even think myself fruitful, and then recently my courses had been sparse, and I was sure I was in the change of life, certainly no longer able to bear children.'

'Oh, Martha! You of all people know there are a million reasons for courses to disappear. You've lived with a midwife for two decades.'

'I know,' replied Martha.

'Why can't you marry him, though? He lay with you, he is a grown man and he knows the risks,' Anne bent to check Jeremy.

Martha pressed her hand to her forehead. 'He said he was pleased I could no longer have children, as he could never bear to lose a wife in childbed again.'

'I see.' Anne slipped her finger into the corner of Jeremy's mouth and detached his latch. 'Well he has no choice now, and you know how rare it is for a woman to die in childbed. The fact that he and John Allen are both widowers is nought but a sad chance. How many women have you seen laid over the years and how many deaths?'

She switched the baby between her ample dugs.

'It's not me who would need convincing of this, though, is it?'

The two women looked at each other.

In John Allen's house, Mary was having an uncomfortable time. Although John had welcomed her inside, he was clearly troubled beyond common grief. He eventually revealed that he couldn't get it out of his head that if only Mistress Smith had called for proper help when she saw his Anne a couple of weeks before she went into labour, she might have lived. What sort of treatment was giving his wife some peas, and declaring her cured, for goodness' sake? The more he spoke about it the angrier he became.

'I said to our Anne, "there couldn't have been much ado if munching on a few peasecods was the remedy!" and she agreed. It did nothing but make me a laughing stock. Plenty were quick to comment that a wife needing peasecods must have a husband found wanting in providing his wife with her due comfort, as if she wasn't even big-bellied.'

Shocked at his outburst, Mary explained it wasn't to do with what it was that his wife craved, but about the staying of the craving, and described the power of the mother's imagination and how terribly dangerous it was for women to suffer unfulfilled longings.

186

'Aye well,' he replied. 'But if we believe that, how can she have just let my wife bleed to death? I thought she was the most experienced midwife for miles around. I thought they called her the gossips' choice because all the women cried out for her, and yet she allows a healthy young mother's life-blood to trickle out of her without doing anything to stop it.'

'John, this is your grief talking,' Mary said. 'Mistress Smith called for the chirurgeon as soon as it was obvious we needed more help. He was useless in the event and couldn't move the child. If only you could have seen how my mistress toiled. She nearly broke her own arm getting him out. She settled the chirurgeon's bill too.'

'Happen she did that from guilt.'

'Goodman Allen. That is a terrible accusation. You know Alderman Robbins supplied the money. He asked Mistress Smith how he might help, and she advised him that he could pay the bill if he was so minded.'

'I'm just saying it as I see it, and there are others who agree with me in this row, I can tell you.'

Mary shook her head. She was quite unable to comprehend this view. 'Well, I am sorry.' She sat unable to think of anything to say for a moment. Then she roused herself. 'I am not prepared to sit and listen to this nonsense, so I'll bid you good day.'

Leaving his house, Mary knocked on Anne Jones's door, and let herself in.

'You'll never believe what John Allen is saying!' she cried, straight away. 'He asserts that Mistress Smith was negligent in her care for his wife. After all she did. I can't believe it.'

Much to hers and Martha's surprise, Anne replied, 'Aye and he's not the only one to think so. There's a fair few folk around here who agree with him, though I dare say his anger will abate with time.'

'You?' Martha queried.

'I didn't say that,' barked Anne, 'but I have wondered. Anyway, that's enough of that. What are we going to do

187

about madam here and the pickle she's in?'

Still on the subject of John, Martha let out a harrumph and reminded Anne that she had been pleased enough to consult with Mistress Smith that afternoon about Toby's teeth.

Mary answered Anne's question.

'There's only one thing to do. Anthony Higgs must be told at once, and he must answer for his actions.'

'Shall I ask Sam to talk to him?' said Anne.

'No, I'll do it myself,' said Martha, resigned. She stood up. 'There's no time like the present, I suppose.'

Mary decided to walk back to the Three Doves alone to clear her head. On her arrival she found young Ned in a foul mood behind the counter.

'What's the matter with him?' she asked Lucie.

'I told the master about Ned's antics at the Black Bull and he's had a sound beating and been forbidden to go out until further notice. Martha not with you?'

'No, but she bade me tell you she'll be home presently.' Mary felt sickened by the guilt of being less than truthful with her friend and teacher.

Chapter Nineteen

The atmosphere in the Three Doves was strained all evening. As Martha hadn't returned, Lucie had served supper, and afterwards Jasper had read from the Bible and asked them to answer theological questions. Ned remained surly all evening and became even more so when Jasper informed him of his decision that the apprentice's truckle bed was to be moved to his and Lucie's chamber until further notice.

The next announcement was a shock for Lucie, as Jasper declared that he had been praying and reflecting on the money the King had sent during the summer. The two bright guineas had been in the locked metal chest in his chamber since they arrived; Lucie had given Martha and Ned their share from her own money. Jasper told them that God had helped him reach the decision that this money should go into the parish funds for poor relief. The Stuart court's profligacy and loose morals, not to mention rumours of its attachment to popery, were everything Jasper opposed, and while he was proud that his wife's efforts had been recognised, he felt they were unable to accept the money.

'This decision has been a long time making, husband,' Lucie said. 'I took it for granted that you were reconciled to my reward, since you had not mentioned it since the day it arrived.'

'That's true, but the extravagant fee Lady Calstone sent lately troubled me anew. We both work hard and take a fair fee for our labour. All we asked from the Manor was that

189

they should settle their fee and not that they should give us large sums, presumably to assure our discretion in the other matter.'

Lucie noticed Ned's ears pricking up and wondered what he was thinking. Given his recent rioting in the alehouse, she was seeing the lad in a fresh and not very positive light.

'Furthermore,' Jasper continued, 'I was disposed to pray on the matter, and the answer revealed to me was that we should accept your customary fee – with something more for your additional troubles – and the later treatments we dispatched, and then the rest should also go to the parish poor funds. It will make provision for the winter months, when the parish is called on most for relief.'

'As you wish,' said Lucie demurely, but with regret. She might be unchallengeable in the birthing chamber, but accepted without question that Jasper was master of his own household. That included her earnings. It was fortunate that the painter she had retained was no longer coming. She did have some pin money saved from her household allowance but having the Calstone and royal money to keep would have been a significant addition to her personal fortune.

Ned spent the rest of the evening making a nuisance of himself as he dismantled his bed frame and dragged it piece by piece up the first set of stairs, deliberately letting the long lengths bang on the stairs as he heaved it up. Lucie felt weary and again wondered if the couple ought to stop training apprentices after Ned and Mary had completed their time. Surly youths and a calm household did not always go together. She was amazed too that the boy dared risk another beating, carrying on in such a fashion, rather than showing some humility at his chastisement.

As the family were rising for bed, Martha came through the door completely drenched and clearly distressed. Lucie told Jasper and Ned to go on up while she helped Martha dry out and warm up. Mary ran to get Martha's nightdress, and Lucie helped her strip off her wet clothes. She removed Martha's dress, and unlaced her leather stays. Her servant was wet through beyond this and shivering, so even her shift had to come off, and Lucie rubbed her down with a linen towel.

When Martha was safely changed into her nightdress, and was supping a warming drink, her red hair hanging loosely over a linen towel around her shoulders, so that it might dry before the fire, Lucie asked, 'When were you going to tell me?'

Martha cast an involuntary glance in Mary's direction, which did not escape Lucie.

'You knew, too?' The midwife sat down heavily in her chair. 'Well, then, start from the beginning. Seems you are like Sarah of scripture after all, to quote your own words back at you, but I'm not going to judge, Martha. Goodness knows you're more like a friend than a housemaid. It staggers me to think that you of all women should find yourself in this plight. And to hide it from me, too!'

Martha's tears started flowing again. She told Lucie what she had told Mary about her friendship with Anthony Higgs and how it had become more than that over the past few months. She told her how she'd thought she was safe from conceiving a child because of the cessation of her terms, and even boldly reminded her mistress how she too had reached that conclusion. She said that Anthony had asked her to wed him on the day Goodwife Allen died, which was the conversation Lucie had questioned her about, and that finally this evening she had told him her belly was filled with his child. His reaction had been every bit as bad as she had anticipated.

'I see,' was all Lucie said.

'Oh, Mistress Smith, it was fearful! He was astonished at first, and then he said I'd tricked him. He became horrible angry with me and shouted out that I knew he could never bear to lose another wife in childbed. We argued about it for a while, and since then I have walked around and around. I couldn't tell what else to do.'

'Will he marry you, did he say?' Lucie asked.

191

'He will. He said he was honourable and would do his duty, but everyone would hear how I had fooled him into it by getting pregnant while telling him I was barren.'

'He can get over that. It takes two to make a baby. He knows that and he's had his pleasure and now must do his duty by you. I'll go and speak to him tomorrow and smooth this out,' said Lucie.

'No!' exclaimed Mary, a little too loudly. 'I meant that it might just be better to let Martha settle the matter.'

Lucie raised an eyebrow: there was clearly more to this than either woman was willing to confess.

'It makes no matter,' said Martha. 'I am resolved to go away. I have some money saved up – enough to tide me over until the child is born. Then I shall pass myself off as a widow, and seek a new employment where the child may accompany me.'

There was no time to discuss the merits, or flaws, of Martha's plan, for they were interrupted by a knock at the back door. It was Anthony Higgs, asking to speak to Martha. He seemed to sense immediately that the three women had been discussing what had happened.

'Martha, may we talk in private?' he asked, his head down.

Lucie nodded her permission, but reminded Anthony that Martha had suffered enough grief for one evening, and so he should not distress her further. She handed Martha one of the candles from the mantelpiece, and bade her pull her shawl round herself more closely for there was no fire in the next room.

Anthony nodded, and he and Martha went through to the shop, from where Lucie and Mary heard him immediately beg Martha to forgive him. At length, he and Martha came back through to the kitchen.

'I am pleased you are reconciled,' Lucie said when she saw that they were arm in arm.

'Martha Jones has agreed to become my wife,' said Anthony, smiling proudly.

Lucie reminded them that they would have to get married by licence in the next couple of weeks because advent would soon be upon them and it was not fitting to marry in that season. Within a few days, she would be losing her housemaid and her companion of nearly twenty years.

'I'm not sure I can afford a licence,' Anthony admitted, 'so we might have to wait until the New Year and have the banns read after Christmastide is over.'

'No,' said Lucie. 'That won't do, and people will talk as Martha begins to show. If you will allow me, I'll make a wedding present to you of the five shillings which the licence will cost. You can be married in the next few days if Dr Archer is satisfied.'

'Thank you, Mistress Smith, but I still have the five shillings you gave me from the King's reward, so we shall use that,' said Martha, tears springing back to her eyes – Lucie supposed from exhaustion and relief.

Once Anthony had taken his leave, Martha collapsed on one of the chairs in front of the fire. Her passions were all in disarray. Lucie asked Mary to go through her bag in the scullery for the powders she carried to make a calming draft for Martha. While Mary was out of the room, Martha began to tell Lucie what had passed between her and her fiancé. Having thought on their earlier conversation, and, he said, sought counsel in the bottom of a tankard at the Bull, he had seen how harsh he had been. He confessed that he'd taken the risk in lying with Martha, knowing the consequences, because he desired her and she him, and he knew, just as he had known when he proposed marriage, that she would make an excellent step-dame to his two children. Martha said she had been about to respond that she understood, but Antony had put his finger to her lips to hush her as he argued that the fact he had proposed before he knew of the babe was evidence of his love, and if she would still have him, he would be proud to take her for his second wife, and the sooner the better.

Lucie was satisfied with this outcome, but warned Martha

that the master must not learn of her big-belly. 'It's not right for husband and wife to keep secrets from each other, but in this case I fear he will not judge the matter as mildly as I have done. We'll wait until after you are safely wed and mistress of your own household, before he learns the truth. Mary, you and I shall have words about your part in all this tomorrow. But for now, goodnight ladies.' She picked up her candle and made her way wearily to the stairs, relieved to find both Jasper and Ned sleeping soundly when she got to her chamber. It was a miracle the men had slumbered through the stir they'd kept downstairs. Rather than kneeling to say her prayers before climbing into bed, she got in and closed the curtains, wriggling out of her day dress and stays in the privacy of her bed. Only then did she begin asking the Lord's forgiveness for deceiving her husband. It was one thing to plan a pleasant surprise like having the shop front painted, and entirely another to collude in a hasty marriage like this. She resolved to tell him the couple desired to be married before the long advent season and not elaborate on why unless asked directly, then she'd not be able to lie.

By the time Jasper rose from his first sleep and went downstairs to have a drink and to read for a while, Lucie had not yet dropped off. She pretended to be sleeping, lest her deception showed in her manner. *More dishonesty.* What was happening to her?

She had always expected Martha to leave her one day for a marriage, but not under a cloud like this. While she had laid women in all walks of life, from fine ladies to hedge whores, doing her duty without fear or favour according to the oath she had sworn before God, she hadn't considered she'd be laying her own Martha within a few short months, and losing her to the life of a weaver's wife in Warley Lane. With a ready-made family to care for, too. Lucie tormented herself through the long dark night wondering how on earth she had failed to see a pregnancy in her own household. What was wrong with her? Perhaps she was losing her touch. Perhaps she should look to retire. Her confidence was shaken already after the sad death of the Allen mother and child. If word got out her maid had concealed her big-belly from a midwife of thirty years' experience then she'd have no work anyway. Who'd trust her judgement?

Another thought struck her: she must remember to ask Martha what her plans were for the Mallet girl, whose schooling she funded. Would she be able to carry on with that? It would be a shame if the child must stop her schooling when she was doing so well, by all accounts. Another problem in want of a solution.

Chapter Twenty

'This day I laid the wife of Joseph Townshend.'

The next morning a message came from the farm just beyond the Bromfields'. On Jenny Bromfield's recommendation, Dorothy Townshend had asked her husband to send for Mistress Smith to attend her. Ned was dispatched to the blacksmith's and returned a few minutes later with Dapple. The blacksmith had told him to caution his mistress to take care, as he had just given the mare new shoes with frost-nails to prevent slipping on icy roads.

'That's good, Ned. Thank you for telling me.' After her recent misadventure on the way to Calstone Manor, Lucie was very grateful for this advice. Luckily, her bruises were finally easing, since Jasper had given her some new ointment which had gone a long way to soothe her pains, but she had no wish to add to them. 'When we return Dapple we must ask how much we are in his debt for the winter shoes. If he adds it to our monthly stabling account, we can make sure it is settled promptly.'

She decided to go alone, as she was still angry with Mary, and felt her deputy's presence would impede her work. Ned cheered up somewhat, seeming to realise that – for once – the midwife regarded Mary with disfavour, and not him.

Lucie was glad of a reason to get out of the Three Doves for a while. She had told Jasper about Martha's impending wedding and answered his questions as truthfully as possible in the circumstances. Jasper was naturally

197

concerned that formalities had not been observed and that Martha and her betrothed had not sought his blessing before proceeding. Lucie knew from experience, including Jasper's recent decision about the money, that this could be something he would brood upon, and then he might get cross and say things that would lead to his discovering the whole truth. All things considered, it was fortunate that this call for her attendance had cropped up.

At the farm, the room was packed with attendants waiting on Dorothy, and Lucie was dismayed but unsurprised to see Mother Henshaw among their number. The two women usually stayed out of each other's way, with the hand woman attending to the rural births and Lucie mainly staying within the town boundaries. A confrontation was all she needed in her current frame of mind. The inevitable twisting started up in her guts again.

'No apprentice to order around today, Mistress Smith?' said the hand woman in a sarcastic tone. As she had never trained formally, she could not train others and was always at risk of being prosecuted by the church for working without a licence.

'No, Mary is otherwise employed,' Lucie replied. She did not add that Mary was tasked with the ironing Martha would normally be doing, both as a punishment, and in order that Martha could go with Anthony to see the Rector.

Dorothy had sharp pains but was walking around trying to ease them, propped up by Damaris Todd and her daughter-in-law Hannah. Lucie asked her to get on the bed, so that she might examine her. Of course, Mother Henshaw decided to quibble and argue there was nothing wrong with standing to give birth, and indeed that it was the normal country way.

'Be that as it may, I am not asking to deliver Dorothy now, just to touch her to see how she does. I hope you have no objection to that?' Lucie said tersely.

In fact she vehemently disapproved of women giving birth standing up. She would happily use the chair or stool as often as practical, but she favoured the woman sitting on the edge of her bed supported by her gossips. But that wasn't the matter at issue here.

On examination, Lucie found Dorothy's womb was completely open, so she tore the membranes with her fingernail. The waters gushed out, and Lucie found that her finger slipped into the bend on the child's thigh, since it was breech. Despite this, Lucie manipulated the child into a better position, took a firm grip of the ankles, and had the body out in moments. She wrapped the visible parts of the baby tightly in a sheet to keep it warm, and tried to push from her mind disturbing visions of Anne Allen's child in the same position. But with Dorothy's next pang, she eased out the head, and the child howled, as if making an objection to her undignified arrival. Lucie had seldom been more relieved to hear such a lusty cry.

'You have a hearty maid, Dorothy,' she told the new mother, with joy in her voice.

'Head first too common for you?' taunted the hand woman.

'Instead of carping, why don't you look after this little girl? She has come into the world so quickly, she finds it all very surprising, I expect,' Lucie said.

At the sight of the pink and lively girl, Jenny Bromfield let out a small gasp, obviously struck by the contrast with her own recent delivery, before composing herself. Lucie patted her arm and reassured her that it would be her turn next to have a healthy child.

'I hope so, Mistress Smith, for I think I have already caught again,' Jenny replied, as the midwife turned back to the new mother.

Soon the after-burden was out in good order, and Lucie made the mother comfortable, and readily accepted the cup of Farmer Townshend's homebrewed groaning ale. After making her final checks on the new baby girl, she took her leave, with instructions to send for her in case of complications – not that she expected any for her careful skill meant the mother had not so much as a graze on her privities.

This was just what Lucie had needed to take her mind off more painful matters. On a whim she decided that, since she was two thirds of the way to Calstone Manor, and in no hurry to return to the Three Doves, she would ride there and call in to see how Lady Calstone fared.

Lucie was admitted straight away when the baroness was notified of her visit, and a servant guided her through the maze of rooms to Lady Calstone's suite. It seemed the medicaments previously sent had afforded some small relief but not enough to make her entirely comfortable.

'It's fortunate I called in. I'll have Mister Smith prepare some different treatments and we'll keep trying,' she reassured her patient.

'Do stay and have some refreshments with me,' Lady Calstone invited. Although there was a gulf between them in terms of rank, Cecilia seemed to find Lucie very easy to talk to, and she said that, to her, life in the country was really quite dull. At sixteen, her daughter-in-law was just another child to attend to. Lady Eleanor had been raised to be indulged and was not at all interested in motherhood. A period as one her Majesty's ladies-in-waiting would do her a great deal of good, Lady Calstone told Lucie, and said she had written to her husband, requesting that he approach the Queen's household to that effect.

Lucie found that, quite contrary to her expectations, she too enjoyed chatting to Lady Calstone, over a cup of spiced wine and some knotted, sweet jumbal biscuits fresh from the oven. She found herself telling her all about Martha's sudden wedding to the weaver and how sad she was about parting with her after all these years. Obviously, she did not impart the reason for the urgency: that would be a confidence too many. On hearing this news, Lady Calstone asked what height and size Martha was, then rang for one of her maids, and asked her to look amongst the waiting gentlewomen's wardrobes to see if there was a gown which was ready for casting off and might be suitable for Martha. It would need to be a plain one, because of Martha's station in life, and not made from a rich fabric. In no time at all, the maid returned with a fine woollen suit of clothes which was both without ornamentation, and in a subdued colour. It would be easy for a skilled seamstress like Martha to adapt this into a wedding gown to be proud of, and she would own the best dress she'd ever had afterwards.

Lucie took her leave, and Lady Calstone personally walked her through the long gallery and down the sweeping oak staircase. Then she insisted Lucie took the coach home with a groom bringing Lucie's mare after them. Since there was no practicable way for Lucie to ride with the suit on top of her birthing bag, she accepted with thanks, joking that she had used the Calstone coach as much as its rightful owners this past few months.

When she entered the Three Doves, Jasper said, 'Did you just alight from the Calstone coach again? I thought you had been to Townshend's farm.' Although late afternoon, Jasper had not gone to the coffee shop, not being willing to leave Ned to his own devices.

Lucie outlined the events of the day, telling Jasper how she had successfully delivered a little maid speedily even though she was a footling, and then gone on to visit Lady Calstone. She explained that she had promised to send some alternative treatments for her back with the coach. Jasper asked what was in the package, and Lucie explained it was a dress one of the servants at the Manor had finished with, but which had plenty of life left in it, and so it had been offered to Martha to alter and wear.

'You prattled to Lady Calstone about our servant's wedding?' Jasper asked with incredulity. 'Why would she wish to hear about that?'

'I think she is sometimes lonely at the Manor. In fact, she seeks a position at court for her young daughter-in-law, as she is not good company at present. She needs to meet more people and become more . . . I think her Ladyship's word was "conversable",' Lucie replied. 'She encouraged me to share my news, and graciously sent this suit of clothes as a wedding gift.'

She quickly changed the subject to Lady Calstone's unfortunate ongoing battle with the disease her husband had visited on her. Jasper decided to step up the treatments. Instead of a drink made from the exotic wood, he would infuse it into a plaster to place on the area directly. The treatment needed skilful making and called for the fat of an adder, which he'd have to send to London for, with fresh beetles and butter. Lucie would need to go back to the Manor to see it applied the first time, since the plaster included some verdigris, which was meant to turn white on contact with the venereal disease but stay green if the problem was something else, and so provide confirmation that Lucie's diagnosis was correct. The couple were in agreement that it was unlikely they were going to get this awful disease under control without using quicksilver, but that would definitely bring the matter into the open and that was the last thing Lady Calstone would desire.

Martha and Mary were in the kitchen preparing the evening meal. The house was spotless. Clearly both women had been working especially hard all day, probably wishing to avoid incurring Lucie's further wrath for any reason whatsoever. Lucie enquired if Dr Archer had been minded to allow her to marry by licence and Martha confirmed that the marriage was to take place on Monday the twenty-seventh of November, as this would give him time to have the licence drawn up. Lucie then showed Martha the suit of clothes that had been sent from the Manor, and Martha was quite overwhelmed.

'Oh sweet goodness!' she said. 'I have never had such a fine suit of clothes. I can't believe it is meant for me.' The wedding was starting to feel very real.

Checking that the door to the shop was firmly closed, Lucie

told Martha she would need to take extra care with a first pregnancy in her forties. She was likely to feel very tired soon. There was an additional complication, in that forty-two was a climacteric year, one of the crisis points in life, so this too needed to be considered in all aspects of her care.

'You are more likely to get wrinkles on your belly too, being not as soft of skin as a younger wench would be. To avoid this you could start to wear a clout covered in almond oil under your shift, if you wanted,' Lucie advised.

Martha responded that she was past the age when a few wrinkles on her belly would trouble her, and she admitted that she felt as if a weight had been lifted from her shoulders now Lucie was aware of her condition. Lucie then dismissed her, in order that she might speak to Mary in private.

Lucie did not mince her words. She made it clear that she was extremely displeased that Mary had not come to her as soon as she learned of Martha's situation. She spoke in a hard tone to the young woman, reminding Mary that had she been hastier in her decisions, she might well have sent her home for this insubordination. She did not give Mary the chance to defend herself. When she had finished her speech, she paused, to take a sip from her cup of small beer. The younger woman stood in front of her, hands clasped demurely in front of her apron, head bowed. Nevertheless, Lucie had to plough on until she possessed the entire truth.

'Martha's situation is not the only matter you are concealing from me, is it, Mary Thorne? Pray why exactly do you wish me not to visit Warley Lane?'

Mary flinched at Lucie's unaccustomed formality, and her eyes pricked with tears. Lucie knew her deputy held her in the highest esteem, and that made the dishonesty even more concerning. She was determined to press on.

Mary's shoulders fell.

'Mistress Smith, I fear it is not my place, but ... but there is some slanderous gossip circulating in the weavers' cottages, and I wished to spare you. That is the truth. I am so sorry.'

'Gossip?   About me?   Is this concerning Martha's condition?'

She had been walking towards her armchair to rest, but Mary's shocking news stayed her and she stood stock still waiting for her deputy to elaborate. The truth was worse than she could have imagined. Goodman Allen was questioning her actions and her care for his late wife. She sank into her chair and sat in silence for a few moments, taking this in. She knew his words most likely rose from grief, but the situation needed tackling immediately. She was doubly horrified when Mary at length plucked up enough courage to tell her that John Allen's doubts were causing his neighbours to wonder if there was any foundation for his claims. There would always be those who said there was no smoke without fire.

Lucie felt the need for solitude and decided she would go to her chamber to think alone. She instructed Mary to go up ahead of her and light the candles, and when her deputy returned Lucie made her way up the steps, telling Mary she did not wish to be disturbed on any account. Lucie noticed the girl had thoughtfully set the fire, and had closed the shutters, too.

Rather than take her seat by her desk, she placed her bolster on the boards beside her bed and knelt, the better to think and ask for divine guidance. She'd hoped that, although the King's restoration was not the political change she herself would have wanted, the resolution of the national turmoil would make the world a calmer place as she moved into her later years. Indeed, it had seemed so for a little while. Now the plague was running rife, suggesting God's displeasure with the citizens of the country; her only child was living amongst the very pest too; the country was yet again at war – this time with the Dutch rather than itself; she'd had a series of disputes with that hand woman, who'd long been a thorn in her side; she'd been called to deliver the godchild of the King; she'd lost a woman in childbed; her maid and companion was leaving her, not in the best circumstances; and now she was having her skills impugned. What a year 1665 was proving to be. The comet last December had been a sign, all right.

She prayed hard for the strength to bear her burdens with humility. She also knew she would need the counsel of her husband, which was hard, since she was deceiving him about Martha's true condition – the very untruth that had caused her to threaten to send her own dear deputy away. It was a sad quandary. By the time she roused herself to rise, slowly and painfully as her joints had quite stiffened, she saw that the fire Mary had started was dying out for want of tending.

Chapter Twenty-one

Jasper had asked Lucie to tell him, item by item, the whole of Anne Allen's story, from the first visit and the longings she'd had, to the day of the birth. He even sought a summary of Goodwife Allen's previous deliveries, which had been entirely straightforward and duly recorded in Lucie's journals. He asked Lucie if her conscience was clear, and she said yes, confirming that she had done everything within her power and knowledge, and prayed at each stage for God's help and guidance. Jasper sat and considered the case for a while, then said she must try not to feel anxious, for her behaviour had been irreproachable, God would ensure that the truth came out, and John Allen would learn to repent of his slander.

On a more practical level, the apothecary determined that they should go to the Rectory without delay to speak to Dr Archer. Since Lucie was licensed to practice by the church they should make sure the Rector was aware of the complaints and rumours and see if he was able to help them. The mention of the Rector reminded Lucie to tell Jasper the date of the marriage ceremony was now fixed for the following Monday.

'That is not possible,' Jasper replied, to Lucie's surprise. 'That is the twenty-seventh, and I have a note in my almanac saying that's the day of Mistress Wallis's licensing. You and Martha are to travel to Grantby the day before. I've already told the blacksmith to have your horse ready and hired one of his for Martha to take. She must change the day. You gave your word and must go.'

In all the confusion, Lucie had completely forgotten about Alice. Of course, Martha could not go all the way to Grantby on horseback, in November, in her condition, but Jasper couldn't know that. Martha, too, had evidently forgotten all about their appointed day. The thought of Martha in Grantby reminded Lucie that Martha must have been with child when they went to the gaol. Well, that explained her claim to be suffering from sickness caused by the coach. Even if the Rector agreed to move the ceremony back a couple of days, some way must be found to dispense with Martha's presence in Grantby, and to persuade Jasper to permit Lucie to go on her own.

The next morning, the couple set out first thing for the Rectory, Lucie still unsure what she could say about Martha and the need to postpone the wedding date. Mistress Archer's maid showed them in, and when Dr Archer joined them, he confirmed that he had already heard the troubling gossip, and that he planned to make a pastoral visit to John Allen that day, in an attempt to resolve the matter. He too asked Lucie to go through the whole case from start to finish, and she once again began with her visit to Anne in early October when she was bleeding, and how she stayed that effusion of blood by getting her the peas she had a craving for. Luckily for Lucie, the Rector had the utmost faith in Mistress Smith, who had delivered his entire brood and whom he considered a pious and trustworthy woman in every respect. Lucie then told the Rector she was due to testify in front of the Bishop on Monday the 27th at her former apprentice's licensing. Unfortunately, the wedding day could not be changed, as the Rector was away on business for the rest of the week – some problems with the tenants on land the church owned a day's ride away – and advent would have begun by the time he returned. Lucie was thrown into a state of unspoken turmoil by the need to choose between attending the licensing or the wedding. She stroked her belly, without being mindful of it, at the anticipation of gripings.

The Rector solved her dilemma by reminding Lucie that she had already provided a written testimonial for the licensing. Lucie remembered how she had told Mistress Archer about this a couple of Sundays ago after church, conversing about Alice, who Mistress Archer remembered well. Dr Archer advised Lucie to write to Grantby immediately, so that she could get the letter to the postmaster that morning. That way her apologies for her absence would reach Alice before Monday; he very generously said she should blame him for being unable to change the wedding day. This made Lucie feel even worse, and she found it difficult to look the Rector in the eye. Like Jasper, Dr Archer could not be made privy to the reason for the urgency of Martha's wedding. But at least the Rector's advice avoided piling up lies upon half-truths.

It was market day in Tupingham and the town was alive with the sounds of traders with carts selling poultry, wildfowl and rabbits, along with dairy produce, oatmeal, herbs and spices. There were stalls with coarse cloth and hemp and women walking with baskets of everything from buttons and ribbons to hot pies. The market keeper was patrolling the town square maintaining order, and made sure every seller stood in their allotted place and had paid their toll to the town council.

At the stall selling wooden-wares, Lucie stopped and picked out a couple of large bowls, four smaller bowls for porridge, a chopping board, two drinking goblets, and a wooden stirring spoon. Jasper raised an eyebrow at the large purchase, but Lucie reminded him that Martha had neither dowry nor parents to help her, and after almost twenty years of looking after them and their family, she deserved a generous wedding present. Jasper countered that surely the widower Higgs had a full set of household items from his first wife, but Lucie said she wanted Martha to start her married life on the right foot with her own things. The seller agreed to deliver the order to the Three Doves.

As they walked the short distance to the shop, one of the traders, a farmer's wife from a couple of miles outside the town, grabbed Lucie's arm.

'Might I have a moment of your time, Mistress Smith?' she said. 'I am with child again and need some advice.'

'Of course, Goodwife Todd.' Lucie recognised her as a gossip at the Townshend birth. 'Why don't you follow us back to the Three Doves, so I can see you immediately?'

Safely back in her kitchen, Lucie looked at Hannah Todd.

'Judging by your bigness, I'd say you have but a month to your time. Is that right?'

'Oh no, I yet want four months, Mistress Smith.'

Lucie was very surprised and asked Hannah to accompany her to her chamber, so that she might touch the woman's belly while she lay flat on the bed. When Hannah removed her dress, Lucie was shocked at the tightness of the laces on her leather stays. By pinching her in from breasts to navel, her corset was forcing the lower part of her belly to jut out in a way that looked not only unnatural but unhealthy.

'Why on earth are you laced so tightly?' Lucie asked.

'It's my husband's mother's doing. She insists upon it,' Hannah replied.

'Damaris? I thought she would have known better.' Lucie told her this was a great error, and that she ought to allow herself as much liberty as possible.

Hannah was very relieved and said, 'That sounds like good counsel. I'm sick and faint three or four times a day, and that's why I wished to consult you.'

She then asked if Lucie could speak to her husband about it, since it was his mother's advice and he was eager for her to follow it.

Hannah went on to explain that she had been pregnant twice before and in each case she had laboured for a week and given birth to a dead child. Her husband had insisted that this was because she hadn't laced herself tightly enough. Lucie ordered Mary to help Hannah adjust her laces and put her clothes back on. When Hannah left, she said she would ask her husband to come to the Three Doves so that Lucie could speak to him.

Half an hour later, Farmer Todd came in to request an interview with Mistress Smith. He listened to what the midwife had to say and agreed he would allow his wife to loosen her stays, in light of her opinion and experience. He explained that he had only persuaded her to bear the lacing because he was desperate for a living child, and that his mother meant well. Lucie was at a loss to imagine what advantage anyone thought a woman might receive from severe lacing. Lucie told him that the female body had been designed to expand with the child growing in the womb and if women were laced too tightly the bowels and other organs would be squashed, so it was little wonder his wife had been sick and fainting.

Later that day, Jasper returned home from his customary retreat to the coffeehouse in a foul temper. Normally the aroma of coffee and tobacco which accompanied the apothecary home was a welcome one, as it signified Jasper would be in good cheer. Not today. While at Hearne's he had found that what seemed like the whole town was discussing the case of Anne Allen, with half questioning his wife's skill and the other half being vocal in her defence. Not only that, but Ned's behaviour was attracting comment, being cited as an instance of the growing problem of apprentices making a nuisance of themselves in town. The worst of the gossip surrounded Martha, though. News of the application for a special licence had spread, and there had been many bawdy comments about the haste of the wedding. As one of Jasper's fellow aldermen enquired, since Martha had waited until she was in her forties to wed, why could she not wait until after Christmas and get wed in timely fashion? Jasper was deeply uncomfortable at finding himself and his family the talk of the town. He had even seen what looked like pity in the eyes of one of his oldest cronies.

The kitchen was piling up with gifts for Martha from townspeople who had known her for years. The box of wooden items had been joined by a fine pair of leather tankards from the tanner and his family, while the blacksmith had sent a toasting fork and a pair of candle holders. Lucie was knitting in her hearth-side armchair and enjoying watching Mary arrange the packages into manageable piles so she could run up the two flights of stairs to store them in her chamber. While doing so, she mentioned that the baker had sent word that he would supply a bride cake on Monday. This didn't improve Jasper's mood.

'There are rumours in the town that Martha is in haste to wed as she is with child. Can you affirm that this is not the case, wife?' It was the very question Lucie had been dreading. She put her wool down, and her hands rubbed at her belly.

'No, my dear, I fear I cannot, for the rumours are true, I'm afraid. But she is not the first and won't be the last to wed in that condition.' Lucie tried to quell the nervousness in her voice.

'And you thought to keep this from me with tales of her wanting to marry betimes to avoid advent?'

Lucie looked down, and fussed with her apron. 'No, that was not false. If they are not wed soon, they will have to wait over a month to be allowed. I didn't tell you the whole story, that's true, but that was to spare you pain, Jasper.'

'Did you think I would like it better to be a laughing-stock for the whole town?' Jasper paced the room angrily, his choler dangerously high, and showing in his reddening face. 'Martha must go.' Bending, he jabbed a pointed finger towards his wife. 'I'll not have her under my roof another night.'

'Oh no, please! Jasper. Not this,' she plucked at his

212

sleeve. 'Think on all she has done for us over the years. Helped nurse our poor children, cooked and cleaned for nigh on twenty years … no, we couldn't be so cruel!' tears pricked the backs of her eyes as Jasper pulled away from her touch.

'I am resolved. She should have remembered her place in our family before she lay with that weaver. She was no green girl who had her head turned. She will not be getting married from my house now.'

With that pronouncement, Jasper stalked off to the shop, giving Ned a clip round the ear for idling in the doorway.

Lucie covered her face with her hands, unable to believe what Jasper had just said. Lowering her hands again she turned to her deputy, who had been hovering in the shadows of the dark kitchen, and asked, 'How in God's name can we tell Martha she is no longer welcome in her own home?'

Mary calmly suggested that since the wedding was only four days off, matters might be smoothed over if Martha took care to keep out of the master's sight. This was worth a try, and they resolved to warn Martha when she came back from the shops. The women carried all the wedding presents up the two flights of stairs between them, in the hope that keeping them out of sight would help take the wedding off Jasper's mind.

In the event, though, as soon as Martha entered the Three Doves, Jasper raged at her, declaring she was no longer welcome in their home and should gather her things and leave. Lucie heard her husband's raised voice and hurried through to the shop in the hope of intervening, but the sight of her appeared to make Jasper angrier.

'Go and take a room at the Boar, Martha, and stay there,' Lucie whispered to her deeply shocked maid. Lucie blinked back her own tears. 'You'll be quite safe and comfortable. I'll come and see you tomorrow.' She rummaged in her pocket for some coins and pressed them into Martha's hand, with a pat.

Before she was able to leave, Jasper, who had followed the

213

women into the kitchen, saw Martha pick up the grey dress she had been working on, and this set him off again.

'That's nice! A woman who's first betrothed was slain at Naseby by Prince Rupert's godless rabble, now getting wed in a lousy cast gown from the courtiers at the Manor. There's a fine thing, I'm sure. What do you suppose your Oliver would have had to say about that?' he spluttered.

'Husband, that is too much,' Lucie chided. As she spoke, from the corner of her eye she saw Martha, sinking to the ground in a swoon.

Jasper's anger was frightening to all the women. The war was a long time ago and they'd had to move on. Lucie's view was that harbouring such bitterness would not help anyone, but Jasper – like many parliamentary men – felt utterly deflated by the unravelling and failings of the commonwealth they had so vehemently supported. For the Cavaliers not only to be back but living extravagantly on the public purse, flaunting their new prosperity in the faces of those who had not only fought but beaten them, was hard for proud men to bear.

Having said his piece, he turned and stomped through to his storeroom so he did not have to look at the women any longer. He appeared entirely unconcerned about Martha's faint. He did, however, prepare a sponge dipped in the vinegar of the elder flower, and sent Ned to the kitchen with it.

When she came round, Mary having loosened her stays and Lucie holding the sponge under her nose, Martha jumped to her feet, eyes wide with horror. Abandoning the dress, she ran from the house in only the clothes she had on her back. Lucie indicated to Mary to go after her, for Martha was in no state to be running down the high street on her own.

When she returned to the Three Doves an hour later, Mary told Lucie that rather than go to the coaching inn, Martha walked all the way to Warley Lane and to Anthony's cottage. Mary had watched her safely through the door before hurrying home.

If the apothecary thought that turning Martha out would dampen the gossip, he had got things badly wrong. His actions merely confirmed the rumours, and, to make matters worse, in the minds of those who already found grounds for suspicion in the events surrounding Anne Allen's death, the harsh treatment of their maid confirmed that Mistress Smith lacked compassion. That she had no power to overturn her husband's ruling was neither here nor there.

The next morning, Anthony arrived at the Three Doves, having borrowed a cart in which to collect Martha's worldly belongings, including the pile of wedding gifts.

All the tension meant Martha's wedding was a subdued affair. It took place at three in the afternoon on a very frosty Monday, after Anthony had completed almost a full day at the loom. The church was freezing, and their breath was visible as the small congregation spoke to one another. Jasper declined to be a witness as had originally been planned, and Lucie's deputy surprised everyone by stepping up to do it. Although she couldn't yet write properly, she had been practising her letters, especially her signature, which meant she could sign her name in full. Samuel Jones, Martha's cousin and nearest relative, gave her away and was the other witness, signing his name with a mark, and the parish clerk filled in his details for him. Many of the people who lived in Warley Lane declined to attend, claiming they were still in mourning for Goodwife Allen, and that it wasn't appropriate to celebrate a wedding. It might rather have been that they preferred to avoid an awkward meeting with their long-time midwife.

Lucie had not seen her maid since she left home in such haste, but had to admit that Martha, pale and tired as she was, looked radiant nevertheless. Her fierce red hair had been brushed until it shone, and hung loose down her back.

She wore her normal dress, evidently Mister Smith's words had cut her so deeply that she could not bring herself to wear the dress she had been given. Indeed, she had asked that Anthony leave it behind when he'd collected her belongings. That request had broken Lucie's heart a degree more, Jasper had been so uncharacteristically cruel to Martha. Having two of the people she was closest to at loggerheads was a miserable prospect.

After the service, the small party went to the Rectory to toast the happy couple, and the Rector and his wife did their best to make the occasion a merry one. The baker had provided a wonderful, richly fruited bride cake, and Mistress Archer had produced a fine spread with venison pasties and a jugged hare. Mary gave Martha and Anthony a beautiful quilt she had been working on for months – originally meant to be a New Year gift for her parents – deciding it would be perfect for Martha's new marriage bed.

Jasper did not even ask how the wedding had gone. However, he and Ned dined on a wedding pasty each – Lucie noted how he did not turn the celebration food away. After they had finished their supper, Lucie cleared the table, and took herself off to bed.

Chapter Twenty-two

'This day the wife of Thomas Round was laid by
Mother Henshaw.'

A difficult week passed in the Three Doves, with the midwife
and apothecary maintaining only a terse politeness towards
each other. Lucie missed Martha immensely. Even on a
purely practical level, life was much harder without her. It
had only been one week, but looking after her mothers,
helping in the shop, and having to manage all the household
chores made each day feel heavier, even with Mary on hand
to help. They would need to see about a new maid-servant as
a matter of urgency; at fifty-seven, Lucie was sure she could
not keep the workload up. Then, with a start, she realised
she was no longer that age, for two days after Martha
married was the anniversary of her own birth and she had
quite forgotten in all the turmoil. She was now fifty-eight.

At the end of the week, a letter from Simon arrived,
sending birthday greetings to his mother, with a laced
handkerchief enclosed as a gift. The letter also had ten
shillings inside as a wedding gift for Martha. He had better
news about the contagion to relate, for the plague had
caused only three hundred and thirty-three deaths in
London the past week, a steep drop from the previous week's
six hundred odd, and the city was beginning to return to
some level of normal activity. It was still hard to believe that

Tupingham and the surrounding area had remained free of the pest so far.

Jasper was cheered by this news and said he had decided there and then to make his customary journey to London after all, taking Ned with him, since he could not trust him to behave properly in his absence. It would be a good opportunity for Ned to spend a few days in Deptford with his mother and sisters, whom he had seen very infrequently since taking up his apprenticeship. Jasper had recently found himself in need of some spectacles for close work, and had been advised to use the spectacle maker in Westminster, who was one of the best in London. Ned was dispatched to the coaching inn to reserve two mounts for the men to ride to the city, since the stage-coach did not run in mid-winter. Lucie's trusty mare would not manage a journey of such length, and in any case might be required by her mistress. Jasper's decision to take Ned with him was an expensive one, for the hire of a second horse would cost a pretty penny, but it was a small price to pay to save the apothecary from the further humiliation he would incur if the apprentice ran riot while his master was away.

Jasper said he had been praying for fine weather. He always looked forward to his annual trip to the city to gather with his friends. They would share successful treatments, debate with fellow chemists and druggists in and around the Society, and read their reports of what was new in the business. There had been many useful discoveries since he'd completed his own apprenticeship in the late 1620s and he liked to keep up with all the developments in his field. Apart from the times when events in the late wars or very bad weather had made travelling difficult, he had returned annually to Apothecaries' Hall just before Christmastide. Lucie had grown used to her husband's quirks, of which making this journey in mid-winter was just one.

She decided she would keep hold of Martha's present from Simon until after Jasper's departure. She would enjoy a visit to Warley Lane to see how Martha had settled in. With Ned going to London too, the shop would have to be closed for the week, so she would at least be free of that care.

When Ned returned from the postmaster's office, he mentioned that the wife of Thomas Round, another member of the cloth trade, who lived near Warley Lane, was at her time.

'How did you learn this, Ned?' Lucie asked. 'Was someone on their way to fetch me?'

'No, Mistress Smith; I overheard two women talking about it in Market Square. They said she had been having throes all night and was making a great clamour with her crying out.'

'Come, Mary, we'd better get down there quickly,' Lucie said. 'I can't understand why no one fetched us sooner. This is most odd!'

'That's the thing, Mistress Smith. The women were talking about how Goody Round was being attended by that Henshaw woman,' Ned reported.

'What?' Lucie was stunned. She had delivered the other Round children without encountering any difficulties, and there had never been any complaints afterwards. She decided she'd better go to Warley Lane straight away to settle this matter.

When Lucie and Mary arrived, Goodman Round was pacing up and down outside the cottage. His breath was visible in the cold winter morning. He was drawing deeply on his tobacco pipe, drinking in the smoke, and looked startled to see the midwife and her apprentice approaching him.

'Good morning, Mistress Smith,' he said, feigning a cheery tone.

'Good morning indeed, Goodman Round! I understand Catherine is having her throes. I take it I may go straight through?' She stepped confidently towards the threshold.

Thomas jumped to bar the way.

'I am sorry, but you have had a wasted journey, Mistress Smith. My wife asked to be attended by Mother Henshaw this

219

time, I'm afraid, so I can't let you in.'

'Mother Henshaw is not licensed to practice in this town, as everyone knows. She is not a trained midwife. Why would your wife risk being delivered by her?'

'Well, I'm not sure it's my place to say, Mistress Smith, but after the sad death of poor Goody Allen, there are many in the neighbourhood who can't tell what to think. While we don't know the full truth of the matter, my wife didn't choose to be delivered by you at this time.'

'This is nonsense, Goodman Round!' Lucie responded. 'May I just satisfy myself that your wife is well and then leave if there is nothing more I need do?

'No, I'm afraid not, Midwife Smith, Deputy Thorne. Good day to you both!'

With that, he went indoors and shut the door firmly behind himself.

Lucie slumped back against the cottage wall.

'What's ado here, Mary? The world has gone quite mad.' From their position under the eaves, the midwives heard an almighty groan followed by the distinctive first cry of a newborn. 'Well, Goodwife Round seems to be safely delivered, in any case, God be thanked,' Lucie kept her voice steady. 'Since we've come this far, let's call in at Martha's new home and see how she does.'

The Higgs family cottage was warm and welcoming. Martha invited them in for a hot drink. Anthony was busy at the loom, and the two children were playing with some wooden animals on the rushes in front of the hearth.

'I feared for a moment that you might have been out gossiping at the Rounds' house,' Lucie said, as she took her drink from Martha.

'They asked me. Anne Jones is there and Jane Croft, and others. I told them I'd have nothing to do with their silly notions.'

'I must tell Dr Archer,' Lucie responded. 'He will have to step in since the Henshaw woman is unlicensed and working in his parish.'

'Yes, but hasn't she always been a law unto herself? I think maybe the Rector is somewhat afeared of her,' Mary said.

'You think he suspects that she will bewitch him?' Martha asked.

'I wouldn't be surprised,' said Lucie. 'But I've known her for longer than I care to remember, and one thing I do know is if she were a witch there'd be little chance of her enchantments being successful. When she births a woman it is only by sheer luck and the grace of God that either mother or child lives. Certainly no proof of her skill.'

'They don't call her "Old Mother Grope" behind her back for nothing! But don't let the master hear you talking about charms and the like, either of you! He thinks talk of witches is superstitious nonsense, doesn't he?' Martha reminded the women. 'Remember that time, Mistress Smith, when I hadn't been working for you long and he caught me running my white feather along the beams in the ceiling and rebuked me so sharply?'

'Oh, yes, I remember! You swore you were dusting the beams but we all knew you were looking for witches,' Lucie laughed.

'Well, you can't be too careful,' said Martha, scooping the little boy, George, onto her lap. 'You see, George, if there is a witch hiding in the rafters, even though you can't see her, she won't be able to help but laugh if you tickle her with a feather. We'll hear her giggling, and she'll give herself away,' she gave George's belly a squeeze to make him chuckle.

Lucie smiled at the young boy's pleasure in his new step-dame's play with him.

'Do you know, though, given how badly things have gone since those hard words between me and Mother Henshaw at the Bromfields' farm at the beginning of summer, I could almost be persuaded she has put a curse on us,' said Lucie.

The three women laughed somewhat uneasily, and George and his sister Jemima joined in, even though they weren't

221

sure what the adults were laughing at.

Lucie decided to change the subject. She asked Martha if she had thought about Cissy Mallet and her school fees. Martha explained that she had paid them up to the end of term and that after Christmas Mistress Robbins planned to seek her father's permission for her to stay on and help teach the little ones, and also to help look after the baby after he came home from his nurse next year. In return she would reside with the school teacher and have her diet provided. She would be about to turn eight by then, and could already read, write and sew as well as any girl two years her senior. Although she wore a patch over her injured eye, Cissy was as active and cheerful as any child in Tupingham, and more so than most. Lucie was pleased, although it had crossed her mind to take Cissy in to train her for a new maid. The girl had always struck her as being very capable, but Mistress Robbins's plan was a better one, if the tanner was minded to agree to it.

After a happy hour in the Higgs's house, Lucie and Mary took their leave. Stepping out onto the freezing street, Lucie pulled her cloak round her tightly. Anne Jones and Jane Croft were walking home from Catherine Round's birthing, and spotted them leaving. They jeered at Lucie and said they were surprised she was so bold as to show her face round there, but she was always sticking her nose in, so they should have expected as much. Lucie was not prepared to accept this slanderous talk, especially from young wives she had delivered multiple times, and drew herself up to her fullest height, puffing out her cheeks.

'Anne Jones, I have delivered all your children, and as for you, Jane Croft, not only have I delivered your children, but I brought you into the world, too. I cannot believe you think ill of me, or doubt my skill. And I am shocked you think it acceptable to speak to me so boldly!'

The women had the grace to look slightly abashed, but then Jane said defiantly, 'Even so, perhaps it's time for you

222

to stop. What went on at Anne Allen's was an odd business. No one thinks you caused harm deliberately but she should have been given proper care when you saw her first, not some nonsense about longings making her bleed.'

'Jane, I am not going to dispute with you in the street, but I will say this: your own mother had a dream that she had cut her hand on a bread knife when she was carrying you, and then you were born with a big red birthmark on your chest, in the shape of a blade with blood dripping from it. It faded when you were five or so, but everyone talked of it at the time. You ask your neighbours and see if I am telling the truth.'

Lucie knew perfectly well that Jane didn't need to ask anyone. She had heard her mother recount the story many times and knew it to be true. Her mother had always impressed on her the power a mother's imagination could exert on her unborn child, using her birthmark as an example. Lucie hoped this reminder would pull the insolent woman up sharp.

'Be that as it may,' she retorted, 'you'll find nobody round here likely to engage your services again.'

'So, you'll risk your lives and those of your children with that unqualified hand woman? You think I should retire but Mother Henshaw who has ten years on me should take on my cases? That's pure foolishness. If your mother was still with us, she'd likely box your ears for speaking to me so, married woman or not.' Lucie shook her head incredulously, as the two women walked on past, arms linked.

Back at the Three Doves, Lucie served dinner and told her husband the tale. Jasper's choler rose again, and he laid down his knife, the shock had put him off his meat. He announced his resolve to go and see Dr Archer straight after his meal, to implore him to act. There was no point in having an ecclesiastical licence to practise and maintain the highest standards, if no action was to be taken against those working without a licence. He was prepared to take the matter to the Bishop himself if he did not get a satisfactory response.

Dr Archer was perturbed, Lucie later heard from Jasper. He'd said he knew Old Mother Henshaw was a difficult sort who acted according to her own will. She had never married, and claimed to have learned the art of midwifery from her mother and all her foremothers. This couldn't be verified one way or the other, for Mother Henshaw had lived in an ancient stone hovel within the woods for as long as anyone could remember, so there was no one who knew her parents. Dr Archer said the country folk readily accepted her help in delivering their children, as she charged low fees and had a knack of turning up when a birth was imminent.

He agreed to give the matter some thought, though at present he felt there was little he could do. Mother Henshaw could be punished by being excommunicated from the church, but since she rarely attended, had no money to pay any fine, and would carry on her trade regardless, this would be ineffectual. He'd told Jasper he had been trying to allay the anger among the people of Warley Lane, and John Allen's in particular, but the fact that Goodwife Round had engaged the hand woman showed there was still much to do. Jasper said Dr Archer promised to continue working and praying to restore peace to his parish.

Here Jasper bowed his head as he spoke to Lucie. Dr Archer he said, had asked him to reflect on his harsh treatment of Goodwife Higgs. He reminded Jasper of the words of St Augustine, that one should proceed *cum dilectione hominum et odio vitiorum*: with love for mankind and hatred for their sins. He had made it the subject of his Sunday sermon, reminding his congregation that Jesus himself did not shun fallen women, but he felt Jasper had failed to apply the message to himself and needed it spelled out more clearly. Jasper admitted to feeling shame at this statement. The Rector also said he had been disappointed in Jasper for not keeping his word to stand as witness, and hoped to persuade him to reflect on his actions. There was too much division and strife in the world in this time of plague, which he saw as a sign from God that the nation needed to be more pious and charitable.

'As he showed me out, he expressed his hope of reconciliation. He made me see that apart from more spiritual considerations, this estrangement would be affecting you badly my dear. I promised to think and pray on the matter.'

Chapter Twenty-three

The day of Jasper's trip dawned crisp and bright. His bag had been packed the night before and contained the new clothes Lucie had stitched for him. He looked very smart in a new camlet cloak, over his thick serge winter coat, and wore his black felt hat. The midwife walked with him and Ned to the Boar Inn and bade them farewell.

'Make sure you apply to yourselves all the same measures against the plague you pressed on Simon. They have served him well, and, God willing, will afford you just as much protection,' Lucie told them. She hugged her husband and gave him a parcel containing the woollen stockings she had recently knitted for Simon. 'Promise me you will have a care in the city, Jasper.'

'I will. And, my dear, I have been thinking, should you wish to invite Martha to our home while I am away, I'll not take it ill. I cannot commend her actions, but I would not have you break off with her forever. You have my leave to see her whenever you wish.'

Lucie nodded; she wasn't sure she trusted herself to speak. Turning to Ned, she gave him 6d to treat himself on the journey, and a parcel with a small gift for his mother inside.

'Remember me kindly to your mother, Ned, and be obedient and dutiful while you're away. We want her to see that we have raised you to be a well-mannered young man while you have been with us.'

Back in her kitchen, Lucie said to Mary, 'Let's treat ourselves! Do you remember when Martha and I went to Grantby and I bought some China tea and porcelain dishes? Well, somehow, all this long while, I've never yet taken the time to try how it tastes. Let's set this to rights straightway, shall we?'

'I'm ready if you are, Mistress Smith. Let's be in the new fashion!' Mary smiled. 'It will be something to tell my parents next time I am home.'

Lucie had another surprise for Mary. Enclosed in Simon's last letter was a penny ballad sheet he had picked up, which he thought his mother might find noteworthy. She had tucked it away until she had a chance to read it properly. Now she asked Mary to light some extra candles against the dark winter day. The ballad was entitled, *The Mistaken Mid-wife, or, Mother Mid-Night finely brought to Bed*, and was to be sung to the tune of I am a Jovial Batchelor, not that either woman had the least notion how that sounded.

The ballad told the story of a midwife who, despite three marriages, had not managed to have a child of her own.

> *A Midwife lately in this town,*
> > *by folly was misled,*
> > *Who many a woman had lain down,*
> > *and brought them unto Bed;*
> > *She to three husbands married was,*
> > *which made her almost wild,*
> > *Because in all that time alas,*
> > *she could not have a Child.*

Because it was common, although not essential, for midwives to be mothers by the time they were licensed, this midwife felt ashamed of her infertility and so, "to take off the scandal of Barrenness", she came up with a scheme to convince people she was pregnant.

A little Pillow she prepar'd,
  which cunningly she plac't,
  And to the women then declar'd,
  she should not be disgrac't;
  Quoth she my time of joy is come,
  I now am big with child,
  I feel the babe spring in my womb
  and thus she them beguil'd.

'It puts me mind of that prisoner I attended in Grantby gaol who thought she could plead her belly even though she had the blood of her courses on her shift.' said Lucie.

The tea was now steeped, and the two women took their first sips of the hot clear liquid.

'Urgh!' exclaimed Mary. 'That's horrible!'

Lucie thought it quite pleasant and drank hers down. 'I can see it would be a refreshing drink on a summer's day,' she said refilling her dish. 'Pray give it another try Mary.'

They turned back to the ballad, which took an even darker turn towards the end. First, the mistaken midwife had deceived her husband by feigning longings for expensive items, and had him provide only the very best child-bed linen, all while he remained oblivious to her wiles. The midwife apparently used the remains of a dead baby she had delivered to stage a birth with the help of some friends. She was found out, of course, and a jury of matrons could see at once that she had never given birth.

'Goodness me!' said Lucie. 'This is meant to be a true tale and it says here that the woman is in gaol to this day. What a wicked thing she did!'

'It sounds as if she was quite desperate,' said Mary. 'I feel sorry for her.'

'Really?'

'Well, a bit at least. The ballad shows how the husband longed for a child, too. He was ready to satisfy all his wife's

229

longings, lest any ill should betide the baby. You should show it to Anne and Jane.'

'I don't think that pair will hear any reason while they are being so silly.' Lucie curled her fingers into her palms. She knew if Jane's mother was still alive, her daughter – married mother or not – would never be so rude to her. Still, the ballad had been useful for teaching Mary more about teeming women and their longings.

Lucie suggested that Mary took a walk to Warley Lane to give Martha the ten shillings Simon had sent, and if she liked, afterwards, she could take Dapple and go and pay her parents an overnight visit. She herself felt a need for solitude.

'Be sure to let Martha know what the master said about her being welcome to call any time now.'

Later, Lucie walked with Mary to the blacksmith's to collect the horse. Lucie hugged her deputy and said her second goodbye of the day. Deciding not to cook for just herself, she called in at the bakery and bought a hot pigeon pie. The she paused, examining the cakes, wondering if it would be fitting to indulge herself. The baker's wife noticed her hesitation and popped a currant bun in the parcel with the pie.

'My gift,' she said.

'Oh, no, Mistress Healey,' protested Lucie, 'it's only a week since you gave my maid that wonderful bride cake as a gift. I must pay for the bun, but thank you. I'll enjoy this tonight.'

'It's my pleasure, Mistress Smith. I've heard the talk in town, but let me tell you clearly without caring who knows it: I'll be in need of your services again in spring and there is no one else I'd trust to lay me.'

'Thank you, my dear. You are with child again? How many is that now?'

'This is number eight. All living, too. I have to be honest and say that while I know I am lucky to receive God's blessings and another child, I'd really rather not have it so again.'

'I understand. It's not for us to question the Lord, though.'

'If men had to suffer as if they were being stretched on the very rack itself, I dare say there would be far fewer souls walking this earth, Mistress Smith.'

Lucie smiled. 'I expect you're right. Good day to you, look after yourself and come and see me now and again, to let me know how the pregnancy does.'

When Lucie got home, she banked up the fire, relit the candles, including a virgin wax one for a better light, and fetched down all her old journals from the trunk in her bedroom. She had decided to spend the evening poring over her notes from past cases to reassure herself that she really had done all she could for poor Anne Allen. If something which might have helped had been missed, it was important she learn the lesson and teach it to Mary, too.

After a couple of hours searching her old records without finding anything to the purpose, Lucie stopped to eat her pie, and poured herself a cup of small beer. As she ate she reflected on what she'd read. Thirty years of birthing hundreds of babies, around two dozen a year. All noted along with the date, outcome, and fee collected. Only a very small number had been lost like Goodwife Allen, more still from problems like fever after the birth, but the vast majority of her women did very well. Some quick reckoning showed she lost fewer than five or six in a hundred. Every single one a tragedy she sought to accept with God's help, but still an enviable figure. That she was regularly being called by women she had brought into the world, to lay them as they become mothers in their turn, must speak for itself.

Lucie's reverie was interrupted by a knock on the front door. Her heart sank, for she had sent Mary away on purpose, so that she could have an evening to read and think undisturbed. She thought about not opening the door, but the weight of her oath bore down on her. If a woman was in need she was duty bound to attend, so she rose from her chair, lifted the latch of the shop door, put her candle in a crevice on the door frame, and went to the front door.

To her surprise, it was not a worried husband or a neighbour, but the Rector, looking very uncomfortable.

'Dr Archer? Is anything amiss? Is Mistress Archer well?' Lucie asked.

'Quite well, Mistress Smith. May I come in?'

In the kitchen the Rector accepted a cup of small beer and explained that he was here to let Lucie know that Goodman Allen had decided to sue the midwife for negligence, in the church court. Dr Archer had appealed to him to reconsider and asked him to give the matter some thought, which he had done, but still he returned to press his complaint. This meant the Rector's hands were tied. He was obligated to refer the petition to the Bishop's office, and it would be heard at the next visitation at the end of January. Lucie pressed her hand to her chest, suddenly finding it hard to breathe. This was the first time in her long career that a formal complaint had been made against her.

The Rector had his arms folded tightly. It was the first time he had heard of such a complaint being raised in the whole diocese, he said. Lucie felt her breathing become shallower.

'In my considered opinion,' continued Dr Archer, 'for what it is worth, while the processes must be followed, I am content it will come to nothing.'

'What will happen if the Bishop finds in favour of Goodman Allen?' Lucie asked, struggling with her breath. 'Would they remove my licence? I don't know what I'd do if that happened. There's plenty as practice unlicensed but that is not my way, nor my mother's before me.'

'I'm not sure what the consequence would be.' Dr Archer shifted from foot to foot. 'Your licence could be revoked, you could be fined, or, um... you might even be excommunicated from the church.'

Lucie gasped. For a God-fearing woman this was a fate almost too horrible to consider. Her mind was spinning. That would mean she wouldn't be able to be buried in the church yard with her three children. She felt as if she was drowning as she struggled to take another breath, falling down and down into increasing darkness. *She was about to faint.*

She needed her stays unlacing – the presence of another woman was an urgent necessity. Dr Archer called out for Mary, before Lucie could make him understand, through her ragged breaths, that she was alone.

'Who can I fetch to sit with you?' he asked, with evident mounting anxiety. 'This has been a terrible shock, I know.'

'Martha, please get Martha,' Lucie whispered.

'Very well, but I'll need to ask someone nearer to sit with you while I'm gone. I have my horse, but it will still take some time to get to Warley Lane and back.'

'No, please! I'll do well enough.' She fought for one breath at a time. 'I want no one else to hear of this yet.'

Martha had been prepared to ride on the back of the Rector's horse to get to Lucie more quickly, but he would not hear of her riding in her condition, so she and the Rector had no choice but to take the half-hour walk to the Three Doves. They managed a pace that knocked a good few minutes off the normal time, but even so when they got there, the shop and kitchen were in darkness. The fire glowed, but Lucie had let the candles burn out. They found her sitting in her armchair, alert but shaking from head to toe. The scene in the room was so very familiar to Martha, yet so distant, now it was no longer her home. She noticed that the fine grey gown she had been forced to leave behind because of Jasper's anger was on the shelf at the back of the room, neatly folded. But she had no time to dwell on these things as she ran to throw her arms around Lucie.

'Mistress Smith, I'm here now!' She threw her cloak over Lucie's body, as much to preserve the Rector's modesty as her patient's, and began deftly unfastening stay laces under its sheltering folds. 'Dr Archer has told me the whole business as we walked here. Pray try not to take on so. I'm sure all this will be resolved. Anthony will plead with John to drop the suit. I'm sure we can resolve this.'

233

The stays came loose, Lucie began to breathe a little more easily, though she was still shaking, and Martha now felt free, if only for a moment, to consult with Dr Archer, who was standing in a corner of the kitchen looking ill at ease – as well he might.

'Your ill tidings have frighted Mistress Smith into a mother-fit!' she hissed in a vicious whisper – she didn't want Lucie to overhear their conversation. 'Her womb has risen into her chest, which is why she can't breathe.'

Dr Archer nodded, saying his dear wife frequently suffered the same symptoms.

'We must give her some stinking thing to smell,' said Martha, 'that will drive it back down again. I'll burn some feathers under her nose, but could you find something that would do her more good?' She reached for a large key that was hanging on a hook in the kitchen, pressed it into Dr Archer's hand, and pointed silently to the door to the shop, indicating that when he went through the door, he should turn right to the locked store-room. She then ran upstairs with a knife to ravish feathers from the first pillow she could lay hands on – which happened to be Ned's.

Dr Archer returned with a bottle which he told her contained *Asafoetida.*

'Stinking gum,' he explained. 'Otherwise known as Devil's Dung.' There was a cluster of sticky brown resinous balls in the jar, full of tiny scraps of leaves and twigs. The kitchen was already permeated with the odour of burning feathers, but still the full force of the drug took them unawares. Devil's Dung did not do it justice. Choking and retching, Dr Archer held the jar under Lucie's nose and let nature take its course. Within a minute she had stopped shaking, and loudly demanded that this frightful stuff be taken out of her clean kitchen without delay.

Having effected this cure, Dr Archer took his leave, but told Martha as she saw him out that it would be as well for Mistress Smith to begin to gather the names of witnesses who would speak in her defence at the visitation, and to ask for letters from those who could not appear in person. He said he deeply regretted not keeping the news to himself, knowing the apothecary had left for the city that morning. However, it had felt too urgent to wait, and bad news had a way of leaking out.

If ever Mistress Smith needed to lean on her husband it was now, Martha thought, yet she would have to supply the want. Any letter sent by post would not go until later that week.

Dr Archer mounted his horse again and set off for home. When the Rector had trotted out of sight, Martha returned to Lucie. She leaned over and hugged her former mistress with all her strength.

'Only a few weeks since, you were rousing me from a swoon, now I had to return the compliment. We must not make it a habit,' she joked weakly. 'We shall get through these trials, Mistress Smith. I'll sleep here tonight with you and I shan't leave until you are yourself again.'

Lucie nodded. Her eyes filled with tears, and she squeezed Martha's hand.

Chapter Twenty-Four

Jasper and Ned arrived at The Dolphin in London after dark on Wednesday evening. Their overnight stop at the coaching inn the night before had been unremarkable. Ned had been on his best behaviour, keen to spend a few days at his mother's house. They were both tired from their long ride, and glad to have reached the city at last. As soon as the hired horses were stabled safely the two men could enjoy some welcome refreshment. Ned was keen to get home to Deptford, but Jasper decided it was too dangerous for the young man to be running around London on a freezing cold night. No wherryman would be at work this hour, and in any case the occupation had been all but annihilated by the plague, so going by water was not a possibility. Ned would have needed to run to London Bridge, and then have over an hour's walk on the south side. Instead, Jasper insisted his apprentice share his bed for the first night; he could set off for home in the morning. Because of the fatigue of the journey, they both were ready for bed after their tasty, hot meal of oysters fried in breadcrumbs.

The following day, Jasper planned to walk to Westminster to track down the spectacle seller who had been recommended to him. Since this took him in the opposite direction to Ned, the men parted company. Jasper had given his apprentice strict instructions to be back at The Dolphin by Wednesday afternoon, ready to depart for Tupingham at first light the following morning.

Ned appeared unexpectedly at the door of Simon's print house. 'I hope you don't mind me paying you a visit?' he said. 'Only when I was walking to the bridge I realised it was more or less on my way.'

'Not at all!' Simon stood back from the door to beckon Ned inside. 'Welcome to town. I wasn't sure if my father would choose to make the journey with the plague still around, even though the numbers of the dead begin to fall. How good it is to see you here. Come, let me show you the sights of my little works. Your visit gives me advance notice of my father's imminent inspection, so I have a chance to make sure all looks spick and span before he arrives.'

Away from the domestic setting of the Three Doves' kitchen where they usually met, Simon saw the younger man with fresh eyes. He spent a very pleasant morning with Ned, apart from one thing: Simon was appalled to hear of the goings-on back home. He must ask his father for his opinion of this when Jasper called in to make dinner arrangements later. Ned begged him to say nothing unless his father raised the matter, for he had promised to go straight to his mother's house when he had parted with Mister Smith. Simon stopped him from saying any more: instead, he offered to buy the lad dinner before he set off home, and Ned happily accepted. They entered a nearby alehouse. Simon took care to make sure that the other customers and the waiting staff appeared healthy before deciding where they should sit. You couldn't be too careful in these dangerous times. Over their meal, Ned confided in Simon that he firmly believed he was in the wrong apprenticeship.

'I truly have no calling to work as a druggist. I know I must see out my indenture because it cost my mother a lot of money to get the place with your father, but I've no wish to spend the rest of my life mixing and supplying remedies all day for disgusting ailments.'

Simon was the right person to confide in, since he understood entirely. He had never thought of being an apprentice to his father, and his father had never raised the matter. As a bookish young man, and a good scholar, he had persuaded his parents to seek a place for him in a print house, and it had worked out well. Like Ned, he had developed a taste for riot and revelry, running about the town with other apprentices, but his master, John Miller, with whom he was now in partnership, had a better idea about raising wilful apprentices, and had brought out the best in Simon in the end. There was no practical advice Simon could offer, but at least Ned would know he'd had a listening ear and had got his frustrations off his chest before going home. Simon walked with him as far as London Bridge, and they laughed together at the thought that, had they had been there two winters before, Ned would have been able to run across the Thames, for it was frozen solid then and a frost fair was held on the river itself.

In Westminster, Jasper had successfully purchased his spectacles. He'd also bought a pair for his wife on her request, as she was finding close work difficult nowadays. Jasper walked back towards the Apothecaries' Hall to meet friends and fellow druggists. He had an appointment to dine with John Battersby, a member of the Worshipful Society, who had a shop in Fenchurch Street; they had engaged to meet at the Hall. The men had known each other since they were both apprentices. As Jasper entered the Hall, he looked upon the portraits of the good and great in his field and, in particular, that of Gideon de Laune, instantly recognisable with his cropped hair and bushy brown beard, who was one of the Society's founders. It had hung over the fireplace as long as Jasper could remember. It felt good to be back.

John Battersby greeted him warmly. The men sat by the fire and discussed the latest events in the dispute between the chemical physicians, the College of Physicians and their own profession, with John bringing Jasper up to date with all the goings on. Jasper mentioned that news of the death in August of Thomas O'Dowde, one of the key players in this controversy, had reached him via his son in the autumn. 'He was a peevish old so-and-so, but London is worse for the lack of his service. For all his faults he was good to the poor, from what I've heard.'

The London apothecary recommended with great enthusiasm a new book on the theme of chemical medicine. The chemical physician, George Thomson, had just published his opinion of the traditional humoral physicians who based their treatments on the ancient writings of Galen. Even the title proclaimed a combat: *Galeno-pale*, or "Wrestling with Galen". John Battersby described some of the highlights in the edition, and how Thomson fiercely condemned the common practice of treating the sick with copious bleeding, which he declared had "destroyed more than Tobacco or the Sword together", and harsh purges, that served only to "cast men into *Purgatory*". Jasper, who often recommended bleeding and purging to his customers, was slightly relieved to learn that the book had attracted several angry responses, which were apparently already at the presses. The dissension was clearly benefiting printers if not patients. He decided to see which of these publications Simon could get hold of while he was in the city. He would take great interest in the argument and counter arguments, and with his new reading spectacles this would be an excellent way to pass the winter months. The apothecaries agreed that the controversy was probably overblown, since in their field they used both the traditional humoral medicines passed down through the centuries and the newer compounds the chemists had developed.

The topic of the plague was unavoidable. Jasper learned that there was now a shortage of apothecaries in London, since so many of their number had died in this epidemic. In

240

the whole of Westminster, from where Jasper had just walked, only one druggist remained. John mentioned that this George Thomson they'd just been discussing also had a new publication on the plague. Jasper made a note to add it to his book order. John told him it was an intriguing examination of the disease, but it also contained some excoriating reflections on the conduct of members of the College of Physicians who left the city when the plague broke out. He said he couldn't see the College taking that lying down: there was bound to be a furious counter publication. Again, Jasper reflected that this controversy was probably doing more good to printers like his son than to the sick.

John left to get back to his shop, but not before Jasper had arranged to visit it during his stay in London. Jasper then decided to take a slow walk back to the Dolphin before dusk fell, and to sup and retire early. He was still a little fatigued from the two-day ride. He hoped Ned had got home safely and avoided getting into any trouble on the way.

The bed in the alehouse was comfortable and the room warm. Before changing into his nightgown, or saying his prayers, Jasper took the precaution of relighting the chafing-dish he'd brought from home, to cleanse the room again and protect him from disease. Very soon the room filled with cleansing scents. Jasper washed his hands and face, changed, and said a short prayer before climbing into bed. He slept better than he had in a while. So much so, that instead of his customary routine of sleeping a few hours before rising for about two hours to read or pray and reflect before returning to bed until the dawn, he slept through the night and was surprised to see daylight seeping through the slats of the shutter when he drew back the curtains around the bed. Despite the long, deep sleep, he didn't feel fully refreshed, and he started to wonder if perhaps he was now too old for such a long ride in the winter months, or maybe it was something as simple as the oysters he'd so enjoyed that first night being somewhat bad.

241

After breaking his fast, he roused himself for the walk to St Paul's to see his son. The sign outside the bookseller's depicted an assortment of books. It was eye-catching and had been repainted since Simon bought into the business. Above the books the sign carried the words, *Miller and Smith, Printers and Booksellers.* The sight warmed Jasper's heart, and he looked forward to describing it to Lucie. On entering he found the shop trading as briskly as could be expected in the half-empty city.

'Well met, sir,' said Simon with a smile, as his father walked up to the counter. Jasper thought his son looked well enough, if paler that he had in the summer months. He wore a cap, but his natural hair was showing, looking like it had not been shorn off after all.

Simon called out to Mister Miller to come from the print house to greet his father.

'Come through, and see the operation,' John Miller said, beckoning the apothecary through the door to the back of the shop. 'Simon, would you mind shouting up to Mistress Miller to ask her to mind the shop, and then you can join us?'

The normally busy presses were much quieter than usual. Stephen, the journeyman printer, was busily checking a large printed proof sheet to make sure the information he'd laid out was in order, explaining to a youth what he was doing. But the contrast between this scene and the last time Jasper had looked in a year earlier was marked. Simon's letters home had told him about the four apprentices who had perished. John Miller said, 'We've only managed to take on young Tom Mason here since we reopened, but although he is only six weeks into his indenture, he is showing promise. He's willing, and that's something rare among today's youth.'

Jasper asked, 'May I take the ledgers over the road to Child's coffeehouse? I'd like to look over them.' Child's was a popular place with physicians and clergymen and one could always secure intelligent conversation there. Once he had studied the accounts, he hoped to learn more from other customers at the coffeehouse about the controversy between the chemical physicians and the Galenists. The apothecary smiled as his son advised him to have a care if he was going into company, and to make sure he only sat near people who looked completely well, and to come away if anyone had any suspicious symptoms.

'You would have me teach my Grandame to suck Eggs, my boy,' Jasper retorted, but promised he would indeed be careful. He carried his plague cake next to his skin and a pomander in his hand to ward off the bad, disease-ridden smells in the city air.

Jasper paid his penny to enter Child's in nearby St Paul's yard and sat in a quiet corner with his drink to study the account books. All seemed well enough. Clearly, the long summer closure would prevent the business turning a profit for this financial year, but they had reserves and should do well enough, according to the figures. As he sipped his dish of coffee, he overheard two men discussing rumours some wig-makers were taking hair from plague victims. *Ah, so that is why Simon has let his own hair grow.* After a pleasant couple of hours in good company, Jasper left to return the ledger to the print house. At the premises he paid John Miller and his wife his respects, but declined to stop any longer as he was still feeling rather disordered and was going to return to his bed at the inn to lie down. He left the list of titles he hoped Simon would be able to track down for him.

'When I get them, do you want to pay the additional sixpence to have them bound with a hard cover, or will you take them only stitched?' Simon asked.

Jasper replied that he would have them unbound, since they were just for his recreational reading, not works he envisioned himself consulting often enough for them to require a protective binding.

'Very well, Father. Would you like me to walk with you back to the Dolphin? You do look a little pale, if you don't mind me saying?'

'No, be assured that I am quite well Simon, thank you. The air in London is thick with smoke compared with Tupingham and it always takes me a day or two to adjust to the change. All the same, I think I will take a hackney carriage, rather than walk.'

'A good idea, sir,' said Simon, holding the door open.

'Farewell, Simon. Until we meet on Sunday. Remember that the morning service is at St Andrew's. Pray do not be late.' Jasper always enjoyed the services at the church assigned to the Apothecaries' Society, and had presumed Simon would join him, as it was their custom to meet on the Sunday during Jasper's annual visit.

'Farewell Father, I hope to have your books by then to bring with me.'

Chapter Twenty-Five

Sunday morning dawned clear, crisp, and bright. Simon was feeling a little the worse for wear, since he had been a guest at Calstone House overnight. Sir Robert had hosted a merry evening for his group of friends and had cut a fine figure in his new silk suit of clothes. The food had been stunning, and Simon had especially enjoyed the neats' tongues and cheesecakes. The wine, generously liberated from Lord Calstone's cellar, had flowed freely. On top of this the party had been royally entertained by a small group of musicians playing fiddles and a harp.

When Sir Robert and Simon woke after their rare night together, it was already well into the morning and Simon was afraid he would be late for the service at St Andrew's. Robbie used his wiles to try and entice his lover to stay, but when he saw Simon was set on keeping the appointment with his father, he insisted on coming along. They only had time to breakfast on a drop of ale and a bite of cake before setting off but it was a speedy journey there in the Calstones' new sprung chariot.

In the church, Simon noted how dignified his father looked in his new camlet cloak. Together he and Robbie walked up the aisle to meet Jasper, who raised his eyebrow as he stood to greet them.

'Father, may I introduce Sir Robert Calstone to your acquaintance? If you recall, mother laid his wife of a son back in May. He and I met while I was at home last summer and we have maintained a correspondence ever since. Does he have your leave to join us at morning worship?'

As everyone was welcome in the house of the Lord, his father moved along the pew to allow them to sit down. Simon told Jasper he had had great success in tracking down the medical titles he'd requested, and some others which were likely to be of interest to him, too. He had left them in his chamber at the shop, and would arrange to get them to his father's lodgings the next day. Simon also reported that he had heard the plague was rife in Deptford town, which made him feel anxious about Ned. Jasper agreed this was concerning news. They discussed whether, having been so exposed to contagion, Ned should stay at home until they could be sure he was free of the disease.

All fell quiet as the service began. It went on for a long time, and both Simon and Robbie struggled to maintain their concentration, but it was Jasper who complained of feeling unwell – short of breath. He whispered that he thought stepping outside to take the air would set him right.

At last the clergyman gave the dismissal. The congregation rose to file out. However, the curate spoke up and asked everyone to wait in their seats for some minutes more. A corpse had been found just outside the main door and must be removed before they could leave. Robbie whispered that he'd wager it was a pauper, hoping to collect a few pennies from the congregation as they left, and he hoped Simon's father hadn't been prevented from taking the air by the dying pauper.

Simon hushed his friend: 'Robbie, don't speak of the dead like that; even the poor deserve dignity in death.' Sir Robert sighed; and Simon was reminded that sometimes Robbie found him priggish.

A few minutes later, the church doors opened and two church servants staggered in with a body wrapped in a blanket between them, one at the head and one holding the legs, with the curate fussing in front waving his arms. In one

246

hand he clutched a pomander. His behaviour struck Simon as rather theatrical. The party went straight though to the vestry. Sir Robert observed that this meant it couldn't have been a pauper as such folk would be left on the road for the next plague cart, regardless of whether or not their demise was caused by the pest. The worshipers were now allowed to leave, but when Simon got up, a parish official asked if he might have a word in private. He led Simon and Sir Robert to the vestry. Shutting the door behind them, the Rector turned to Simon and said, 'I believe the body is that of your father, Apothecary Smith.'

'No!' Simon felt the colour drain from his face. 'There must be an error. My father is in good health. He was a little fatigued by his journey, that's all, and just stepped out of the service for a moment to take the air. He'll be down the road, waiting for me.' If only he could be outside breathing in the fresh, cold air himself. The Rector responded by drawing back the blanket from the corpse's face. There was no error. There was no question but that it was Jasper.

Simon's knees gave way beneath him and he heard himself groaning. He was vaguely aware of being supported under the arms as Robbie and the Rector guided him to a seat. 'No, no. This is not possible, not at all! How did it happen? Was he assaulted in the street? You have sent for the parish constable, I assume?'

The Rector pulled the blanket down a little further and ushered Simon forward to see for himself. He saw that his father's doublet had been opened and his shirt pushed up to his neck. Spreading out from his father's left armpit was a large, black bruise.

'Oh, my God,' Simon felt the weakness in his knees again, which obliged him to return to the chair. 'Plague.'

The Rector admonished him for blaspheming, both in church and before his father's corpse. He was oblivious, struggling to make sense of what he could see. Everyone had heard of people dropping like flies from the pest, while

247

seeming well right up to the moment of death. There were even stories of people dropping while playing with their children in the street, but in truth they were much used to people taking long days to die, in shut up houses, while their locked-in relatives watched and waited for their own symptoms to appear. A few went to pest-houses but they, too, generally waited several days for death.

Recovering his senses a little, Simon was appalled at the actions of the clergy. Pushing himself to his feet and stumbling before he regained his balance, he started shouting.

'Why on earth did you let the congregation leave? The church will have to be shut up for a month. All the people present must be quarantined. Quickly, raise the alarm!' The Rector and his officials looked at one another in a crafty manner, and the Rector nodded to his curate.

'I'm afraid this is not how we have determined to proceed,' the man stated, meeting the Rector's eyes, who nodded his agreement. 'We will not have our church shut up until after Christmastide is over. This is one of the holiest seasons and we have our parishioners to think of. We shall bury your father here in the churchyard this afternoon. If we follow this scheme, his funeral will have all the rites and ceremonies fitting for his station as a well-respected tradesman, a credit to his Guild. Indeed, a man who had spent his whole life devoted to the care of others.' The curate was warming to his theme now, and appeared to be enjoying his moment of power. 'If he were known as a plague death he would be thrown into a common grave with many others. You would not want that for a skilful practitioner of the healing arts as your good father, here before us, was. His death will be recorded as "sudden" in the parish registers, which is true, and no one will have any cause to query the matter.'

Simon slumped back into the nearby chair, thankful that this insufferable man had ceased prating. His fists and jaw clenched with equal force as he fought to suppress the urge to punch him square in his hateful face. *Such dishonesty, and from a churchman too.* Sir Robert saw his friend's passions were roused and crouched down beside him, placing his arm around Simon's shoulders.

'Listen to them, Simon. Think! If you are shut up, who will tell your mother? Who will comfort her in her grief? And would your father, rest his soul, wish to be thrown in a poor-hole without as much as a woollen winding sheet?'

Simon sat in silence for a few seconds, and then turned to the Rector.

'My father would never agree to this. He lived his life embodying the saying, "While you live, tell truth and shame the devil".' He paused for an amount of time which caused the gathered men to shift uncomfortably.

The curate broke the silence. 'Mister Smith, I realise you grew up in a family of healers. But pray be so kind as to tell me how many times you have seen, in person, a body displaying the symptoms of the disease you were so sure you saw on your late father's person.'

Simon regretted his decision not to punch this odious man.

'I have never seen such a case close up,' he admitted through gritted teeth.

'Quite as I thought, and if you recall you told us yourself your father had been a little tired recently. Is it not possible in his fatigue he stumbled and caused this bruise? Perhaps in the unfamiliar chamber of his accommodation? People die every minute of every day and it is not fitting for those of us not skilled in physick to presume to diagnose the cause of it.' The Rector had nodded along to this speech. Simon held the immediate fate of his church in his hands.

The clever wordplay was offering Simon a way to allow the official's plan to proceed without imperilling his soul. It was undoubtedly the case that none of those present had any medical learning. He *could* plead with the officials to send for a physician, although there were but few left in the city, or to summon some searchers to make a pronouncement, but he

249

already knew he would do no such thing. With a deep sigh, he said, 'May God forgive me. I agree to your scheme, but you are to meet the costs of this burial. And my father is to have a proper wooden coffin.'

The Rector agreed, although a deep vein rose on his forehead. His stomach then growled in a way that broke some of the tension and reminded the party that no one had taken any dinner. The clergyman explained that the sexton already had a plot dug out, for an ailing elderly parishioner who had wanted his final resting place prepared ready, being well aware of shortage of space in cemeteries across the city.

'I shall ask my wife to prepare the body for burial,' he added, 'and the curate will bid the carpenter send a coffin over straightway, suitable to Mister Smith's position in life. We shall dine in the refectory, and then I shall conduct the funeral service for your father this afternoon.'

Simon did not want anything to eat, and instead asked for a few minutes alone with his father's body. Sir Robert left him there, taking his leave with a reassuring squeeze of Simon's shoulder, and accompanied the Rector and the church officials to the refectory. For all Robbie's high spirits and pranks, there was a tender side to him, an empathy rare in men of his relative youth.

When he was certain they were quite alone, Simon apologised to his father for not being the son he had wanted. He knew if his elder brother Peter had lived, he likely would have become an apothecary like Jasper – the two were not only bound by strong affection, but by a remarkable similarity in tastes and opinions. And there was the other matter too. At least his father had been spared finding out about Simon's inclinations; he suspected it would have destroyed them both. Next he apologised for the rushed and underhand manner of the interment. Finally, he promised with all his heart to care for and protect his mother. He then fell to his knees and prayed for his father's soul, holding on to the dead man's hand as he did so.

After their meal was finished, the church officials and Sir Robert returned to the vestry. The Rector's wife stood at a distance but explained to Simon that Jasper should be buried as he was, in the clothes he was wearing, and not be laid out in the traditional way, for fear of spreading any disease he may have been exposed to. Of whatever kind, she added hastily. He was to be covered in a flannel winding sheet, tied at the top and bottom, with a few sprigs of rosemary tucked into the folds. At that moment, the curate returned from the coffin-maker, reporting that there was not one to be had for love or money. Simon was reduced to a sense of helpless misery by these tidings, but Sir Robert instantly resolved the difficulty. He sent a message with one of the clerks to his men, who had been waiting with the coach. They would go to the workshop, where the sight of servants in the Calstone livery would have the desired effect. Sure enough, in just a quarter of an hour, the men returned with a coffin. A little large for Jasper, but of good quality timber, and well made.

So it was that at three in the increasingly dark afternoon, Jasper Smith was buried in the graveyard of St Andrew's in the Wardrobe. The church bell tolled to mark the death. Simon instructed the parish clerk to keep a true record of where his father lay, for in the spring he would return to the church with his mother to erect a suitable stone in his father's memory. At the mention of his mother, Simon's stomach lurched and he grabbed for Robbie's arm, to steady himself. She would be going about her normal Sunday routine, attending church – twice probably, if there was no delivery to attend to. She would be looking forward to his father's return the next weekend. She would have no idea of the news Simon would be bringing home.

Sir Robert offered to take Simon back to the print house in his coach, but Simon declined. The walk would do him good.

'We should ride to Tupingham tomorrow, Simon. We can be back at the Three Doves by nightfall tomorrow, if we ride like the wind.'

'We?' Simon queried as Robbie clambered into the chariot.

'No question. I'll not have you going alone after a blow like this. I can bring strong horses from our stable for us to ride. I haven't been back to the Manor since we left together, and I should see my wife and son before she leaves for Court. My father informs me that she'll set out after the New Year celebrations are over. Besides, if I am to keep in his good favour, I should try to sire another grandchild for his Lordship soon, before he grows tetchy.'

'Robbie, you are quite mad,' cried Simon. 'But how will we obtain certificates to travel at this short notice? You know, thinking about it, my father and Ned would likely have been denied certificates to leave the city to return home because of my father's stomach pains and lethargy.' His voice trailed off as he became lost in his thoughts.

'Well that's what comes of being scrupulously honest isn't it? His own worst enemy, if I may say so. Why would you declare any indisposition to the Mayor's clerk?' Robbie looked exasperated at the thought. He grabbed hold of Simon's shoulders with both hands and looked directly into his eyes. 'We *shall* leave at first light. I will ensure we do not lack the necessary papers.'

As he turned to face his sombre walk home, Simon reflected that it seemed the younger man could make him smile no matter how dire the circumstances. Still, he was pleased he would be able to get back to his mother so soon, and was glad to have company. The two agreed to meet on the morrow for their long ride.

Instead of taking the shortest way home, Simon walked along the river to take in the clear air. There was much to do before he could leave: he must go to the Dolphin to collect his father's belongings, and to settle the account for the hired horses. He'd also have to dispatch a messenger to Deptford to tell Ned the news of Jasper's death, and to let him know that it would be best for him to stay at home until further notice. Simon had no idea what would happen to the apothecary business. As he walked, he noted that the river was now frozen over, twinkling where the moon lit up the frost. Not enough ice to hold a man's weight perhaps, but enough to stop the watermen earning their living for a few days. It was just as well, he reflected, that the plot his father now occupied was already dug, for there would be no breaking the ground now.

Chapter Twenty-six

Martha was busy washing the sheet from Jemima's mattress; the child must have been disquieted by sleeping in an unfamiliar room. Ned would not be happy when he got home to find his truckle bed had been taken over by the two children, and wet into the bargain!

From the scullery, Martha sent George upstairs to collect all the chamber pots.

'Bring them down carefully, one at a time. Don't mix them together. And mind your footing on the steps.' The child was unused to walking up and down stairs.

Martha had taken a small earthenware bottle from the apothecary store, into which she had placed some bent pins. When George came tottering in with Mistress Smith's pot, she carefully poured a few ounces of urine on top of the pins in the bottle, placed the cork lid on, and tucked it away under the sacking that covered the birthing chair. As she did so, she saw a figure at the back door. It was Mistress Healey, asking if she might have a word with the midwife. Martha showed the caller through to the kitchen, and then took the opportunity to retrieve the bottle of urine from the scullery, saying, 'Come children, let's go into the garden for a minute.'

The ground was hard, and digging was difficult, but eventually she made a hole deep enough to fit the bottle in, and they covered it back over and tamped the cold soil back down. She put a finger to her lips, making the children smile.

'No need to mention this to Mistress Smith, children. It will be a fine surprise for her one day. Come, let's walk to the green and see if the pond is frozen over.'

She walked with a child clutching each hand, smiling to herself. If Mother Henshaw had cursed Mistress Smith, then the buried bottle would soon sort it out. Her mother had taught her the trick when she was a girl. The bent pins would irritate the witch's bladder and drive her to distraction until she reversed the curse.

Lucie had been reflecting that the children had brought life back into the house. Martha had returned from church with them the day before and they were going to stay there with her until the master's return.

'There you are, Mistress Smith!' said Mistress Healey, entering the kitchen. 'We missed you at church yesterday. I do hope you're not hiding away, for you have surely done nothing to warrant that.'

Lucie played with the truth a little: 'No, I was merely feeling unwell, that's all.'

'Are you well enough to spare me a few minutes of your time? When I told you I was breeding again the other day, I should have told you I was afraid something might be amiss,' said the baker's wife.

'Of course, Helen. Follow me upstairs to my bedchamber, where I might examine you in private.' Mary was just back from running some errands, and so Lucie asked her to join them. Upstairs, Mistress Healey told Lucie how she had been having pains and spotting with blood on and off for the last few weeks, but the pains and blood had been much worse over the night that had just passed.

'How far gone are you, do you think?' Lucie asked.

'I'm sure I have quickened, so at least four months. Mistress Smith, can I confide in you? I'm afraid I have brought this on myself and the baby because I was

256

frightened, and even angry, at becoming with child again. I really would rather not have it so, but what if this is a punishment for my evil passions?'

Lucie said she didn't want Mistress Healey to trouble herself with notions like that. Many a good woman found herself unable to welcome every pregnancy, blessing though it was, especially when her home was full of mouths to feed and clothes to sew. She advised her patient to be examined by Mary, who, afterwards, considered the symptoms and the results of her examination, and told Helen that it was her opinion that what was in her womb needed to come out. She was sure it wasn't a child. Helen said surely it was, as she had felt it move. Mary asked Lucie to re-examine Helen, which she did. The womb was already open enough to admit a forefinger.

'I agree with Mary,' she said, 'and we have given you our opinion of your case. You need help to take the contents of your womb away. They will come away by themselves eventually, but you will be wracked with pains until the womb is clean. However, we don't wish you to decide in haste. Why don't you think about it a while and come back if you would like my help?'

Suddenly Helen bent forward, clutching her abdomen. She appeared to be in agony.

'Well, that makes up my mind, Mistress Smith,' she gasped. 'Whatever is in my belly seems to be coming out whether I agree to it or not, so pray help me!'

'Of course, my dear. Let me see what I can do,' and Lucie greased her hand again. Upon this examination she found that the womb was still just open enough to admit one finger. It took some effort but she managed to get the neck of the womb open enough to get a second finger in. She needed to press down hard on Helen's belly to keep the womb steady while she did this.

Mary stroked Helen's hair and tried to comfort her. At times the discomfort was too much, and try as she might, Helen

257

writhed on the bed as the midwife's fingers probed. Lucie spoke calmly, explaining what she was doing. She asked if Helen would like a draft of something to take the edge off her pain, but she declined, saying that it was best to get this over and done with now the operation had begun. Soon Lucie's fingers extracted several fluid-filled bladders. The biggest was the size of a pigeon's egg and the smallest just the size of a pin head. Mary was standing by to receive them in the chamber pot that George had recently returned. By the time the womb was emptied, there were nearly twenty of the parcels, along with a piece of putrefied flesh.

'Was it a false conception, Mistress Smith?' Helen asked in a trembling voice, as her body began to shake.

'No, I don't believe so,' Lucie said gently, wiping her hands on her apron. She turned briefly to her deputy. 'Mary, please would you bring me a thick coverlet for Mistress Healey from the press? She has had a shock and needs to be kept warm a while. When you have done that, please bring up a jug of warm water and some Castile soap.' The cold weather had left her hands rather chapped, and she was disinclined to use the harsher lye soap as was her normal custom. Turning back to Helen she explained, 'I think you must have miscarried a while ago when the child was around ten weeks. The fleshy mass is the after-burden, which continued to grow.'

Examining the bladders of water in the pot, Lucie noticed that one of them was a mass about the size of a hazelnut, this she took to be the miscarried foetus.

'What you felt was not quickening but these bladders moving inside you. The womb is clear now. When you have laid here a while, and I can see your humours are settled and the shaking has stopped, you should go home and to bed until the bleeding stops in a day or two.' Lucie packed Helen's vagina with clouts to ensure that the cold air did not get into her womb while she walked home.

Lucie sat at her desk, writing in her journal as Helen rested. After an hour or so Helen got up from the bed, a little

258

shaky, and Lucie said she would ask Martha to walk her back to the bakery, but not until she had joined the family in a dish of hot chocolate. The warm, sugary brew would help abate any remaining shock at the procedure she'd undergone. Helen began to shed a few tears, but Lucie reassured her there was nothing to reproach herself for. Mary came up and helped Helen back down the stairs and into a seat by the fire in the kitchen, and then she went back upstairs to strip the bedclothes. It was lucky that Lucie had had the foresight to lay several sheets down before carrying out the examination, thus the mattress was unaffected.

Later that afternoon, Lucie found herself worrying again about the complaint against her. Anthony had agreed to speak to John and to let them know how he got on that evening after work. Mary, devastated to have been away when the Rector had come bearing such terrible news, was determined to make up for it by surrounding Lucie with kind attentions, making sure she wanted for nothing, and keeping up a conversation to try to distract her from her anxiety.

———————————•◆•———————————

At six in the evening an exhausted party, consisting of Simon, Sir Robert and his man, arrived at the Boar in Tupingham. Apart from a rest at noon to allow the horses to eat, drink and recuperate, the men had ridden hard all day, setting out before the dawn. Sir Robert had decided he and his servant would stop at the inn overnight, so he might be refreshed before finishing his journey to Calstone Manor in the morning. At the inn, Simon had hugged his friend and shook the servant's hand, thanking them for their company on the long ride, before starting the walk to the Three Doves. His legs felt like jelly after so long in the saddle, but he must press on. He had arranged with John Miller that his father's belongings would be packed and sent along in a wagon to the Boar. John would also make sure Ned knew about his master's sudden death. He'd told Simon to take all the time he needed before returning to London.

As Simon approached his childhood home the street was in darkness, and he almost failed to notice that the new sign was hanging proudly outside. The lantern he had picked up at the inn lit the sign as he turned into the ginnel, preparing to enter by the back door. Never had a shop sign seemed so poignant. The pain hit him all over again and he needed to wait a few moments before proceeding, and steel himself for the task before him.

As he lifted the latch to the back door, a small child he didn't recognise greeted him. At his pressing, the little girl introduced herself as Jemima Higgs. She appeared disgruntled at his presence.

Lucie came into the scullery to find out who the little girl was talking to. Seeing Simon, she stopped dead in the doorway.

'Simon, is it really you? This is twice in a year you have taken me by surprise! Your father is with you?' her eyes searched behind him.

'Oh mother, I am so sorry!' Simon's voice cracked. He struggled to get his emotions under control. 'There is no easy way to say this. Father is dead. He died without warning at church yesterday.' Barely above a whisper, he added, 'He is already buried.'

Lucie's legs gave way under her, mirroring Simon's own reaction the day before. He caught her in his arms.

'How can this be?' Her voice was muffled against his chest.

Simon told her what had happened, still holding her tight. 'At least it was quick, mother. He would have felt no pain, and coming from the church he must have been in a state of grace.'

Lucie caught her breath, and swooned once more. Simon half carried, half dragged his mother into the kitchen, and the safety of her armchair.

'But why was he buried with such haste?' she asked at length. 'He should have been carried home.' She moaned softly. 'You know we have reserved the plot here, beside your brother and sisters. This is too much. My mind is fuddled. Please start again from the beginning. Mary and Martha need to hear it, too.'

Simon felt lost. He took a moment to gather himself before answering. 'Yes, Mother, of course. Ladies. I am ashamed I blurted this news in the scullery before I'd even crossed over the threshold.' As he began repeating the events of the last day, slowly and with more sensitivity than at the last telling, Martha poured a cup of small beer for them all and tried to get Lucie to sip hers. Explaining the hasty burial, Simon said: 'It's not permitted to take bodies across the country with contagion still abounding in the city, Mother. I am so sorry. If I could have, I would have returned him to you.'

'Is that what killed him?' Lucie asked in a small voice, as Martha and Mary glanced at one another anxiously. 'I asked him not to go. I didn't want you living amongst it either. Oh, I can't bear it!' she cried, bursting into tears. Simon fell to his knees in front of his mother's chair and hugged her close.

Lucie looked searchingly about her, and Simon only understood what she was looking for when Martha explained that she had tucked the two children up in bed. Breaking away from his mother and standing, for he could not bring himself to sit in Jasper's armchair, he continued and told the three deeply shocked women the agreed version of the story. If they knew of even the possibility that the plague had killed Jasper, they would be appalled that Simon had not gone into quarantine. He struggled again with doubts now he was in his mother's kitchen, yet, he had played the scene over and over in his head on the long ride, and still came to the conclusion he would take the same decision again. He did not *know* beyond all reasonable doubt of what his father perished.

It was eight in the evening before Anthony arrived. Martha

quickly told him the terrible news, before showing him through to the kitchen. This was not the time to tell the midwife that his conversation with John Allen had, if anything, made matters worse. John had accused Anthony of siding with the midwife to keep in with the Smiths, and of being too intent on his own concerns to spare a thought for those who were less well provided for, now that he had a wife again. John was more determined than ever to pursue his suit to the church court. Apparently, Simon had yet to learn this other bad news, but it could wait for another day now.

Anthony sat up long into the night with Mistress Smith, Simon, Mary and his wife, with the family sharing reminiscences about the apothecary and the good he had done in the town in his long years as the local druggist. There were so many people to inform, and so much to do. Lucie mentioned that Henry, next door, would be devastated, for he'd known Jasper as both man and boy and had a deep respect for him. Anthony knew this was true of Old Tom, too. Perhaps the old townsman's war-induced fuddled mind was a blessing in this one case. Lucie agreed and reminded the group how patient Jasper had been with Old Tom, giving him soothing drafts when he'd come into the shop agitated and shouting nonsense. Jasper, of course, had remembered Tom in his prime, a fine man and the one who'd taught him to fish in the river before Jasper had left Tupingham to take up his apprenticeship.

Anthony comforted Martha, who was deeply saddened that Mister Smith's last words to her had been so cruel, but was resolved to dwell on the good times. It was decided that Anthony should stop the night: it was too late and too cold to walk back to Warley Lane. He and Simon would share Martha's bed, with George tucked in with them, and Martha would sleep with Lucie, to try and be a comfort to her. Mary would take the truckle bed and have Jemima in with her.

Chapter Twenty-seven

Christmas day was always observed quietly in the Smith household as a Holy Day, but this year was understandably subdued. Martha, Anthony and the children had returned home, but would be eating with the Smiths after church, a meal to be brought by the Rector's wife. The whole town had been shocked at the loss of a man who had been not only their apothecary, but a leading alderman. To make matters worse, because Jasper had already been buried in London, the good folk of Tupingham could not attend his funeral. Such a service would have enabled them to begin their mourning in the accustomed fashion. Dr Archer had done his best to make up for this by preaching a moving memorial sermon for Jasper on the Friday after Simon's return.

Lucie had found *The Young-Man's Warning-Peece* on Jasper's desk. The old book was dated 1636 – the same age as their marriage. A brief look through had shown Lucie that Jasper had underscored a number of passages and she soon realised he must have been using it in an attempt to reform Ned. One passage jumped out at her above the others: it was about the way the subject of this book, another apothecary, charged his patients. The way it started could have been written for Jasper:

> *Sought to far and nigh was he. The sober sought unto him, because of his sweet temper seasoned with successefulle skill ... The thrifty sought to him, because of his gentle rates upon his care and*

cures. He would not suffer them to spend all they
had upon Physitians. And the covetous sought to
him, because if something pleased them not, he
would (for the most part) take nothing for what he
did.

Both Jasper and Lucie took pains to charge only what they
knew their patients' purses could bear, but the line about not
charging for a treatment which did not satisfy his patient
made Lucie smile through her misty eyes. While she had
been known to refuse a payment, Lucie was not sure her
thrifty husband had ever gone quite that far, but his patience
with the sick, and his fair rates for everyone he served rang
true. She had passed the book to Dr Archer, who had
incorporated the passage into his own sermon.

Lucie had attended the service in her new plain woollen
mourning dress, provided by the seamstress expeditiously.
Simon had worn a smart black bombazine suit of clothes.
Lucie had not had the strength to query where this outfit had
appeared from.

It was a relief that for the twelve days of Christmas there
was a break in the hostilities over the case of Goodwife Allen.
All but John Allen freely offered their condolences, and food
had been arriving at the shop regularly, so there had been no
need to cook anything. Helen Healey, who had recovered well
from her recent ordeal, told Lucie she felt terrible to think that
while she was being treated, Jasper was already lying in his
grave.

Simon had received a letter from John Battersby in
London. He offered to take over the remaining years of Ned's
apprenticeship, upon agreeing a fair fee. With so many
qualified practitioners lost to the plague, it would likely be a
long while before Tupingham would have another
apothecary. Simon suspected that, even if Ned continued to
doubt that he had a calling to be an apothecary, he would
find the life of a London apprentice offered more consolations

than Tupingham could provide: it was to be hoped, however, that the effect of Jasper's sudden death and the need to please a new master would keep his riotous tendencies in check.

Lucie had received an affectionate letter of condolence from Lady Calstone and Lady Eleanor, including an invitation to travel to the Calstone property in the North of England with the family next spring, should she feel a change of air would be helpful. Simon was invited, too. Lucie was touched by the offer but had no thought of accepting. To do so would have Jasper surely turning in his grave.

Jasper had made a new will two years previously, when Simon was offered the partnership. The new document took into account the money Jasper had invested for his son and this was deducted from his inheritance:

> *In the Name of God Amen 22 Day of November 1663, I Jasper Smith of Tupingham, being in good health and memory praise be to God, and being unwilling to be busied about earthly things when death approacheth do make my last will and testament in the manner ensuing. First as becometh every Christian declaring that I firmly believe the wonderful mystery and power of the Trinity and willingly and joyfully assign my soul unto the hands of my Creator and Redeemer trusting to have remission of all my sins and everlasting happiness both of soul and body through his merits and mercies to me. and my body to be Interred in my plot at All Hallows besides my children Peter, Sarah and Hannah already with God, with such final Ceremonies as is convenient. I do appoint my named Executrix, my much beloved wife Lucie Smith, to discharge all payments and duties due.*

Lucie had been surprised at how well she was to be provided for, for after fees and small bequests. Simon was left 100l in

265

ready cash, while she had just over 200l, as well as all her husband's goods and chattels. The lease for the Three Doves was paid until the end of the financial year on Lady Day in March, so she need be in no haste in her search for a new home. Small bequests included 5l for Martha and 2l each for Mary and Ned. There were also sums allotted to buy mourning clothes for Lucie and Simon, mourning rings for three of Jasper's fellow aldermen and coffeehouse cronies, and some charitable bequests. As Jasper had set aside ample funds for his funeral, these could be diverted to Simon, to reimburse Sir Robert for the expense of the hastily procured coffin, with the remainder being kept towards the expense of the headstone the following year.

Around the large table for the Christmas meal in Lucie's kitchen sat the Higgs, the Archers, the Smiths and Mary. The meal, cooked by Mistress Archer, consisted of beef ribs, roasted pullet, plum porridge and mince pies. Lucie had little appetite but took a bite of each to be polite.

The rest of the Christmas season passed quietly. The Smiths were invited to the Robbins' New Year's party as usual, but this was a formality and they declined, as etiquette dictated during mourning. Lucie had sent for the carpenter to take the sign back down as she couldn't bear the sight of it outside Jasper's shop, he had not set eyes upon it and never would. The sign pole was left empty.

After New Year, the household decided to reopen the shop. There was a large stock of ready-made remedies, balms, ointments, and dried ingredients in linen bags for infusing, and this might as well be available to townspeople in need, rather than decaying on the shelf. Once these ran out the shop could be shut up. They would move out at the end of March.

On Twelfth Night, a cake arrived from the Manor with a kind message from Lady Calstone. The cake's appearance was a reminder that January was progressing – Lucie's thoughts returned to her hearing. Half of her wondered if she should defend herself at all. While some midwives worked into old age, she now had enough money to ensure that if she took a couple of rooms for herself and a maid, and lived carefully, she could see out her last years in tolerable comfort. At other times, she would either dismiss the notion of yielding without resistance as a temptation to shameful sloth, or, rather less piously, feel angry at the insult offered to her high standing as a midwife. Thirty years and more of study and experience! Her emotions also swung between relief that Jasper hadn't known about her summons before he died, and bitter desolation that he wasn't there to be her support.

Lucie and Simon discussed the matter at length, before deciding it was time to gather supporting statements and letters of recommendation in advance of the hearing. Lucie was to petition the townspeople and Simon went to make sure Mister Collins the chirurgeon was prepared to testify about the sad events. In fact he was bound to testify, being a key witness, but it was as well for Simon to find out exactly what he intended to say. They had two weeks to prepare.

Lucie's first stop was at the schoolroom, and she asked to speak to Mister and Mistress Robbins. As they were her long-time friends, Lucie had assumed their support would be unconditional. However, Suzanne said it was difficult for her to take a side since her son, little Jeremy, was out at nurse with Anne Jones, who was supporting John Allen. Although grateful for Lucie's ministrations during her childbirth, and certain she would call on her again next time, she was nevertheless unwilling to testify at the visitation. Lucie reminded her that if she lost her licence – or worse – then she would not be in a position to deliver any more Robbins babies. This did not sway Suzanna, who said she had to think of her son before all else.

There was a similarly dispiriting result at the Black Bull. Peggy Dill, whose children had all been delivered by Lucie, also thought it would be bad for business to publicly take a side. George Dill, her lump of a husband, had nothing sensible to add either. Better news was to be had at the bakery, for Helen Healey was determined to have her say. The more she thought about it, the more convinced she had become that Lucie and Mary's swift action in ridding her of her dead child the previous month had saved her life, and she wanted to put her feelings on record.

Simon, meanwhile, had finished at the chirurgeon's home and ridden off on his mother's mare to Calstone Manor. He would ask for an interview with Lady Calstone in the hope of persuading her to send a letter to the Bishop, attesting to his mother's skill and integrity. A recommendation from a lady of such high rank could only help.

Simon noticed the flush creeping up his lover's neck at his unexpected appearance. Shyly, Robbie invited him into his suite of rooms. Ornate tapestries portraying classical scenes hung on the two main walls.

'A relative?' Simon cocked his head towards the portrait of a stern-looking elderly man in merchant's garb, glowering down at them. 'He has a look of you when you are in a dark humour.'

'Charming!' This was Robbie's great-grandfather, builder of the Manor. The goblets and fruit in the painting hinted at his success as a wine importer. 'Speaking of which, can I offer you some canary sack?'

Over a glass of the sweet wine, the men discussed their news.

'You are looking very well, Robbie,' Simon heard the relief in his own voice.

'I am indeed. The country air suits me, as it clearly does you, too.'

They looked deeply into one another's eyes. Their gamble with their health and others' had paid off.

Sir Robert's man returned to confirm that Lady Calstone was happy to give them an interview. Sir Robert led his friend down the dark-wainscoted long gallery, towards his step-mother's chambers. 'Did you know they built these corridors for those of a delicate disposition to take exercise when it was inclement?'

Simon shook his head, and pulled a face.

'You should see the one at the Trusts' mansion,' Robbie continued. 'Twice this size, maybe bigger. My Lady Northerton used to walk up and down with her women, gossiping away for hours. Old man Calstone had a passion for mimicking those above his rank, and so obviously had this built into his house. And here we are at Cecilia's chambers.' Robbie knocked on the door.

The room was warm, and bright. Lady Eleanor was not present but baby Charles was in the room with his nurse, who had been showing his grandmother a small mark that had appeared under his chin.

'Your son has a teething rash, Robert,' Lady Calstone said.

Robbie took the baby in his arms and made him chuckle by pulling silly faces. 'Thank you Agnes, you may take the child back to the nursery,' he said after a short while.

After the introductions were complete, Lady Calstone insisted on hearing the whole of Lucie's story from start to finish.

'It is so cruel even to think of a hearing when your poor mother is in mourning. It is most unseemly for the Bishop not to dismiss the matter out of hand,' she said. 'From your account your mother did all she could, sent for the chirurgeon in good time and was diligent afterwards. I see no case to answer.'

'Thank you, Madam,' said Simon, squinting as a beam of light from the low winter sun caught the crystal of Lady Calstone's dangling earring. 'Nor do I, but I suppose the Bishop is obliged to consider a petition where death is concerned.'

Lady Calstone shifted in her chair, looking as if she were in some discomfort. 'Well, you may tell your mother I shall write to him this very day. Your mother's skill at the birth of my grandchild, and in various family matters since, has been second to none. If the letter does not take effect, you may tell your mother that I shall attend the visitation in person.'

Sir Robert cleared his throat, before chipping in, 'I'm not sure my father would permit that, my Lady.'

'His Lordship has been kind enough to trust my discretion in these matters,' replied Lady Calstone curtly. 'He hasn't been home since May, and since the plague has kept us away from London, I have scarcely seen him all year.'

'Even so, he's expected here very soon, isn't he? I understand he is to accompany my dear lady wife to her position at court.'

Lady Calstone considered this for a moment, once again adjusting her position in her seat.

'You could attend the hearing, my dear,' she said at length. 'After all, Mistress Smith brought your son safely into this world.'

'Very well,' said Sir Robert.

Back in the long gallery, Robbie used his charms to try and persuade Simon to stay a while longer and play a game of Ombre. 'My man will make up the third player, say you'll tarry a while,' he implored. But Simon declined.

'I will show you out in person then.' Robbie led Simon back down the sweeping staircase. 'I must say my bombazine suit of clothes flatter your colouring rather more than they do mine,' he added, smiling, once they reached the bottom. 'I'll do anything for you, you know.'

'I don't mind why you do it, so long as it's done,' replied Simon wearily. 'My mother does not deserve this. But God knows, between your kindnesses on the occasion of my father's untimely death, and this, I shall be in your debt forever. I am grateful to you for the loan of the suit too. I knew it must be from you as soon as I opened it.'

'You must consider it a gift and keep it. And in return perhaps you might do me the honour of taking a turn in the coach one afternoon. I do so look forward to our rides,' he added with a wink.

'Indeed.' Simon turned to him at the door. 'Goodbye, Robbie. I hope it's not long till we can be together again.'

When Simon arrived back at the Three Doves, the shop was in darkness. Neither his mother nor Mary was at home. The midwifery bag and bundle of linen which were always ready were missing too, so they must be at a delivery. It seemed at least some of his mother's women remained loyal. He hoped they would not be out long, for it was already late, and bitterly cold. At least his news from the Manor would provide a good welcome for his mother when she returned home. After cutting himself some slices from a large ham on the kitchen table and taking a jug of ale, he added a log to the fire and sat in the armchair to eat his meal. Without consciously thinking to do so, he realised he was sitting in the place his father had occupied on the countless evenings he had waited up for Lucie to return.

Chapter Twenty-eight

The morning of the visitation arrived, following a wet and stormy night. Lucie hoped this wasn't a bad omen. Mary was still sleeping, tucked up beside her. Simon was asleep in the attic bedroom. She hastened down the stairs to find her shawl and pull it about her, for the morning was chilly. The fire was almost out, with no Martha or even young Ned around to have it blazing in the grate ready for the family rising. When the visitation was over, whatever the outcome, Lucie resolved to engage a new maid-servant. At the table, she sipped a cup of small beer, and steeled herself for what lay ahead. If only she had Jasper by her side. Often irascible and difficult, he would have been unreserved in his public support for her. He would also have been appalled by those of Lucie's women who had either refused to speak in her support or, worse, were supporting her accuser. She strongly suspected this would not be so if Jasper had been here to press her case to their husbands, and to remind them what they owed Lucie for her past care of their families.

When Simon emerged some while later, he had a small parcel in his hand. 'Mother, did you ask Father for some spectacles for yourself when he was buying his own pair? For amongst his things sent from London, I found these. They are not the ones he bought for himself; he showed me those while we waited for morning service to begin in St Andrew's.'

He handed her a small pair of reading glasses. She had not opened Jasper's bags yet and hadn't been aware that Simon had either, but these glasses seemed to be a sign that her late husband was looking after her from beyond his grave. She sniffed and brushed a tear from her eye. Popping the glasses on she looked at her journal – thrilled by how much clearer the magnified hand was to read.

'Oh, Simon, it does my heart good that you found these. Your father was always so kind and took such care of me. And with all his business in London, he remembered to buy some spectacles for me. I feel that he is with us yet!' With the declaration, she instantly burst into tears.

Simon took her into his arms and, taken by surprise by this outburst of passion, found himself weeping too. When their paroxysms had ceased – and they had made good use of their handkerchiefs – he felt much calmer, and ready for business. 'Now, what time must we be at church?' he asked.

'The hearings begin at eleven o'clock. The Bishop and his party stayed at the Rectory last night and will spend the morning reviewing parish matters before hearing any cases. I'm not sure what other business will come before him, but we should learn my fate by suppertime.'

Taking deep breaths to calm herself, Lucie returned to her bedroom to dress in her mourning gown, to which she had become very accustomed these past few weeks. Mary, too, had a dark, sober dress which Lucie had ordered for her after her master's death. The trio arrived at the church in good time, despite having to wait for Lucie to avail herself of the privy at the end of a row of houses, until her gripping and looseness ceased. Dr Archer and his wife were waiting to greet them. The Rector had dark circles under both eyes. Visitations happened only every three years and were something of an ordeal. The Bishop's officials reviewed all the church and parish records to check that everything conformed to the latest decrees.

Martha, now very visibly pregnant, was waiting at the church with her husband. She was one of the witnesses, having served as a gossip at the birth, along with Jane Croft and Anne Jones. Both of these women were present, but stood together away from Martha. Much to Lucie's delight, Alice Wallis was also at the church.

'Alice, you keep surprising me, my dear!' cried Lucie, hugging her former deputy.

'Simon kindly wrote to me to tell me of Mister Smith's sad passing. He also put in a line or two about the troubles you were having. I wanted to come in person to support you and to condole with you,' Alice said.

'You are too kind, especially after I failed you when I didn't come to your licensing. It was a grief to me, but Martha had to be wed before advent, so we had little choice.'

'You have never failed me! I had the six women I laid to speak in person for me, which was plenty, but your letter about the work I did when I was your deputy found great favour with the Bishop.'

'How did you get here? Did you ride this morning? You must have had to set off in the middle of the night, and we had that terrible storm. Tell me you weren't out in that and for my sake!'

'No, it was most strange. I meant to ride here, but yesterday the Calstone coach appeared in Grantby and some servant came to my home and told me I was to ride with them. I was a guest at the Manor last night, and came here with Sir Robert this morning. He told me his mother had insisted he come, since you laid his wife last year. I didn't get to meet the great lady, for I went to bed with one of the nursery maids, but this girl told me herself how highly my Lady regards you. And looking at our Martha, I see quite clearly why she needed to wed with such haste. Who would have thought it?' said Alice, with a fond smile. 'She looks very well as a married woman, and her present condition agrees with her!'

Lucie didn't know what to say. She was a little overwhelmed at all the support she was receiving. It was then she saw Sir Robert, who had been in a corner of the church, talking to her son. She went over to the pair and thanked Sir Robert for his consideration. The young aristocrat looked as resplendent as ever in a colourful silk suit with lace embellishments. The contrast between him and Simon in his mourning suit was stark. Their conversation was interrupted by the arrival of Mister Collins, the chirurgeon, who was in a foul humour, having been summoned to attend and so lose a morning's custom. He had as much to lose as Lucie, for he had attended the same case, and could face the same wrath of the church if it was deemed they were at fault.

The Bishop's clerk came over to know if they were ready to proceed. There were a number of matters to hear after this one – petty slanders, local disputes, and one case of fornication. The Rector reported that Goodman Allen was not yet present; the clerk said he would be allowed five more minutes, after which the case would be dismissed. This delay allowed time for Mistress Healey the baker's wife to arrive, fired up to have her say. With a minute to spare, the church door opened and in walked John Allen, accompanied by Sam Jones and the Allen children – no doubt brought to display their motherless condition.

'Forgive us, we were in the graveyard, praying for the soul of our departed sister, Goodwife Allen,' said Sam.

Watching his face, Lucie sensed that Dr Archer thought the weaver was perhaps enjoying his supporting role a little too much, and he seemed to feel sorry for the poor children, tagging along to make a show. The Rector cast a significant glance towards his wife, who clearly shared his sentiments, and she took them into the Rectory, planning to leave them, Lucie supposed, in the care of her maid. Lucie suspected Dr Archer would have some hard words for Allen and Jones after this day was over.

The Bishop's clerk called for order and everyone took their seats. To Lucie's initial relief the Bishop was not present for this stage of the hearing. The clerk explained that he would hear the deponents while their evidence was written up by the secretary, and the Bishop would decree if a full hearing was needed when he had read the written reports. If he decided one was needed, he would order it when all the cases before this court had been heard. Lucie gasped and reached for Simon's hand. She had no idea this purgatory could go on for days. John Allen was the first deponent to be called. He began by telling the Bishop how his wife had flourished during her previous teeming times, and that he had no fear of this one until around six weeks before the end, when his wife's indisposition became apparent. He explained that on the morning he had fetched the midwife, his wife's private bleeding had got worse and she had suffered horrible pains, being sure her throes were upon her. She had two children already so knew the signs, and her friends, Goodwives Jones and Croft, agreed. He said that instead of delivering her, the midwife and her deputy were more concerned with making food and changing linen. Mary let out a loud gasp, and made to rise from her seat at this version of events but was hushed by the clerk, who motioned for her to remain seated.

Allen continued that his wife did well although the indisposition continued, albeit slowly, until the day she died. He then told the court how his wife's waters had gone, and the baby was coming. He received accounts of his wife's progress from his neighbour Goodwife Jones, he said, nodding to Anne, so he knew things were looking ill for her and the child, but he was shocked to the core when, in the afternoon, he was told to go to her bedside to say his farewells. He did concede that Mistress Smith and her deputy treated his wife and child with the utmost respect following her passing, but couldn't seem to resist adding that in his opinion this was probably from guilt.

'That is your whole testimony, Goodman Allen?' the clerk asked.

'It is, sir,' John replied stiffly.

Lucie was called upon. Straightening her body as best she could, despite the trembling that ran through her, she raised her chin and told her story.

'I have known the deceased for many years and delivered her of her other children,' she began. The sense of calm she had experienced in Goodwife Allen's chamber washed over her, and she raised her eyes to offer up thanks. In a clear and steady voice, the one she had called up at hundreds of deliveries over the years, she explained to the court how seriously a woman's longings should be taken, and that neglecting them could have dire effects on mother and child. She contradicted Goodman Allen's testimony by saying that Mary had examined the woman, and then she had done so herself, but neither had found any sign on her person that she was at her time – this was why she asked many more questions until she got to the bottom of the matter. She then explained how she deduced that Anne Allen's pains and bleeding were caused by longings, and made the appropriate recommendations. She told the court how Mary had gone to get the peasecods Goodwife Allen desired beyond all else from the garden at the apothecary shop, and how she herself had made food from the produce. Although no voice was heard, a slight breeze, composed of a dozen indrawn breaths, rustled through the echoing church at this point, as some of the men present, and even a few women, recognized a double meaning.

Lucie was vaguely away of some sniggering at the back of the nave. There was a crowd there who had come for the entertainments afforded by the bawdy cases due to be heard next and were growing impatient. One of their number clearly fancied himself a comedian and began whistling a tune which Simon later told her was well known in the alehouses as "In Peasecod Time". The Bishop's clerk was obviously used to this type of behaviour. He raised his hands.

'Silence. I am sure we all know the jests the name of this vegetable carries. I should not have to remind you that we are here to hear about the death of a young wife. There is no cause for levity.'

At the clerk's signal, Lucie then continued to the day of Goodwife Allen's death. She was uncomfortable about talking about such private matters as the birthing chamber in this forum. Indeed, it went against every part of her modest nature. But she knew she must press on if she was to clear her name. In a clear tone she testified that Anne's womb wasn't opening, but there was a heavy blood loss, and that after only half an hour she made the decision to send for the chirurgeon. The clerk asked for clarification at this point, and asked if Mistress Smith carried the irons and hooks needed to remove a dead child. She confirmed that she did, and had last used them in early summer at the Bromfields' farm. She explained that she could not use them on this occasion as she, rightly, believed the child yet lived. She described the rest of the birth and the agreement she and the chirurgeon reached about the cause of the deaths of mother and child, which was that the after-burden had become detached from the womb.

Mister Collins was called up next. He swore on the Bible, and then stated he had got to Warley Lane less than a half hour after being fetched, and that he examined the patient and decreed there was no way to get that child out without damaging both mother and baby beyond all repair, so in his opinion nothing profitable could be accomplished and nature must take its course. He then told the assembled people how this was not good enough for Mistress Smith, who tried valiantly to get the child out with her hands. He said that he was struck with admiration for the midwife's skill and forbearance, and that she was right, for the child was born living and so could be baptised on the spot.

John Allen jumped to his feet, yelling that none of that would have been necessary had the midwife delivered his wife when she was first called out. The clerk ordered him to sit and compose himself, and asked Mistress Smith to go back over the first consultation. She explained again that Goodwife Allen had no signs of labour upon her and that this

279

was her deputy Mary's view, too. She then told the court that she had known of women ruined by unskilled midwives forcing them to give birth before their time, and she would never countenance that.

The chirurgeon was allowed to finish his testimony. He confirmed Mistress Smith's statement. Again, John Allen rose, and cried that this was not good enough, and that the midwife and chirurgeon were in league against him. Mister Collins, angry in his turn, retorted that if Mister Allen had been a better husband and father he would have made sure his wife's cravings were satisfied, and his neglect was undoubtedly what caused the womb-cake to deteriorate and start to peel away from the womb wall. Quick as lightning and before anyone could stop him John Allen jumped up and ran towards Mister Collins, fists raised, shouting, 'How dare you try to put the blame on me?'

He looked likely to reach the chirurgeon, but Lucie stood in his way, and seized his hands. She spoke to Goodman Allen firmly but gently, with the tone that had commanded numerous women in their travails over the last three decades.

'John, this is not the way. And Mister Collins, your accusation is not just. Goodman Allen knew nothing of his wife's longings.' John dropped his fists, so Lucie loosened her grip but held onto his sleeves. She continued testifying.

'Mary Thorne and I had to coax the truth from her, as she didn't want to admit she longed for anything. No one is to blame, certainly not John here. This was God's will and it is not for us to question Him. The Lord knows how hard what he asks of us is. I am finding this too, with regard to my late husband.'

John slumped, and his whole body shook with his sobs. He looked utterly broken standing before the midwife as she held his arms. Lucie guided him to a seat, just as she had done for Simon or Peter when they had had a childhood hurt. She sat down beside him and took the widower in her arms and soothed him, his head on her shoulder, gently rocking him like a small boy, until the sobs subsided. The clerk adjourned the proceedings while this went on.

'Oh, Mistress Smith, will you forgive me?' John said eventually, after blowing his nose. He worried at the handkerchief in his hands. 'I am so very sorry. My grief sent me quite mad. I don't know how I will survive without my wife, but I was very wrong to blame you. I see that now.'

The clerk came over and asked if everyone was ready to continue. John Allen cleared his throat. He declared that he wished to withdraw his complaint. He acknowledged that the midwife, her deputy and the chirurgeon had acted with the best of intentions, and he wanted to record his sincere apologies. It seemed to Lucie that God Himself had moved within John Allen at this moment and reclaimed the lost soul. The clerk left the nave to confer with the Bishop in the vestry. He returned moments later and called the court to order. A ripple went through the audience as the Bishop himself appeared before them. He stood in place of the clerk and announced that if the complaint had not been withdrawn he would have dismissed it in any case. He had heard enough from his desk, and was reassured that the midwife and chirurgeon had done everything possible to preserve the life of the deceased and her child. He asked the two to inform his clerk if they wished to enter a counter suit for defamation, but Lucie immediately said that wouldn't be necessary, although Mister Collins looked as if he would otherwise have been minded to. The Bishop thanked all the other witnesses for coming out in the bad weather, saying he was sorry they had been put to this trouble, and dismissed them.

The clerk came over to ask Lucie and Dr Archer to remain behind, and took them over to his desk. Lucie reached for Simon to accompany her. The clerk said he was sure that the Bishop would wish him to reassure Lucie that she left the church with her reputation for skill and integrity intact, and that the written testimonials which had been sent ahead were full of her praises, but there was nothing in them that his own knowledge of her did not confirm. He noted especially that Lady Calstone had written in her support. He also said he was moved by her compassion for her accuser, which was a sign that she was a good woman. Finally, he told her how he remembered her from his last visitation, and that he had been pleased to receive her statement in support of Midwife Wallis, which had made his decision to grant her licence so much easier. Lucie's face flushed. Finally, the clerk said she would not be required any further during this visitation, and asked Dr Archer to note in the records that he was satisfied that all was in order with the midwife. Lucie and Simon turned to leave, and the clerk and Dr Archer walked back down the aisle behind them. On the way, the pair heard them discussing that the Bishop was minded to excommunicate Mother Henshaw in the afternoon proceedings, for practicing without a licence. Lucie glanced up at Simon with a rueful smile, but remained of the view that the gesture was pointless – Mother Henshaw answered only to herself, and probably wouldn't care a whit.

At the church door, the Smiths' party was waiting. John Allen and his supporters had already left for Warley Lane. Lucie learned that Sir Robert had also left in his coach, taking Mistress Wallis with him, so that after he was dropped at the Manor the coachmen could take her back to Grantby. Lucie was sorry that she had not had the chance to thank them both and take her leave appropriately. She resolved to take a trip back to Grantby when her mourning period ended, to spend time with Alice properly. Mary and Martha both expressed amazement at the turn of the morning's events. John had withdrawn his complaint in a manner as sudden and vehement as his original accusation.

'The only explanation is that we saw the Lord at work this day,' Lucie concluded, 'for we were gathered in His house.' She gave each woman a sincere hug in turn.

Martha had another possible explanation of her own. She

thought maybe the witch bottle she had buried in the garden at the back of the Three Doves had worked its charm and broken any curse Mother Henshaw had cast on the midwife. Perhaps one day she would admit what she had done, but today wasn't that day.

About this book

Like all historical fiction this book is a mixture of facts taken from the historical record and things I have invented. For example, my apprentice or deputy (as trainee midwives were known) midwife, Mary Thorne, takes her name from a real historical figure, a midwife who received her licence to practice on 10 September 1724. She was based in the Worcester area. See Appendix 1. Some of the names used in this book are taken from her evidence in support of her licensing. Mary listed the names of ten men whose wives she had successfully 'lain' or delivered, and she signed the document with her mark.

Midwifery licences were issued by the church rather than any medical regulatory authority. Prospective midwives needed six women to testify in person that they were competent. The fact that Mary lists these clients by giving their husbands' names gave me the creative licence to imagine their deliveries and circumstances, and so while I have borrowed their married names, all other details are fictitious. Some other minor characters are taken from real life, too. The physicians Dr Burnett (doctor to the diarist and naval officer Samuel Pepys) and Thomas O'Dowde were real figures, and the apothecary John Battersby did indeed have a shop on Fenchurch street and was also a friend of Pepys. O'Dowde's daughter Mary did take over his practice and wrote a book, *Medicatrix, or the Female Physician*, vindicating him from his detractors, which was published under her second married name, Mary Trye, in 1675.

Details about midwifery and recipes for cures are largely taken from Jane Sharp's *The Midwives Book*, published in London in 1671, which was the first guide to midwifery published by a named English midwife. In her book, Sharp claims to have worked as a midwife for some 30 years, like Lucie Smith. We know nothing more about Sharp's life. While Sharp's book is made up of material copied from existing works, such as those of Daniel Sennert and Nicholas Culpeper, her distinctive and sometimes lively tone does come through. One of my favourite parts is when she mentions a man who complained that his wife's vagina had grown loose after childbirth: perhaps 'his weapon shrunk and was grown too little for the scabbard' (p. 53).

I've also taken character names and events from another midwife's memoir: Sarah Stone's *A Complete Practice of Midwifery* (London, 1737). Stone was originally from Somerset where she trained under her own mother, a well-reputed midwife, Mistress Holmes, during a six-year apprenticeship. Sarah Holmes married apothecary Samuel Stone on 29 November 1700 in Bridgewater. So she married on Lucie's birthday and the same week as Martha, although apparently not for the same reasons as couples were still being wed in advent at Sarah's church and their first child, another Sarah, was not baptised until 17 October 1702.

She began practising in her own right in 1703. The Stones moved to Bristol and then to Piccadilly in London, before returning to Bridgewater in the 1740s. The Bromfields' stillbirth is one of hers as is the story of the peasecod longing, although her patient lived, and Lucie's did not. Although Sarah trained for six years under her mother, she argued that midwifery apprenticeships should be standardised to three years.

Many babies were delivered by hand (or handy) women until the twentieth century as they were more numerous than midwives. While the one in the book is suspected of witchcraft, because she is an older, self-sufficient, difficult woman, neither hand women or midwives were routinely assumed to be witches and were of all ages. Belief in witchcraft was declining in the post-Restoration era, in line with Jasper's views in the novel, but amongst the populace there were widespread practices to guard against witches and their spells.

As unlikely as it might seem, none of the recipes for cures has been made up. If they are not in *The Midwife's Book* then they have been sourced from the Wellcome Collection, which has made their recipe books available to all in digital form. Often these were recorded in commonplace books like the one Lady Calstone keeps. Readers are urged *not* to try any of these at home! It is true, too, that the Restoration ushered in epidemics of syphilis and other sexually transmitted diseases.

The apothecary shop where Lucie and Jasper Smith live and work is identified by a sign with three doves – this was the sign of an apothecary's shop in the sixteenth century on Bucklersbury Street, in the City of London, where apothecary William Normevyll worked (see Thomas Raynalde, *The Birth of Mankind*, 1545, 108r-v, who recommends this shop to his readers). So I borrowed his sign. It is little wonder an apothecary like Jasper would seek out new books and practical measures against the plague since fully a fifth of the population of London (some estimates suggest 100,000 people, a third more than the number officially recorded) died in the Great Plague of 1665 alone. Some churchmen were reluctant to record the true numbers of plague deaths, and non-conformist congregations did not complete records. However, events and characters at St Andrews in the Wardrobe are fictitious.

Some of the events and happenings in the story, such as the weather, or the plague figures, or otherwise are adapted from entries in diaries such as that of Samuel Pepys or Ralph

Josselin. For instance, on 26 July 1664, Pepys was at a gossiping or party following the birth of a child to his relatives, the Joyces. While he was there, he took the opportunity to ask the assembled women for advice, because he and his wife were unable to conceive a child. The advice Lucie gives is the advice Pepys received, with some additions from Jane Sharp's book.

The ballad Simon sent his mother, *The mistaken mid-wife, or, Mother Mid-night finely brought to bed*, was a ballad printed in Restoration England, but some years later, between 1674 and 1679.

At this time, the legal year ran from Lady Day to Lady Day (March 25). So in Lucie's notes all the events in this book occur in 1665.

Note on medical theory

Most people understood their body through what is known as the doctrine of the four humours (blood, phlegm, black bile or melancholy, and yellow bile or choler), with each humour, or fluid, having its own characteristics (blood was hot + wet, phlegm cold + wet, black bile cold + dry, yellow bile hot +dry). Humoral balance was linked to personality traits and other physical and mental characteristics. The body was consequently seen as a fluid exchange system where the humours needed to be kept in fine balance to ensure good health.

Men's bodies were assumed to be hotter and drier than women's colder, wetter, leakier bodies. These ideas had come down from ancient pre-Christian Greek and Roman writers. Disease was nearly always put down to an accumulation, excess, or corruption of one or more of these humours. Treatments like blood-letting were used to remove any diagnosed excess of this humour. Medicines could be simples, that is, single herbal ingredients, or compounds, such as the mixtures Jasper makes up in his shop.

In the sixteenth and seventeenth centuries other medical theories grew in popularity. The German-Swiss Renaissance physician Theophrastus Aurelius von Hohenheim, self-styled Paracelsus, set out to create a truly Christian medical framework, the chemical medicine that men like Thomas O'Dowde and George Thompson practised. This system proposed that the cosmos was composed of three active substances or chemicals: mercury, sulphur, and salt. Ill health in this new model was the result of dysfunctional chemical processes in the body, and it was thought that diseases were specific entities that would afflict different people in the same way. Largely, the chemical cures melded into humoral medical practice and humoral theory continued to be the main way of understanding the body for at least another century.

Appendix 1

Statement in support of the licensing of Mary Thorne, 1724

The Wife of Samuel Jones

The Wife of Joseph Bennet

The Wife of William Robbins

The Wife of Joseph Townshend

The Wife of Olifor Hill

The Wife of Thomas Cooper

The Wife of William Hill

The Wife of Thomas Round

The Wife of William Pardoe

The Wife of John Woolrich

The Wife of Samuel Brook

The Wife of John Hill

Mary Thorne midwife her Mark 10 September 1724

Herefordshire achieves, list of midwives used and oaths. MSS BB80 & HD5/1-4

My thanks to Alun Withey for alerting me to this record.

Glossary

After-burden – placenta or afterbirth

Apothecary – dispensing chemist

At her time – at her due date

Caudle – a nourishing custard, often made with milk, eggs, wine, sugar and spice

Chirurgeon – barber-surgeon

Clyster - enema

Coats – amniotic sac

Costive - constipation

Courses – menstrual periods

Druggist – dispensing chemist

Dugs – breasts or nipples

Ell – unit of measurement approx 18 inches long

Flowers – menstrual periods

Hand or handy woman – unlicensed midwives without formal training

Humours – bodily fluids

Jakes – toilet

Jalap – a purging medicine

Navel-string – umbilical cord

Neck of the womb - cervix

Pangs – contractions or labour pains

Physician – medical doctor

Privy - toilet

Privities – women's sexual area

Quickening – the moment a mother first feels her foetus move in the womb. Believed by some to be the moment the soul entered the baby's body.

Secrets – women's sex organs

Secundine – placenta or afterbirth

Stays – corset normally made from boned fabric, but sometimes of leather for the less well-off

Terms – menstrual periods

Throes – contractions or labour pains
Watching - insomnia
Womb-cake – placenta or afterbirth
Wrinkles – stretch marks
Yard – penis

Acknowledgements

There are so many elements that have aligned to make this novel possible. Firstly, I need to thank Elaine Hobby for introducing me to the seventeenth-century midwife Jane Sharp back in the early 2000s, when I was an undergraduate in her class. This introduction was life-changing. Elaine went on to supervise my PhD research which made extensive use of this text. I have been lucky enough to have spent many years since researching and writing about matters related to reproduction in the early modern era, often in partnership with Jennifer Evans.

I want to thank Kerry Featherstone and Jonathan Taylor for the practical help both generously gave. Separately, both encouraged me to attend the 2019 States of Independence publishing fair in Leicester and it was there I came across Wild Pressed Books. I'm grateful to Sarah Fox for sharing her knowledge of midwifery licensing and church courts in early modern England.

I have had so much encouragement and support to move forward with this project from family, friends and colleagues including Catie Gill and Deirdre O'Bryne, and that means more to me than I can express. My mother, Lynne, and daughter-in-law, Kelly, both had early sneak previews of the opening chapters and both demanded more, which gave me the heart to press on.

One woman needs acknowledging further. Carolyn D. Williams worked with me on the pre-submission edits, where she used her expertise in the period to make suggestions for wonderful extra details and colour which have added authenticity to the story. She went far beyond a proof-reading brief and I am grateful for all her efforts, her enthusiasm, and the way her questions challenged me to make the draft the best it could be.

It has been a great pleasure to work with Tracey and Phil at Wild Pressed Books. Tracey 'got' the book immediately, so I knew my story had found its proper home. Tracey's thorough, insightful and patient edits and suggestions have not only infinitely improved my debut novel, but taught me such a lot too. Tracey has also produced the cover art, based on Michael Sweert's 'Head of a Woman' (c1654) now in the Getty Museum's collection.

About the author

Sara Read is an academic who specialises in the cultural and literary representations of women, reproduction and medicine in the seventeenth century, and a lecturer in English at Loughborough University. She has published two academic books: *Menstruation and the Female Body in Early Modern England* (2013) published by Palgrave Macmillan and *Flesh and Spirit: An Anthology of Seventeenth-century Women's Writing* published by Manchester University Press (2014). She has written a popular history of women's lives, *Maids, Wives, Widows: Exploring Early Modern Women's Lives, 1540-1740* (2015) and co-authored *Maladies and Medicine: Exploring Health and Healing, 1540-1740* (2017) published by Pen and Sword.

In addition to her academic articles on the subject of matters relating to reproduction in this era, Sara regularly writes for magazines and periodicals.

The Gossips' Choice is her debut novel: They say write what you know, so that's what she did or, rather, she wrote what seventeenth-century women knew. See more on sararead.co.uk or follow Sara on Twitter @saralread.

Lightning Source UK Ltd.
Milton Keynes UK
UKHW041328290620
365747UK00002B/111